STEPPING UP TO LOVE
LAKESIDE PORCHES SERIES BOOK 1

KATIE O'BOYLE

SOUL MATE PUBLISHING
New York

STEPPING UP TO LOVE

Copyright©2013

KATIE O'BOYLE

Cover Design by Niina Cord

This book is a work of fiction. The names, characters, places, and incidents are the products of the author's imagination or are used fictitiously. Any resemblance to actual events, business establishments, locales, or persons, living or dead, is entirely coincidental.

All rights reserved. No part of this publication may be reproduced, stored in a retrieval system, or transmitted in any form or by any means (electronic, mechanical, photocopying, recording, or otherwise) without the prior written permission of both the copyright owner and the publisher. The only exception is brief quotations in printed reviews.

The scanning, uploading, and distribution of this book via the Internet or via any other means without the permission of the publisher is illegal and punishable by law. Please purchase only authorized electronic editions, and do not participate in or encourage electronic piracy of copyrighted materials.

Your support of the author's rights is appreciated.

Published in the United States of America by
Soul Mate Publishing
P.O. Box 24
Macedon, New York, 14502

ebook: 978-1-61935-270-4
Print book: 978-1-61935-507-1

www.SoulMatePublishing.com

The publisher does not have any control over and does not assume any responsibility for author or third-party websites or their content.

For my inspirational friend John

whose 90th birthday brunch

on the porch at Belhurst Castle

sparked the idea for the characters

and stories of Lakeside Porches.

Acknowledgements

Heartfelt thanks to Debby Gilbert for taking a chance on Stepping Up To Love and for guiding every phase of the publication process. Warm hugs to my test readers—Chrissie, Tracy, Jackie, Debbie, Anne and Martha. Respectful bows to the writers who critiqued sections of this work, from the Lilac City Rochester Writers and the Golden Pen contest. Special thanks to Nina Alvarez and Joy Argento for their expert workshops at Writers and Books.

Chapter 1

A barrage of ice pellets on the windshield roused Manda from the sleep of the dead. She poked her head out from the cocoon she'd made with her hooded parka. Her muscles hated her as she fumbled for the micro flashlight on her key chain and stole a look at her wristwatch. Three thirty. One hour since the last time she'd checked. At least she was getting some sleep. And she was safe.

Just a few hours ago, Manda had slammed out of the designer home on Cady's Point at ten o'clock and driven aimlessly until the gas gauge caught her attention. With no more gas to spare and no place else to go, she'd pulled into the parking lot of the Manse where she worked, and tucked her car between the half dozen staff vehicles.

Even though the main lot offered more protection, she knew her car would stick out like a sore thumb among the dozens of luxury vehicles driven by the guests. Kristof might or might not be looking for her, but it was a sure bet she'd be in major trouble if Manse security spotted her rusty, twelve-year-old VW Beetle hobnobbing with the Jaguars.

Security was tight at the Manse Inn and Spa; she hadn't figured out how to get into the spa showers to make herself presentable for work in a few hours. She had hoped Remy would be on the premises by seven, an hour ahead of the administrative staff. The big boss usually arrived at eight thirty, but he'd been known to make an early morning sweep every few months to keep everyone on their toes. Probably the kitchen staff might be there even earlier than Remy, but she had no "in" with them. Remy owed her; she'd filed his personal taxes for him last week and he hadn't paid her yet.

Last night she wished she had that money to get something to eat, but maybe it was going to work out after all. A spa shower would help with her bruises and the spasms in her pelvic area. Don't think about the pain, she told herself. Think about the steaming shower, the fluffy towels, the fragrant body lotion.

A spasm along her inner thigh made her cry out. *Who am I kidding? I am in major trouble here.* Way more than a shower could fix, she admitted to herself. *God, if you're paying attention, I really need some help here.* She kneaded the cramp until it eased.

Manda listened while the tattoo of ice pellets slowly gave way to a steady rain. Wind swirled around the car, whistling through every crack in the seal of the windows. She fell asleep with a comforting thought. *I didn't drink tonight.*

A jangle of keys against the window roused her just before dawn. She opened her eyes and saw Remy's face peering down at her. He motioned to her to get out of the car and come with him. "Quick!"

Manda gathered her purse and her wits the best she could and crawled out of the car.

"You have lost your mind?" Remy scolded her, his French accent making the words comical. "*Merde*! Did you drink all night and pass out in your car?"

"I had a fight at home, Remy. I drove back here and slept in the car. Or tried to."

"You are hurt, *ma petite*," he realized. "Who did this?" He snapped to his full height of five foot five and declared, "I will kill him!"

Manda laughed in spite of her pain. "Remy, can you let me in to take a shower?" He was brandishing an imaginary sword with the hand that should be opening the back door to the spa. "Please, I'm going to faint if I don't get out of this wind."

He commanded, "Come, *ma petite,*" and grabbed her arm. She cried out in pain. Remy winced, too. He let her lean on him as they made their way through side door, past the massage rooms, into the locker room and the showers beyond.

Remy made a show of opening the frosted glass door for her and motioning her into the elegant bath enclosure with a flourish.

Manda leaned back against the cool tile wall and wiggled out of her shoes. "You are my hero, Remy," she told him. "Thank heaven it wasn't raining when I left the house. I'd have died of hypothermia."

Remy helped her out of her coat and surveyed her ruined clothes.

Manda's spirits sagged even further. "How am I going to get dressed for work?"

"I bring you everything you need, *ma petite*. Here are towels, tiny bottles—lotion, shampoo, you take what you need. I go through the lost and found and bring you nice clothes. Clothes for a lady," he said, humming his way back toward his office.

Manda turned on the shower as hot as she dared and sat for a moment on the wooden bench of the shower stall, stripping off her torn clothes and letting the steam warm her. She hoped Remy could find something that would cover the bruises. Pants and a long-sleeved top maybe. She would leave it to him.

Halfway through the shampoo, she heard him tap on the frosted glass door and slip some clothes onto the hook in the dressing area. "I owe you, Remy," she said over the noise of the shower.

"Shhh!" he commanded. "I know nothing!" he declared and hummed his way back through the locker room.

The bubble of laughter that rose in Manda turned into a flood of tears. She let them flow and mix with the hundred-degree simulated rainwater pouring from the ceiling.

Finally warm, and thoroughly clean, shampooed, conditioned, citrus-scented, and far less achy than she'd been, Manda turned off the water and drew back the linen curtain dividing the shower stall from the dressing area, and screamed. Standing at the glass door was the big boss. Remy's boss. Her boss's boss. She wasn't sure, but Joel Cushman was probably everybody's boss.

"Geez, Joel, I thought you were a pervert!" she yelled at him. *I can't believe I just called Mr. Cushman "Joel." I am in so much trouble here.*

"Manda? What—?" His voice cracked like an adolescent.

Manda stifled a laugh. His eyes were drinking in her body as though he couldn't believe what she'd been hiding under her baggy clothes. *Drink your fill now, Joel, because I am off men for life.*

"I thought you were a criminal. What are you doing in the shower at seven fifteen in the morning? And stop batting that curtain around."

Manda tried desperately to grab hold of the linen shower curtain, flapping this way and that in the current created by the open door. "Do you mind?" she scolded him.

Giving up on the curtain, she crossed her arms and turned her back on him. *He probably likes that view, too.* "Could you hand me a towel, please, or get out of here?" *Why am I yelling at the boss? Seriously dumb, Manda.*

He was silent now, which was worse. *What is he doing, standing there, looking at me?* Panic overtook anger, and she turned back to look at him.

He had dropped the admiring once-over, and she saw he was taking a second look at her purpling bruises. Silently, he handed her a towel from the top of the stack and looked her in the eye.

Manda wondered if he could read the shame and fear clouding her vision.

Joel cleared his throat and ordered, "In my office. Five minutes. Dressed." His jaw was hard as he turned on his heel.

Manda wrapped herself in the towel and reached for another to dry her hair. The black linen slacks and blue silk shirt Remy left for her fit perfectly and caressed her skin. After Kristof, she never wanted another man to touch her, but the silk and linen felt beautiful and, more importantly, made her feel beautiful.

Joel stood fuming at his office door. He directed Manda to the chair that squarely faced his intimidating desk. After glaring up and down the hallway to clear the area, he gave the door just the right amount of slam. He turned on her and cut through the preliminaries. "I got the plea from Remy to go easy on you, but I'm not inclined to do that." He perched on the corner of his desk and glared down at her. "What were you thinking, living with this lothario professor in the first place? Aren't you supposed to be a student? A top-of-your-class business major, the kind we're proud to employ at an upscale inn and spa? Do you get that's not consistent with shacking up with some divorced sot that doesn't know how to keep it in his pants?" He bet that was language she never expected to hear from Joel Cushman.

"I so don't deserve that!" Manda glared at her boss and he glared right back. He wanted to wring her neck, her beautiful bruised neck.

"And please," she continued, "quit yelling at me. I've had enough explosions." She choked on the last word. She pressed the back of her hand to her nose to stop it running.

Joel crossed the room, grabbed a box of tissues, and tossed it at her. "Use these."

"Thank you." She pulled two out of the box and dried her eyes and nose.

"Nice clothes. You need a scarf. Ask Remy for one. You've got three minutes to save your job."

She got her voice under control but not the tears. "I came to Tompkins College on a full scholarship—tuition, books, room and board. I did really well, made Dean's List freshman year, yada yada. Scholarships were cut across the board sophomore year, and I only had tuition support from then on."

Joel flinched. He knew all about that, because he'd voted for those cuts, with the understanding that the Presidential Scholars—the best and brightest—would be given some options to make up for the shortfall. Someone had dropped the ball on the follow-through; he made a mental note to track it down.

"I didn't want to get a loan or drag out my program if I didn't have to. I answered an ad by Mrs. Lothario Professor Kristof," she snipped at him, "as a live-in, part-time housekeeper."

Joel snorted and muttered, "Housekeeper."

Manda snapped, "I don't need it, Joel. I mean Mr. Cushman."

"Joel. Go on."

"I had no means of support and no time to find any. I wasn't going to give up on college if I could find a way to continue." She drew in a sharp breath and put a hand on her stomach. Her face paled, and her forehead creased with pain. Manda took a few deep breaths and tried to get back some control.

Joel was not doing well in the control department either. Mangled jumbo paperclips littered the rug where he'd missed the wastebasket. He tried again, his voice more reasonable this time. "So, what were you a nanny?"

Manda shook her head. "No, she kept the children with her always, except for a private child care person. It was my job to fix the evening meal every weekday and do some minimal day-to-day straightening up."

"You cook." He failed to keep the skepticism out of his voice.

"Lorraine—Mrs. Kristof—wasn't looking for a gourmet chef. Just someone to fix nice salads and light, healthy meals for her — and her husband if he ever came home. The kids were on special diets, and she had a nutritionist handling all of their meals. The biggest need was to keep the toys and stuff picked up and the place looking"—she rolled her eyes—"'serene and lovely'. How hard is that? I did that for a year, and it was great. I lost weight and got fit swimming and biking all over Cady's Point. It gave me a place to live and enough money for books. That summer I got an internship here, and it turned into a part-time job, but the money wasn't enough to get my own place or even share an apartment, plus books, fees, food, computer—"

"I get it. Go on. You stayed on at the Kristof palace on Cady's Point."

"I didn't find out until after the holidays last year that Lorraine had filed for divorce. She apparently traded the house for the kids. Over the holiday break, she and the kids moved to England and I came back to a half-empty house and a different employer." Manda's eyes widened and she sucked in a breath.

"Mr. Lothario Professor Kristof," Joel supplied. "Go on."

"A very angry." Manda could not continue. The silence dragged on. Manda seemed to be fascinated by her hands.

Joel did not like the sound of her breathing, shallow and labored. Her hands were trembling, and he could see bruises on her wrists and lower arms.

Fear replaced his rage. "Manda, what's been going on in that house the past fourteen months?"

Incapable of answering, Manda folded into herself, trembling.

"Okay, we're finished, for now. Tell me what you need."

She just shook her head. He moved carefully off the desk and crouched down beside her chair. "When is the last time you ate a meal?"

"I don't know," she said in barely a whisper.

"Can you eat something?"

She nodded gratefully.

Joel's call to James in the breakfast room landed them a private table, a full breakfast, and a pot of coffee. Joel worked on his smartphone while Manda worked her way through a plate of eggs, a bowl of fruit, and three croissants with strawberry jam and butter. When she pushed the plate away, he silenced the smartphone. She sat, eyes down.

Joel sipped his coffee and studied her, wondering how a bright, beautiful Presidential Scholar could turn into a basket case without anyone at the college seeing it. Stellar grades, no doubt; was that all anyone paid attention to? He tapped a nervous rhythm on his coffee mug. No one at the Manse had seen the decline either, including himself. He watched Manda run her tongue over her lips, nervously, not seductively. That mouth of hers should be laughing, flirting, teasing. "You're a business major?" he asked, testing to see if she was ready to talk again.

"Accounting," she said and cleared the frog in her throat. "Business and accounting."

"Why?"

She turned puzzled eyes toward him. Beautiful, sapphire eyes. "Why?"

"I'm not a numbers guy. I can't imagine picking accounting as my major."

She let out her breath in a soft chuckle and smiled at him. "Numbers are fun. They're like Tinker Toys or Legos. You can line them up, build them on each other, manipulate and transform them, calculate them within an inch of their lives, and they just go right on being whatever they are. They'll tell you the right answer whether it's what you want to hear or not." She shrugged. "They have integrity."

Hidden message? he wondered. So she was giving him the right answers and she had integrity? He'd see about that.

Joel's eyes bore into hers, but he kept his voice casual. "Figures don't lie; liar's figure. Is that how it goes?"

"Got it in one."

He held up his right hand, and she gave him a high five. He challenged, "What famous person said that?"

"No clue. But she was right."

He laughed and threw her a curve. "Are you one of the liars?"

She shook her head and held his eyes. "I'm just one of the figurers."

"So, you love numbers but you didn't pick Math?"

"Too theoretical for me. I like to see how things operate."

"Do you like what you do here?"

She nodded with enthusiasm. "Being in the middle of a business is interesting, and Dan is a great supervisor. Well, you already know that. He is always willing to explain why things are done the way they are and to give me new work to challenge me."

Joel wanted to sip coffee and banter with her all morning. Too bad they had a pile of problems to fix right now. Maybe after this was over, and it would be over, he would see to that, maybe they could try this again. He shifted in his chair, and she seemed to pick up on his signal that the easy part was over.

"Thank you," she began, "for breakfast and for making me laugh. It's been a long time. And I'm sorry I snapped at you earlier. The day wasn't going real well for me."

"I got that." Her hair had dried in loose curls, and a few fell onto her forehead. He watched her push them back and saw them fall forward again. Part of him wanted to mess them up. He pulled himself up sharply.

Manda took a deep breath. "About your question," she prefaced, "the terms of my employment changed after Lorraine—Mrs. Kristof—left, and I didn't know how to handle it. What changed first is that she had paid me an allowance for groceries, and that stopped."

"So, Kristof never paid you? How did you pay for food and books?"

"I paid for them myself. Sometimes—" she hesitated.

"Go on," Joel ordered.

"I do people's taxes for them sometimes, and they pay me in cash. That helps."

He didn't care if she was being paid under the table. "I understand. What else changed after Lorraine left?"

"I was stupid and all alone out there and I let myself be pressured and threatened into being . . . available whenever he wanted me."

"Sexually?"

She nodded, without meeting his eyes.

His heart raced with anger. "Threatened how?"

"At first it was about kicking me out of his house, but it wasn't long before he realized that wasn't much of a threat, and I know I shouldn't have stayed. But by the time I realized it, he had me convinced he'd fix it so I'd lose my scholarship if I didn't do as he said. I was just so scared about that. I started drinking more, drinking a lot, to just get through another night; to just keep the lid on, get the grades, and graduate."

She took a deep breath and put one hand on her stomach, as if willing it to settle down.

Joel knew James would have a fit if she hurled on the white linen cloth.

"And I guess I wasn't properly humiliated or degraded enough or who knows." She had lined up three spoons, and now she flipped one off the table. "So," she started to say and had to catch her breath. "It got physical and then violent and then sick and," she shook her head, unable to go on.

Joel consciously relaxed the white-knuckle grip he had on his coffee mug. "Manda, did Kristof give you the bruises I saw in the shower this morning?"

A strangled sound came from across the table.

He watched Manda's composure disintegrate and tried to detach from her anguish, knowing they had to name it and deal with whatever had happened. And yes, they both had to deal with it. Partly because it was his responsibility as her boss, and partly because he served as a trustee of the college, although he wasn't going to tell her that. They'd be lucky if she didn't sue the whole college.

"Manda, have you talked with your parents about what's been going on?"

She shook her head. "They're both dead," she managed to say.

He knew how that felt.

"My aunt took care of us before college. She died a few years ago."

"How old are you?"

"Twenty-two."

"You said your aunt 'took care of us.' Who's 'us'?"

"My sister Lyssa. She's in Austin, at UT in a doctoral program in economics. Also heavy into weed. It's hard to have a conversation with her, and, well, she's not able to help."

"You said weed?"

Manda nodded. "Since she stopped drinking. She calls it her marijuana maintenance plan."

"Where have I heard that before?"

"I thought she made it up." Manda's face was wet with tears again. She'd saturated her napkin, so she snuffled her nose. "I just wanted to finish college and that's all I knew how to do. I know I messed up."

She looked him in the eye and he saw no guile there.

"Joel, I need help. I don't know how to fix any of this."

Joel fought against his inclination to put an arm around her, comfort her pain. He wished he could erase whatever had happened to hold her prisoner and finally drive her out of the swanky million-dollar house on the lake into the icy rain to spend a sleepless night in her wreck of a car.

Manda's hands were shaking even though they were clasped together on the tabletop. Joel reached across the table and covered her hands with his warm ones. She did not pull away. "Manda, it will be all right," he reassured. "You will be all right. People will help you."

She choked, "I am so sorry. I have disrupted your work and Remy's and probably embarrassed you in front of everyone here."

He squeezed her hands. When she winced with pain, he pulled his hands away but let his fingers just touch hers. "This is not about me. And no one is watching us." He had seated them so he had full view of the dining room and she had as much privacy as possible. "There are two diners reading their newspapers, oblivious, sipping their coffee; everyone else has left; and the staff knows to leave us alone."

He thought he heard her whisper, "Thank you."

He tapped her right hand with his finger. "And I know you are afraid of a lot more than being fired."

She met his eyes, and he saw how intensely blue they were and how filled with fear and something worse. *Desperation*. He knew how that felt as well.

"I am going to get us fresh coffee. Then I need you to help me lay out some next steps. Another croissant?"

She nodded. "And butter and strawberry jam, too, please."

He smothered a laugh. "That's my girl."

He took his time, stopping to ask the remaining diners about their breakfast and their stay. On his return he juggled two mugs of steaming coffee and a plate with a buttery croissant so fresh and appetizing he wished he hadn't banned all pastries from his food plan.

He saw that she had commandeered a stack of crisp white linen napkins. A soggy pile beside her plate gave evidence she'd blown her nose with gusto using half a dozen of them. She had soaked one napkin in her glass of ice water and was holding the compress tight against her eyes. James would have a fit if she left mascara stains.

"These are the world's best croissants," he announced. He scooped the pile of soggy napkins onto her empty plate and set it aside. He watched with relief as she set down the makeshift eye compress, free of makeup.

He knew he needed to be scrupulously professional right now. He sat down with deliberate slowness, unbuttoned his cashmere jacket, and crossed one elegantly tailored leg over the other, a Joel Cushman trademark move. A question flashed through his mind. Which Joel did Manda like better, the one that was smooth and in control or the one that mangled paper clips and made her laugh and pushed her to be honest? *Get over yourself, Cushman.*

"Are you going to fire me?" Manda wanted to know.

"I'm not sure yet." He took a long drink of coffee, and set down the mug. "Either way, you are not off the hook."

"I know." She pulled off one flaky layer of her croissant and slowly ate it.

He watched in fascination. He didn't think she was toying with him, just being methodical as accountants were.

"I just started with the easy one," she said, and spread butter and jam on the rest of the croissant.

"Are we talking the easiest layer of the croissant or…"

She laughed and shook her head.

Encouraged, he said, "Let me start with a simple question, and I'm looking for a brutally honest answer here." She had the most beautiful eyes. Why had he ever thought she was a frump? Manda Doughty had sounded like Manda Dowdy to him, and it fit. He'd never looked past the baggy, shapeless clothes and the over-sized eyeglass frames. "You're not wearing your glasses," he realized.

"I think I left them in the shower. And least I hope that's where they are. But that wasn't your question."

He sat up straighter and tried to put his mind back on business. Where was he going? Ah, the drinking. "Manda, I know that most nights you go directly to the bar with some of the staff and have a strong scotch before you leave the Manse. The bartender jokes with you when you ask for another and says he'll have the cops tail you. You laugh and leave without a second. And probably have more when you get home—am I right?"

She nodded, stunned. "A lot more. More all the time."

"But last night you stayed late in the office. What were you working on?"

"I hadn't been productive for a couple of days," she confessed, "and I wanted to finish some work Dan needs by the end of the week."

"Did you finish?"

"Yes, I left a note for Dan and went home around nine or a little later."

"I understand you didn't stop at the bar for a scotch, even though your friends were still there."

"Do you know what everybody drinks?"

"I do. It's a habit that has paid off."

Manda looked like she wanted to ask him about that sometime.

Joel went on, "I'm thinking whatever went horribly wrong last night—that explosion—had been building up. And you'd had enough. Last night when you went home, you walked in there sober and put an end to it for yourself, no matter what. Does that sum it up for you?"

Manda sat rigid in her chair like a bird trying to be invisible to a hawk. Joel knew he had nailed it for her.

When he let out his breath, she answered, her voice incredulous. "Exactly. That is exactly what it adds up to. How could you know that?"

"Why yesterday?"

"I was done. I knew the only possible way my life could change was if I didn't have that first scotch after work and then get drunk when I got home. Does that make any sense?"

He nodded. "Tell me more about that." He sat back and saw her relax.

"I had to stop living the way I was living, doing what I was doing. And yesterday—" she shook her head. "I don't know why it was yesterday. Nothing was different. Except I…" Her voice trailed off. When she spoke again, it was with conviction. "I just knew if I didn't stop drinking nothing was going to get any better."

She shook her head, apparently at a loss to explain it any better. "When I saw Kristof was home, I left my coat and my purse in the car, and I was hoping I could grab my laptop and get out without any trouble. Dumb me, I didn't plan it any better than that."

"Not much of a bail-out plan," he said lightly.

There was that soft smile of hers again and those eyes, sad enough to melt a heart. She was looking past him now, toward the display for the wine cellar, not seeing the hand-picked bottles on the velvet-covered perches and the hand-lettered signs, seeing instead whatever had happened after she went through the front door of the Kristof house on Cady's Point.

Joel gave her a minute and then prompted, "So you went home sober and everything exploded?"

"Yes, he was there, and there was no escaping a confrontation." She tried to meet his eyes but looked away, shame dulling her gaze. "It was so clear this time. I could see how he operated. I refused to play the sordid game. He got angry. And I still refused." She was breathing in little gasps now. "And refused. And finally he exploded, and I fought. I fought for my life. No matter what, I was going to get out of there, and I did."

Joel reached his hands toward her without touching her.

"When I finally got free, I ran and didn't look back."

"So is that the end of it?" he asked, meaning the end of the relationship with Kristof. Because if it wasn't, he was going to be really sad with the realization that this beautiful, smart, funny woman was a lost cause.

"It has to be the end of it. I can't live my life that way. It's not who I can be and should be and want to be."

That wasn't the answer Joel needed to hear. "So you're not going back to Cady's Point?"

She looked like she was considering it.

"Or are you?"

"I will figure out a way to reconstruct the work on my laptop and how to finish my courses without books or notes."

"Or clothes or makeup or a warm bed."

Manda rolled her eyes as if he was being dense. "I have a bigger problem." She looked him straight in the eye. "What I meant when I said it had better be over is that my parents were both alcoholics, and it killed them, and I'm pretty sure I'm one, too."

From the way her voice shook on the word "alcoholic," he knew it was the first time she'd identified herself as one.

"What I became in that house this past year, drinking more all the time to pretend it wasn't happening… I need this nightmare to be finished." She looked him in the eye. "That's not what you wanted to hear from the Manse's accounting assistant, is it?"

He let out his breath all at once and gave himself a mental slap. Manda Doughty wasn't looking for a date with Prince Charming. She needed a substance abuse counselor, and she was looking for an employer's response. He gave her the best one he had. "If you start drinking again, you're history here. If you do the footwork to stay sober, I will support you in any way I can."

"What footwork?" she started to ask.

"Sir, will there be anything else for you and the lady?" James called from the doorway.

Manda said under her breath, "The lady, right."

"Thank you, James. The lady and I are just finishing and will be out of your way momentarily." Joel stood up and helped her to her feet. It did not surprise him that she swayed at first. He kept his hand on her back as they walked out of the breakfast room. "Task number one," he directed Manda, "you will check the shower for your glasses. Can you do that?"

She nodded.

"And I will find out if Professor Kristof is at home. As soon as the way is clear, we will drive over there to retrieve your laptop, etc. and then drop you at the college for a long talk with the substance abuse counselor." He was already punching buttons on his smartphone. He sensed resistance. "Any argument so far?"

"No argument, but I need a bodyguard."

He searched her face and remembered the bruises on her arms and belly and back and thighs. She was right; Sir Lancelot on a white horse was not the solution. "I'll take care of it. Find your glasses; make a list of everything you want to rescue from the house; prioritize it, because you'll have very little time to get it and get out. I'll meet you out front in one hour." He tapped her watch. "Eleven o'clock sharp." He gave her a gentle push toward the spa, and signaled Remy to let her pass into the guest locker area.

Joel stood a moment watching her, trying to make sense of the beautiful, bruised, naked woman in the shower, dressed now in someone else's classy clothes, admitting her alcoholism, and doggedly trying to complete her semester's work at the college, come what may.

Manda Doughty was tempting, but the whole package was too hot to handle.

Right now he needed to do some serious digging into her story and re-think all his assumptions about his junior accountant. And involve the authorities. And dig into Kristof's extracurricular activities. And the Presidential Scholars debacle. He gave Remy a brief, "Thanks for your help with this," to tell Remy that letting an employee use the spa showers was not the biggest problem today.

Remy nearly shook with relief. "Anything else I can do, boss?"

"Find her a scarf or something." Joel took a back stairway to his office, the smartphone at his ear.

Joel speed-dialed the office of the president at Tompkins College. "Wendy, it's Joel. I need time today with the president on an urgent matter."

The unflappable secretary offered, "One o'clock?"

"Beautiful." Joel pitched a jumbo paper clip in the direction of the wastebasket and missed by a few inches. "Please organize a conference call at two for as many trustees as you can manage." The next shot hit the wall. "And I need to be connected to the provost's office immediately."

"Lydia is with Professor Kristof until noon on an urgent matter."

Joel absorbed the information. "Then half of my agenda will come as no shock to her."

"I can schedule you for noon in her office. I'll have lunch sent in for both of you."

"Good. Salad and iced tea for me." Joel tried again, and the paper clip ricocheted off the wall into the basket. "Who would I speak with to have a student see a substance abuse counselor, the sexual harassment liaison, a physician, and a therapist in that order this afternoon?"

"I will set that up for you, Joel. May I tell them the name of the student?"

"Manda Doughty." He spelled it. "Honor student, senior, works for me at the Manse."

"That's a new one. I'll get back to you with her appointment times. Any parameters?"

"Starting shortly after noon, running no later than four o'clock. I need to have her see an eye doctor for a new pair of glasses at four."

"Am I scheduling that?"

"I am. Is Tony Pinelli on today?"

There was a delay while Wendy looked up the daily schedule for campus security. Joel opened a few more jumbo paper clips to just the right angle for smooth sailing; he pitched one and it dinged the side of the basket.

"Tony is not on today." Wendy's voice held a question.

"Good. I will have him deliver Manda to campus for her first appointment and return for her in time for the eye doctor."

"You had me worried there."

"Tony is part of the solution. One more thing, Wendy, and this may be impossible, I understand, even for a miracle worker like you."

He heard her chuckle across the connection. "Lay it on me, Joel."

"I need a safe place for Manda to live for the remainder of the semester. Can you find a place on campus?"

"I'll do my best. Assuming I succeed, I'll need an account number to cover this," she added tactfully.

"Pick one and I'll cover it." The paper clip landed squarely in the wastebasket this time. "Thank you, as always, Wendy."

The next call was to his friend Tony Pinelli. "Need you to transport a student," Joel prefaced, "and do a little AA twelfth step work and body guarding at the same time."

"I'm your man," Tony agreed without question. "You coming with us?"

"If I can get away, yes," he said at first. "Or not. I'm not sure I want her to know I'm in AA at this point. Listen, pal, I know when we talk to a drunk about the AA program for the first time, we're advised not to do it alone, but she's already convinced about her alcoholism."

"So it's more of a 'get acquainted with how the AA program can help her.' Sure, I'm cool with that. Are you serious about the body guarding?"

"She's got a body covered with serious bruises, and she's terrified. I'm counting on you to find out everything you can about what happened to her last night. I'm meeting with the provost at noon about the professor in question."

"Why noon?"

"Because the provost is in a closed session with him until then. I need you to be here at the Manse by eleven and out of the Kristof house by noon."

Tony whistled. "Kristof? News to me," he told his friend. "And our mission is?"

"Retrieve as much of her stuff as she wants and document anything you can about what's been happening in that house."

"You called the cops yet?"

Joel's stomach took a dive. "No. I'll do that."

"Have someone meet us at the house or at least be in the area. You talked with Lorraine yet?"

"My next call. Gotta go, pal."

Joel put in a call to Lorraine Kristof at her ivy-covered mansion in the Thames valley west of London. Next, he arranged an emergency visit for Manda to his own eye doctor at four o'clock. "Check her vision and have her pick out new, very chic frames. This is on me, Paulette. Anything you can do to make this an upbeat experience for her will be much appreciated."

Joel hesitated, gathered his courage, and made the next call. "Chief, Joel Cushman. Thank you for taking my call. One of my employees, who is also a student at the college, has made me aware of a crime committed against her by her employer, who is also a professor. I don't know where the definition of domestic violence begins and ends; she was until yesterday his live-in housekeeper, and the home was the scene of the crime. The college will investigate from the standpoint of sexual harassment, but I believe this also involves you." He inhaled deeply, held the breath, and exhaled to clear the turmoil in his stomach.

"If there has been sexual activity between the employer and the live-in employee, whether consensual or coerced, then yes, we do need to be involved."

"I understand it was coerced." Joel noticed his knuckles were white, and he willed his fingers to let go of his coffee mug.

"Joel I can hear how difficult this is for you. I need you to answer some questions now, and we will need to talk with the student as soon as it can be arranged."

Joel responded to the police chief's questions as directly and completely as he could. They agreed a car would be in the area when Manda went back to Kristof's for her things later this morning, and they agreed Manda's interview would be handled by a policewoman at the college during Manda's round of appointments this afternoon.

"Joel, I hear your tension." His old friend asked, "What's your biggest worry that I can address?"

"Her safety first. Also, the publicity. Both the impact on the young woman, who is fragile at this point, and on the college."

"We'll determine the right measures to safeguard her. That's our job, and we do it well. I'll do what I can around the publicity. It's not the first time I've heard this professor's name, and nothing's been in the media yet."

"You've heard his name in connection with this student and this situation?"

"Not at all. Between you and me, he's a smooth operator, well connected. If he's come to your attention, though, he's making very big mistakes. We'll get him. The report from you and from the student will help."

Joel let out his breath as he hung up from the call. His hands were shaking, but he knew he wasn't finished with his mental to-do list. What was he missing?

He called catering and arranged for breakfast in his office at eight o'clock the next morning, dictating Manda's preferred menu and his own. He put in a call to his attorney; he would leave it to the president to engage the attorneys for the college.

He walked to the window and looked out at the woods, still choked with snow. The bare trees were quiet right now, but he had seen robins this week, so spring was not far away. The minutes stretched on without a return call from Lorraine or his attorney. The hour he'd given Manda to get ready was running out.

Joel decided he needed his workout in the fitness center more than he needed to accompany Tony to the Kristof home. He would give Manda a positive send-off with Tony. Even though it was against the rules, he'd take his phone to the weight room. He needed Lorraine Kristof's input for his discussions with the provost, the president of the college, and the trustees.

He reached for another jumbo paper clip. "Catherine," he called to his secretary, "I'm out of paper clips again. I'll be in the weight room from eleven to eleven forty-five and at the college for several hours this afternoon. Reschedule whatever you can."

On his way out, he saw Catherine staring at him.

"Please," he added. "And why not take a long lunch today."

Manda was waiting at the curb when he stepped through the front door into dazzling sunshine. He told her, "My good friend Tony P. is on his way, and he'll drive you to Cady's Point. I have a crisis."

"Ran out of white linen napkins?" Manda guessed.

Joel grinned. "If we can keep you out of the dining room, we may make it through dinner." What was it about this woman that made him laugh in the face of life-changing circumstances for her and professional crises for him? "You didn't find your glasses in the shower?"

Manda shook her head.

"No one had taken them to Lost and Found?"

Manda shook her head again and scanned the drive. A truck had turned in from the highway and was making its way up the tree-lined avenue. "They weren't in my car either."

Joel wondered if she'd lost them at the house last night. He decided not to push it. Let Tony find out.

He gave Manda the itinerary. "Tony will help you retrieve your things and keep them in his truck until we know where everything's going. He'll drop you at the college, where the substance abuse counselor is expecting you. Others at the college are on the hunt for housing for you for the rest of the semester."

"Joel, I can't afford it."

He squeezed her shoulders. "You're not responsible for the tab."

"Who is?"

"It's being taken care of. Don't fight it," he told her.

She opened her mouth to protest but closed it again. "Thank you," she said humbly.

"And if it doesn't work out living in the dorms, I expect you to tell me. Sooner rather than later. I need you to keep your priorities straight," he ordered.

She repeated their agreement. "I will keep my mind on my courses and on my work, and I will stay away from booze in any form."

"Good. Go," He propelled her toward Tony's battered white truck. "Check in with me first thing tomorrow. Eight o'clock sharp."

Manda waved her understanding.

Joel reached a decision. Whether Lorraine approved his plan for compensating Manda or not, this was his one and only opportunity. As Manda pulled open the passenger door, Joel called back to Tony, "Look for the bike. We can park it here for now." With that, he hustled back inside.

Manda contemplated the giant step up into the cab.

"You okay there?" Tony asked. He held out a big square hand to her. She took his hand and let him draw her up onto the seat. "You know me from the college," he introduced himself. "Tony Pinelli. I work Security, and I teach the self-defense classes."

"Manda Doughty," she told him. "Your class saved my life last night."

Tony had pulled away from the curb, but he slowed at her statement and threw the truck into park. If this woman was lying, he wanted to know it now. He tested, "Should I be carrying?" He saw the fear in her eyes and noticed a bruise on her neck that wasn't quite covered by the jazzy silk scarf.

Tony climbed out of the cab, unlocked a box in the back, rummaged through, and tucked his gun under his jacket.

"Anything else you need to tell me about this mission?" he asked as they resumed the drive.

"Does your cell phone take photos?"

He nodded.

"Unless the cleaning crew has been there already today, you'll see what I want recorded."

Tony maneuvered the truck onto the highway and pressed the accelerator. "Planning to sue the guy?"

She shook her head. "I want some documentation. I don't think he's finished with me, and I need to protect myself."

"I'll bet this cleaning crew knows a few things," Tony offered. "Any idea who they are?"

"No, and I'm sure they're well compensated to keep quiet and remove the evidence."

"So, we need a plan for today," Tony told her. "Joel is sure Kristof is in a meeting at the college until noon. That gives us about an hour." He was betting Manda didn't know the level of Joel's involvement. Nor would he, Tony, clue her in. "That may seem like a long time to grab a laptop, but when it comes right down to it, can you make fast decisions about what's most important to take and what you can do without?"

She nodded.

"Where are we likely to find a bicycle?"

"Garage. I don't have a key, though."

"No problemo. I moonlight as a private eye." He finally got a smile out of her.

"From the looks of this truck, you moonlight as a carpenter."

"Joel said you were bright."

"Time I started using my brain instead of hiding my head in a bottle of scotch."

Tony told her, "We call that denial. It makes everything worse."

"You think? I was in deep, and the only part I knew how to handle was studying and working. I just pretended the bad stuff would go away."

"How'd that work for you?" Tony said with a knowing smile.

Manda wasn't smiling. "Except for studying and working, drinking took over my life."

"You flunking out?"

"No, I'm still getting good grades, and my boss likes my work. Unless Joel decides to fire me."

"I think that's up to you. You hold up your end of the bargain, he'll hold up his."

Manda let out a sigh of relief. "Thank you for saying that."

"You are one brave chick, if you don't mind my saying so."

She rolled her eyes at him.

He insisted, "It took a lot of guts to come clean with the big boss about what's been happening. And to come back with me to the scene of the crime. What's so funny?"

Manda laughed. "The 'brave chick' thing. More like 'desperate.' I'd skip this mission if I didn't know my glasses are somewhere in the living room and my laptop is in my bedroom. I can't believe I drove without my glasses last night. I am seriously near-sighted."

"Were you drunk?"

"No, for a change."

"I'm pretty sure I heard you tell Joel you're planning to stay away from booze."

Manda nodded and looked unsure about what to say about that.

Tony told her, "I've been sober six years. Went to AA. Best thing I ever did."

Manda swiveled toward him. "No way."

Tony grinned. "Way."

"What's it like?" she pumped him. "Do you still go to meetings?"

"Every day I can." He told her about his first AA meeting, the sense of belonging he felt right away. "Everybody drank like I did and reached the point where they couldn't go on drinking and have any kind of a life."

Manda was nodding, though she didn't seem ready to disclose any more details about her drinking.

He told her people welcomed him and wanted him to stay sober and be happy and useful like they were. "I'll take you to a meeting this weekend if you want. There's a hot dog meeting in Canandaigua Saturday night at seven."

"Yeah, I'd really like that. What's a hot dog meeting?"

"They serve hot dogs at the end of the meeting."

Manda laughed. "Some things are what they sound like."

"You're right, we have our own vocabulary. You'll get used to it. And, listen, no funny stuff out of me. I'm not looking to jump your bones. I've got a girlfriend. She might even come with us."

Suddenly Manda dissolved in tears. She choked out, "Are there any girls my age at meetings?"

Tony reached under the seat for a grimy box of tissues. "Yes, guys, too, but you'll want to keep your focus on recovery for a while. Stick with the women." He watched her pull tissues out of the box as if she were planning for a flood of tears. "You go right ahead and cry, honey. You don't ever have to feel this bad again."

She let the tears flow while Tony drove seven miles down the lake road and a mile on the gravel access lane to Cady's Point. He pulled out his cell phone and speed-dialed Joel for a cryptic update.

Manda was still blowing her nose when Tony stopped the truck, hopped out and opened the garage door without a key. He disappeared into the first of four bays.

Moments later he gave a shout from the cavernous depth. "Do me a favor, Manda. Open the back of the truck. One bicycle coming up."

When he emerged with a shiny yellow Georgina Terry custom hybrid, Manda shook her head. "Tony, that's not mine. It's Lorraine's."

"Lorraine ain't coming back for it. You like it?"

"It's great, but—"

"Joel asked me to get it. Let's not waste time," he told her. "Where's your room and your stuff?"

"Around the back, but there's too much snow and crud to cart stuff from the back door. The best way is through the front."

"That's using your head," he praised, but he was worried. She was trembling all over. He didn't think it was withdrawal so much as delayed reaction to trauma. He wanted to keep her focused and busy. "Lead the way, Manda," he said with a comical arm wave toward the front of the house.

Manda walked ahead of him to the limestone portico. She fumbled with her key until Tony took it from her hand. He made short work of the lock, and pushed open the heavy teak door.

"You weren't kidding," he breathed when he saw the wreckage. Two chairs lay where they'd been hurled. Vases and glassware were shattered, a table overturned. The place stank of liquor spilled from a bottle used as a weapon.

Tony kicked his way into the room, snapping photos as he went. He spotted what he was looking for on the hearth. When he picked up Manda's eyeglasses, ground to a mangled mess, he felt in his gut the full force of what she'd gone through in this room the night before.

"I know you were hoping to find these intact," he said as he turned back to Manda.

She had her arms wrapped around herself, shaking, leaning heavily on the doorframe, her face white, her breathing ragged.

"Come on, honey," Tony urged. "Look at me, Manda."

She met his eyes but did not budge.

"The war is over, and we're walking through this together for the next forty-five minutes." He beckoned with his right hand. "I need your help, if we're going to accomplish what we came to do. Now walk toward me."

She came forward, eyes on him, not daring to look anywhere else. He tucked the mangled glasses in his jacket pocket, reached for her hand, and wrapped his arm around her shoulders. "You show me the way to your room. Let's be quick."

While Tony stuffed her clothes and toiletries into a duffle, Manda disconnected her printer and router and laptop. "We'll take these to the truck and come back for the books. I spotted some boxes in the garage. Let's move." It took two trips to collect all of Manda's books and notebooks. He could see her trembling again, but he knew there was more she wanted to collect. This was their only chance.

As he shoved the box of books onto the truck, Tony suggested, "Let's take a five-minute break right now. I want you to calm down, use your head, and decide what else you have here that you need. We will have exactly fifteen minutes." When she didn't argue, he walked around the truck and lit a cigarette.

Manda sat on a boulder at the edge of the driveway, pulled her knees to her chest, and focused on her breathing. She remembered a long walk she'd taken in the snowy woods before Lorraine left. She thought of the bike rides in the morning, and the evening swims in the lake. It had not always been a nightmare. After a few minutes she felt her heart beating normally again.

She slipped off the boulder and watched Tony stub out the cigarette. She squared her shoulders and told him quietly, "I'm not a thief, and I don't feel right taking Lorraine's bike, but I am owed some other things. Lorraine gave me a food budget, but for a year I've been paying out of pocket. There are things in the kitchen I can use and towels and sheets in the linen closet near my room."

Tony looked at his watch and proposed, "We'll split up. I'll grab the linens. Two boxes enough for the kitchen?"

While Tony packed up the linens, he heard a car crunch on the gravel drive. From the window, he saw two officers emerge from their cruiser. One was his friend Lou. Tony raised the window, leaned out, and waved them over.

"We're almost finished here," he told them. "We want to be out of here by the time Kristof gets back. You'll want to have a conversation with him and see the state of the living room." He shook his head, still not believing the scene.

"The chief says Miriam will be talking with the young woman this afternoon," Lou told him. "She's a real pro talking with women who've been involved in domestic violence and sexual abuse."

"Good. Manda's a nice kid. Look, let me finish and get her out of here."

"Right. We're continuing to the end of the lane—the usual run—and then coming back here to the house to wait for Kristof. Good seeing you, Tony."

Manda worked quickly in the kitchen, pulling her most-used cookware, utensils, bake ware, recipes, and spices, her favorite apron, mitts, and towels. She carted her first box out to the truck and hurried back. The second box was for the pantry, which held bags of rice and flour, jars of pepper sauce and green chilies, her favorite chicken stock, Lorraine's crackers and tea from England that Kristof never touched.

She was halfway across the kitchen with the box when she heard Kristof's car skidding and spraying up gravel as he swung into the driveway. "Tony!" she screamed. She judged she could not make it through the media room and out the back door ahead of Kristof. "Help me!"

She set down the box and looked for the nearest weapon. The designer bronze teakettle on the six-burner range was heavy with water. Holding it with two hands, she knew she could fling it at Kristof and do damage. Where was Tony?

"Caught you!" Kristof shouted with triumph from the front entry. His eyes shone as he crossed the space to the kitchen; she knew he was high on something.

Manda listened for any sound that would tell her where Tony was. She had to trust he was there for her. She planted her feet and drew in a steadying breath as Kristof entered the kitchen.

He came within range, and she hurled the heavy kettle at his head. He fended it off with his arm but roared with pain. The blow forced him to pause and test his injured arm. He eyed her with hate. "This time you're dead!"

Manda felt her stomach contract. She took one step back and saw Tony emerge from the media room, gun drawn. He planted himself halfway between Manda and Kristof.

"You're on video with that threat, professor. I have stills of the living room showing what went on here last night. And the police are on their way back up the lane as we speak. Back off now."

"Or what? You'll shoot me, Pinelli? You'll lose your job for discharging a weapon in the line of duty."

"Not on duty for the college now, Kristof. This young woman's employer believes she is danger. From you. If you do not cease and desist, I will discharge this weapon where it will do the most good for womankind."

The two eyed each other, Tony watching for any movement, Kristof eyeing the gun and the direction it was pointing.

In the lengthening silence, neither man gave credence to Manda's quiet statement, "Thanks, Tony, I've got this one." She brushed past Tony, who watched in fascination as Manda slammed her knee into Kristof's groin. She stepped back, twisted to the right, moved her left elbow into position, and unwound a cracking blow to Kristof's temple. The professor dropped without a sound.

Manda grabbed her elbow sucked air through her teeth. "Man, that hurt!" She watched Tony reach toward the body, gun still drawn.

Tony felt for a pulse at Kristof's neck.

"Did I kill him?"

"No way, but he'll be out for a good long time." Tony straightened up and let out a laugh of disbelief. "Wish I had that knee-elbow combo on video. You could inspire next year's entire freshman class."

Manda tried to laugh through her tears. She glanced at the front entry and saw spinning red lights. Two burly men walked through the door. Was she losing her mind?

"Not to alarm you, honey, but the police just pulled in."

Manda felt lightheaded. She tried to listen while Tony explained, "The police are going to have a word with the good professor as soon as he comes to, and you'll be talking with a policewoman this afternoon about what's been happening here. She's absolutely great, and you can say anything to her. We're all going to walk through this with you, honey."

Tony caught Manda as she doubled over, and she felt his arms hold her caringly while she threw up her entire breakfast right beside Kristof's crumpled body.

Chapter 2

Joel's smartphone roused him from a troubled sleep at two in the morning. "What?" he muttered.

"And a fine good morning to you, too, Nephew."

"Justin, where are you?"

"Back of beyond. I got your message on my wall."

"You're too old to use Facebook. Why don't you have an email address like everyone else your age?"

"Hey, I return your call, and you complain about my communication habits. What's up with that?"

"All right. Let's start over." Joel let out a cleansing breath and breathed in another one. "Thanks for getting back to me, Uncle."

"What can I do for you, Nephew?"

"The college that bears my mother's name is harboring a predator who's been beating up on and having his way with one of my employees, and—"

"Not so fast. Is this young woman of age?"

"She's twenty-two."

"And is it consensual?"

"No. It's long-term and coerced."

"Technically, she was free to walk away?"

"Technically." Joel's tone was sour.

"You asked for counsel. I'm trying to point out what others would see in the same circumstances."

"Neanderthals, maybe. The police are prepared to protect her."

"I've never known you to involve the police."

"Are you opposed?"

STEPPING UP TO LOVE | 34

"No. Just surprised. Normally, the college covers up its dirty secrets, and I know that has always bothered you. What's different about this?"

"Is was the right thing to do."

"Do you have a thing for the young woman?"

Joel yelled, "He threatened her with loss of her scholarship, and finishing her degree seems to be the only thing she cares about right now, besides getting sober."

"Ah, so you identify with her as a very young person that needs to get sober?"

"Yes," he snapped.

"And you have a thing for her?"

Joel threw his pillow across the room. "Beside the point."

"Not if you act on it," Justin said sternly. "While she's a student at your college and particularly while she's going through whatever ordeal she's going through, keep your hands off her."

"I know all that," Joel said impatiently. "Look I need your counsel about my options here."

"You have no options for the girl."

"For the college," Joel growled.

He laid out the situation with the professor who had been sexually harassing more students than Manda, according to the provost. Three young women had come forward together last week, and Lydia suspected there were more. "I told Lydia I would support any investigation she or the president believed was necessary."

"This must be a nightmare for them. I'm sure they appreciate your support."

Joel was quiet too long.

"What am I missing?" Justin prompted.

"For one thing, the professor's identity."

"Who is it?"

"Kristof. Lorraine's ex."

"Your ex's ex?" Justin let out a roar of laughter at his own cleverness.

Joel let him have the point without further comment.

"Well, I feel bad for her—Lorraine, that is. When you broke off the engagement, she picked up with this character because he was devastatingly handsome and brilliant—good qualities for the children she desperately wanted to have. Judging by how it's worked out, she should have had him investigated before she married him. Is she still 'newly single'?"

"Newly single and living with the children in the UK in a sleepy valley where several college roommates also have estates. She'll find Mr. Right one of these days. I spoke with her this afternoon, and she confirmed the story. I gave her hell for abandoning her student housekeeper to her lothario husband, and she blew it off." Joel let out his breath in a pained sigh. "You knew her better than I did."

"Yes, but it doesn't make me happy to hear that admission. Watch yourself. She may come back for you now that you've made contact with her."

"Don't go there," Joel warned him. "Listen, there's another matter that is almost certainly unrelated, except it was the beginning of Manda's trouble with the Kristofs."

"Manda is your young woman's name?"

"Yes." Joel got out of bed and paced while he talked. "Three years ago all of us trustees were convinced by some slick talkers to cut the Presidential Scholars program down to just tuition support. The promised follow-through with the students never happened. When I asked Lydia about it this noon, she went so pale I thought she was having a heart attack."

"Lydia being the provost?"

"Who I would have sworn was above reproach."

"Perhaps she is, but she inadvertently received some information and is being bullied into silence."

"I hadn't thought of that."

"Did you get out of her what she knows?"

"No, I dropped it for now. I don't want to be responsible for a stroke or a heart attack."

"What do you think is going on?"

"I think embezzlement is going on."

"I agree, that's what it sounds like."

"And I can't believe we were all conned."

"So your ego is banged up?"

"True."

"What have you done so far, besides querying Lydia who you thought would have no clue?"

"When I met with the president, I mentioned the Presidential Scholars, and he dismissed it as unimportant. In fairness, he had just been informed about Lydia's confrontation with Kristof. We agreed the president would quietly launch an investigation relative to Kristof and the students he has used and abused."

"And Miss Manda's name will be in the spotlight."

"Thanks for pointing that out," Joel said dryly. He leaned his forehead against the cold glass of the French doors to his porch and looked out at the lake.

"Can't be helped," Justin said brusquely. "Does she have assets of an academic or business nature that will get her through?"

"She's exceptionally bright, hard working, and honest. Yes, she'll weather the storm with AA's help."

"So where are we? Working our way up from provost to president to trustees. What have you told the board?"

"At the president's request, I did not tell them about Kristof, but I did tell them about the mishandling of the Presidential Scholars."

"And?"

"They are as angry as I am about being duped. They have authorized a quiet but thorough investigation."

"Good. Who will conduct the board's investigation?"

"The board secretary with—it is assumed—the full cooperation of the college treasurer. We'll involve two people from the ethics committee who are above reproach. The board agrees we will ask for a full accounting by the end of the academic year. June thirtieth."

"Less than four months. Did I hear an 'or else' in that statement?"

"That's where I need your counsel."

"How are you inclined to complete the 'or else'?"

"I expect a full accounting with swift and appropriate consequences to those involved, or I will resign from the board and withdraw all financial support from the Tompkins estate. I will further request that the college either close its doors or change its name."

Justin was quiet, and Joel took the opportunity to get his breathing under control. A full moon played peek-a-boo behind the clouds, and the sight made him smile. It was a full minute before Justin answered, "I support that. I fully support that."

"Thank you. Tell me your thinking."

"I think your mother's ancestors who founded the college were scoundrels, and so are the people who've been running the place ever since then. It is both honorable and inconvenient that you are not a scoundrel. Realistically, I think it's unlikely you will get a full accounting or swift and appropriate consequences for the wrongdoers. Even by the end of the calendar year. Are you prepared to follow through?"

"I don't know yet. I need to think it through before I make any statement along those lines. The economy is bad enough without putting the whole college out of work."

"Yes, I agree. And you do realize these investigations may come to the attention of the media?

Joel wished he could float away on the moon. "I do. Scandal has its own way of crippling a college. So my bottom-line question to you: Is there a way to protect those who are not involved, those who are doing a good job for the students and for the college?"

"That's why we have Unemployment."

"Be serious."

"I will give it more thought, but that may be my best answer. And I want your assurance that you will use your head where the young woman is concerned. Until she graduates and until the investigation is finished, you have no business getting involved with her."

Joel opened his hand and pressed it against the cool glass.

"I know you, Joel. I hear a tone in your voice when you're speaking about her that I have never heard you use. The kind of thing they write poetry about. I need you to use your brain, Joel, the one in your head."

Joel sighed deeply. "I know you don't want to hear this, but I wish you were here, wish you were closer and more accessible."

"I know you need a sounding board, and I know your network is mostly made up of people like me who think in dollar signs, not in terms of people's needs and the importance of the community."

"It's unbelievably valuable to me to have your input and your insight."

"You're handling it well, Joel. Personally I wish you didn't have to deal with the college at all. Part of me wishes you'd resign tomorrow and put your energy into the charitable foundation that I've been neglecting right along with you for a decade. Resign the board and let the chips fall where they may. I never liked that place. And I know it's harder for you because you have a conscience."

"Don't kid yourself, so do you have a conscience."

Justin laughed weakly. "Maybe that's what I'm running from."

"Where are you anyway?"

"London, leaving in a few hours for Indonesia."

"Oil?"

"Oil and other minerals."

"I need you to be safe. And get an email address, will you? They're free."

***

"Checking in as requested," Manda stood uneasily at Joel's office door the next morning. He turned to her, and his eyes lit up. She was glad she'd decided to wear the spa-castoff linen trousers again, paired with a pale gray turtleneck that looked decent tucked in. She stood tall and hoped she wasn't shaking.

"Good, I was getting hungry." Joel pressed the intercom, mumbled something into it and ushered her to a small table by the window.

Manda looked out at bare trees and a fountain shut off for the winter. *Why didn't he have an office overlooking the lake?*

Joel sat across from her. "Have you had breakfast?"

She shook her head. "Tony took me for a burger on the way home last evening. I'll get some groceries this noon so I can fix some meals."

"What's the dorm like?"

"It's a campus apartment for four. There's just one other girl, a junior, and we each have our own room with a bathroom, plus a little kitchen and a living room."

He toyed with his pen. "Is she okay?"

Manda shrugged. "I met her for, like, two minutes; she went off to 'study'; and I was asleep when she got back, which I think was early morning."

Joel's nod confirmed he knew more about the situation than she did.

She let it go. "Thank you for giving me a place to lay my weary head for the next eight weeks, but…"

"But what?"

"It's going to be a while before I can pay anyone back for it."

Joel gave her his "hawk" look, and she went rigid in her chair, at a loss to know what she'd said wrong.

He broke eye contact, toyed with his pen again, and set it down. "That's not necessary."

"Can we talk about this?"

Joel avoided her eyes.

"Joel—Mr. Cushman—"

"Joel."

"Joel, this is hard to say. When I lived at the Kristof's, I was dependent on them for a place to stay."

He was looking at her again with those smoky gray-green eyes that she didn't quite trust.

"It didn't go well for me. I don't want to be in that position again."

She saw a muscle twitch in his jaw.

"Ever. I know three months' room and board is—"

"Covered. Most colleges have a fund for students in good standing who are confronted with a financial emergency that threatens their ability to continue their studies."

Manda stayed quiet. Why hadn't he told her that when she brought it up yesterday?

Joel went on, "The college makes an investment so the student can get on his or her feet and finish the degree."

What he said sounded plausible to Manda, but she still felt uneasy. She knew if she asked further he would deflect her questions, no matter how she phrased them. She looked him in the eye, opened her mouth, and closed it again.

Joel's next words made her think he was on her side, if not exactly on her level. "Manda, no one wants a repeat of what happened. I'll just speak for me. I want you to graduate in May and have a great life. No delays, no more—" he shook his head, "no more worrying about where you're sleeping or how you're going to pay for a meal or replace a laptop."

Manda felt herself tear up. She felt about ten years old. Maybe, like the substance abuse counselor told her, she was just going through emotional withdrawal. Or—what was it?—post-trauma something.

Joel asked her, "What are you planning after you graduate?"

He was smiling now, and his eyes were warm and interested. Manda rallied a smile for him. She didn't trust her voice yet.

"Grad school? Marriage?"

She rolled her eyes. She was definitely off men for life, but she wasn't going to tell him that. "I have some applications in for—"

A knock interrupted.

"Come in, Tina," Joel welcomed the caterer who quickly set up breakfast. Eggs and a basket of croissants, butter, and jam for Manda, an egg-white omelet and dry toast for Joel, a carafe of fresh-squeezed orange juice, and a large pot of coffee. No cream, no sugar, no white linen napkins.

"Will there be anything else, Mr. Cushman?"

Manda covered her smile, glad Tina was focused on Joel. Joel's eyes sparkled, and she bet he was thinking the same thing. "I believe we have everything, Tina. You can shut the door on your way out. Thank you."

"Thank you for breakfast." Manda picked up her paper napkin, slowly, with two fingers.

Joel teased, "We have you to thank for no linen napkins."

"I'm cool with that." She shook open the oversized napkin and made a show of spreading it on her lap.

Joel laughed out loud at the performance.

Manda poured orange juice for both of them.

"Tell me what you know about the Manse rumor mill," Joel directed.

"It's humming this morning. So far I've heard (A) you and I are hot and heavy, (B) you pulverized Kristof, (C) I'm pregnant—lots of speculation about whose baby— and (D) Remy is on probation. You're feeding me again, which is feeding the rumor mill. What's up with that?"

"What's up is that I need to keep close tabs on you, and you need to eat." He waved his fork playfully. "Don't think breakfast is part of the deal after today."

They ate in silence for a few minutes. As Manda relaxed, she realized how tense Joel was. She wished he'd ask her a question. Halfway through her eggs, she caved. "What do you need to know?"

"Counselor first. What did she say?"

"Well, between the counselor and the doctor, I understand that I have the disease of alcoholism, but they decided I don't require detox or rehab."

"And how do they know that?" Joel asked casually.

"The way I heard it is they use two criteria. First, I totally get that I can't drink again without hideous consequences, like losing myself and being totally humiliated, which is exactly what happened. And I know from experience that, for the last year or more, once I pick up a drink I don't stop, even on a good day, until I pass out. So I don't need rehab to know I'm an alcoholic. And I don't need detox because I'm not in withdrawal."

"And what does that mean? How do they know you're not in withdrawal?"

"I guess they measure blood alcohol level and look for symptoms like delirium something?"

"Delirium tremens or DT's."

"That's it. Did you know you can die from alcohol withdrawal?"

Joel nodded. "And who made the determination that you're not in withdrawal?"

"The doctor. One of the doctors I saw."

At Joel's raised eyebrow, she explained. "A campus physician's assistant went through a series of questions and tests for my physical condition in general and alcohol damage in particular, and then I was sent for blood work and to a gynecologist." Manda dropped her eyes and focused on her plate.

Joel sat quietly.

Manda felt him watching her. She went back to her first topic. "And since I know I'm an alcoholic, I plan to go regularly to AA. I'm going to a Saturday night meeting with Tony and his girl this weekend."

"Tony will take good care of you. There's a women's meeting at seven tonight at the Presbyterian Church; I want you there. Ask around for Cassie."

Manda paused with a forkful of eggs halfway to her mouth. How would he know that?

"Please," he added.

"Absolutely," she agreed.

"Are you pregnant?"

"No."

He was so guarded right now, she wasn't sure, but he seemed seriously relieved. She decided not to make a crack about how un-politically-correct his question was. "Then," she continued lightly, "I visited the eye doctor, got a whole new prescription, and I get to pick up my awesome new glasses at eleven today." She added, "Thanks for arranging that." She was guessing about him arranging it.

He didn't deny it. He was intent on his omelet.

She didn't know how he could get dry toast down his throat. She layered more butter and jam on her croissant and saw him watching the procedure. She nudged the jam closer to him and followed it with the butter dish.

"That is wicked," he said. He spooned strawberry jam on his toast. "No fair smiling."

Manda let out a laugh and went back to her eggs. She savored the luxury of being fed breakfast. Two days in a row. Today she would keep it in her stomach.

Joel, she noticed, was pushing a piece of omelet around on his plate.

Eventually he made up his mind about whatever internal debate he was having and told her, "Your new roommate is thought to have substance abuse issues, maybe illegal drugs. It's not for you to rescue her or to tell on her. I bring it up because it may not be a healthy situation for you. Apparently all three roommates left within the past month with no explanation, and they're renting an apartment together, which is a pretty big unnecessary expense, so it must have been a bad situation for them. I'm banking on you not having a drug problem?"

Stunned, she shook her head. Another un-PC question. She had to admire his strategy. He knew how to slip them in and get answers. But, she conceded, he did need to know the answer. She watched him chug his glass of orange juice, a total departure from his usual smooth style.

"I mean it. If that apartment doesn't work out for you, I need you to tell me, and I'll find an alternative."

"Got it. Thank you."

"Did you talk to the police?" Joel asked.

Manda's hand jerked, and her fork flipped onto the rug. She ducked down to pick it up, set it on her plate and pushed the plate aside. "Yes, this policewoman Miriam interviewed me right after the substance abuse counselor. Another woman from the college was with us; I think she handles complaints about sexual harassment. They were both really kind. They asked hard questions, and they're both really smart. I think the police are going to arrest Kristof. And they had me sign an Order of Protection so he can't come near me. And they advised me to protect myself."

"I'm not at liberty to discuss what is happening with regard to Kristof."

Manda had no idea what to do with that statement. How would he know anything more about Kristof than she had just told him?

If Joel saw her puzzlement he did not address it.

What was happening here? He was all over the place. Was he avoiding some topic? What could be touchier than pregnancy, drug addiction, Kristof, the police and DT's? Maybe she was taking up too much of his time. "You probably have meetings—"

"In fifteen minutes," he told her without looking at his watch. "Tony showed me the stills and the video."

So that was it. Manda set down her coffee mug, and Joel shifted in his chair.

"You're not—?"

"Going to throw up again? No," she told him. She let out a breath of relief at the same time he did. On his wavelength again, she told him, "I don't trust that he won't retaliate, and I'm watching my back." She met his eyes. "And honoring my deal with you—keeping my focus on being sober and getting my work done, here and at school. My class work is on schedule, and I'm not worried about doing well and graduating as planned. And if I'm messing up here, I need you—I mean, I know you'll—"

"I'm not worried about your work here. You do a fine job. I'm sorry about violating your privacy with those questions. I needed to know for myself. A lot of us have your back, Manda. Security is all over this thing, and I don't just mean Tony and the police. I mean here at the Manse and all over campus. I want you to check in with Cassie at the meeting tonight and specifically tell her what's going on; that's very important; she'll alert the appropriate people to watch out for you before, during, and after meetings, not just tonight."

Manda tried and failed to get in a question.

"I know you have an Order of Protection. You need it; you're still in danger. And I would be remiss in my duty as—as your employer if I didn't do everything I can to protect you."

Manda didn't know why his suddenly patronizing tone annoyed her, but it did.

"What?" he snapped.

Manda decided he was seriously freaked out by this whole conversation. She wished she knew how to help him out.

She shook her head and apologized. "I get there are things you're not telling me, and I don't think you're trying to treat me like a child."

"You're right on both counts. There's a lot I can't explain right now." He gulped coffee and realized too late, "Hot!" She pushed her glass of orange juice over to him. He took a mouthful and nodded his thanks.

Manda saw that she had instinctively reached out her hand and laid it on his. She heard someone say, "Tell me how can I be most helpful with all of this." Did she say that? And what she was doing touching his hand?

Before she could pull her hand away, Joel set down the juice glass and enfolded her hand in both of his. "Thank you for wanting to work with me on this," he said with obvious relief. "The best thing you can do is let us help you, Manda."

That was it? That's what would make it easier? She was sure her puzzlement showed on her face.

Joel continued, "I realize asking for help is probably a foreign concept to you right now."

She blinked and he smiled into her soul with those gray-green eyes. She felt something go soft in the center of her being.

"I need you to be safe, Manda. That's very, very important to me. Personally, not just professionally."

A knock sounded at the door. In less than a second, Joel had let go of her hand and stood up behind his chair. "I cannot believe this guy," he muttered.

Without waiting for an acknowledgement, someone opened the door. "Harold. Right on time," Joel said heartily, although it was obvious to Manda Harold was seven minutes early and had no business barging in. "Come right on in."

Harold was Director of Buildings and Grounds, Manda was pretty sure. She stood up with—she hoped—grace and dignity and said sweetly, "Thanks for your time, Mr. Cushman." She made a show of wrapping up the last croissant in her big paper napkin and walked to the door. "I appreciate your advice, and I'll keep you posted about the grad school applications." Manda beamed an angelic smile at Harold.

Joel rolled his eyes at her performance and said, equally loudly, "Good deal, Mandy. On your way out, ask my secretary Catherine to have these dishes cleared, right away."

Manda gritted her teeth at the "Mandy" crack, but she thought that last statement was deliberately un-PC, aimed to put her in her place in Harold's eyes.

"Absolutely, Mr. Cushman," she said crisply. Manda couldn't wait to hear what Harold had to tell the rumor mill about the scene he had just witnessed.

Manda was greeted with a different collection of rumors when she returned to campus with her groceries at lunchtime. From the moment she entered the campus apartments, conversations paused and changed to whispers accompanied by furtive glances. She smiled calmly and kept moving; she picked up phrases like "Gold-digger," "Slut," "Deserves to be expelled," and "I'll do anything for Professor Kristof." She fumbled with the key to her apartment and was about to give up when her roommate opened the door.

"It's you. Forgot you live here. What's your name again?"

"Manda." Manda saw that Stacey was still coming down from last night's high. Her hair was flattened on one side, as if she'd just gotten up, and she wore a skimpy tank top and sweats that revealed an elaborate tattoo on her belly. "Cool snake, Stace," she said.

"Thanks for getting food. I'm starved!"

Manda closed her eyes. Her budget did not cover feeding two people.

She set down her two grocery bags and started putting away salad fixings, olive oil, and chicken breasts.

Stacey pawed through the second bag. "Don't you eat anything good?"

"Nope, just healthy stuff. Do you like olives?" She held out her one treat, a container of hot, spicy olives.

Stacey popped two in her mouth, chewed, swallowed, and ran for the bathroom.

Manda heard her retching. She stood still for a moment and thought about it. *God, I hope you've got a better idea than I do right now.* Joel would probably ask her what would get her to her goal of graduating in eight weeks, sober and sane.

She turned on the radio, dialed a light rock station, fixed a salad, and ate it standing by the window in the living room. Then she washed and put away the dishes, grabbed her things, and headed back to work at the Manse. After this, she vowed, she would fix a salad in the morning and take it to work with her. She would simply avoid contact with her snake-belly roommate.

Manda got into a groove the next two weeks: classes in the morning, lunch and work at the Manse, an AA meeting after work. Then home to fix a meal, library to study, and home again to crawl into bed. The one place she did not encounter rumors and name-calling was at her "Happy Hour" AA meeting. She started recognizing faces and learning names. The regulars called her Manda; she could even smile at the good old boys who called her "Mandy."

"Come for burgers with us," a thirty-something woman invited the last Thursday of March.

Manda started to excuse herself but knew she didn't have to study every night of the week. She could probably ace her exams without any more effort, and her projects were ahead of schedule. "Thanks," she agreed. "You're Carol, aren't you?"

"You must be clearing up if you know my name already!" Carol laughed. "How are things going?" They walked out to the parking lot together, and Carol asked her, "Cassie has a few of the men watching out for you. What's that about? You got trouble?" Manda nodded. "Want to talk about it?"

"I guess not," Manda said. "Things are quiet right now, and I'm doing okay. But thanks for asking."

"How long have you been sober?"

"Must be two weeks," Manda said in surprise.

"Has it been hard?"

"Life's been a little hard, but staying sober has not been too bad. When I think about a drink, I remember where it took me. Or I pray, which is what this old guy Charlie told me to do. It works every time. And to be honest, life's a lot less hard now than it was a month ago."

"Good; that attitude of gratitude will really help you. For my money, the best burgers are at Ralph's. Know where that is?" Manda shook her head. "Follow me," she suggested.

Manda laughed, "That's about all I am able to do lately—follow people in AA and do what they tell me."

Carol winked. "Good thinking. It works better that way."

Fifteen minutes later Manda was glad she had come with them. "This is the best burger I've had in my whole life!" she said. Her hands were dripping with juice, and she was pretty sure she had ketchup on her nose.

"I live for these fries every week," the twenty-something woman with the half glasses said. Manda thought her name was Annette. She saw the woman looking at her ring finger. "No husband?" she remarked. Manda wondered what was coming. Not more gossip, she hoped. Annette went on, "I think it's easier to get sober when you're single. I feel so bad for the girls whose husbands are still drinking or who give them a hard time about coming to meetings."

"Guess I'm lucky," Manda said.

"You looking?" Annette asked her.

"I am off men for life." Manda declared.

The table erupted with laughter. Suddenly she felt like one of them. Even though they were all different ages and were leading very different lives, they were all trying to stay sober. She had that in common with them. She felt connected with these women, almost the way she had as a freshman with the other Presidential Scholars.

Manda realized how much she missed spending time with friends and having fun together and supporting each other. It had been too long, and that isolation had cost her.

Carol gave her a wise look. "Good idea to steer clear of relationships for a while. But you might want to rethink that in about a year."

"Why a year?"

"You'll change a lot in your first year of sobriety. Things will look different. You'll be able to handle things you couldn't. And you'll be better at relationships. Barb is dying to tell you about her picker."

The woman her age with the edgy haircut set down her burger and grabbed a handful of napkins. Manda laughed. Maybe she'd tell them the napkin story later.

"My picker!" Barb prefaced. "When I got to AA I could really pick 'em," she said. "If there was a loser in the pack,

I'd pick him. And date him. And be miserable. And get rid of him. And pick another one. And another one. Doing the same thing over and over and expecting different results. Got sober. Traded in the defective picker." Barb picked up her burger again and turned it around for the best bite. "Got me a good picker now." She bit into the burger and smiled.

Annette told Manda, "She got married last summer to a really good guy." Barb was nodding and chewing. "So keep an open mind, but we do advise staying out of relationships the first year. Get into the Twelve Steps."

"Isn't that the poster that hangs on the wall at the meeting? The Twelve Steps. We admitted we were powerless and yada yada."

"Exactly. The steps are designed to be done in order, and they're a proven way to clean up the mess you made as an active alcoholic and change the bad habits and ways of thinking that could lead you right back to a drink. You'll want a sponsor—a woman who's experienced in AA—to work with you on the steps."

Carol added, "Use this first year to get to know yourself and develop a relationship with your God or your Higher Power."

Manda still had no idea what a Higher Power was. She asked them, "What is this 'God as we understand him' thing? Do you all have some common definition of God?"

Carol told her, "Just the opposite. You can understand God your own way; I can understand her my way."

Manda smiled. Apparently people from all beliefs and religions came together in AA. She was glad she wouldn't have to argue about her God or explain him to anyone.

"And it's nobody's business. But it's important that you find a God or a Higher Power, not just to help you stay sober but to guide your life. Did I just lose you?"

"No, actually, I know God's been watching out for me lately." She thought about her prayers in the car the night she left Kristof's. That God had been listening and had dramatically changed her life in a single day. She had a feeling she could rely on that God and ask for help with all of the problems she was dealing with right now.

"Keep talking to your God, Manda, and let Him guide your life. Do you have a sponsor yet?"

"I know you just told me what a sponsor is, but could you say it again?"

Carol said patiently, "A sponsor is a woman you can talk with, who'll read through the Big Book with you, and guide you through the twelve steps. She's someone who's comfortable with her sobriety and who is living the way you'd like to live your life. Sometimes a woman continues to be a close advisor long after the newcomer has gone through the steps using the Big Book, so—"

"I'm sorry. Can you explain what you mean by 'the big book'?"

Annette told her, "Tomorrow we'll make sure you get your own copy of the book *Alcoholics Anonymous*. We call it the Big Book. It explains the program of recovery that men and women have been using for decades to recover from alcoholism, and it really works. For tonight we'll give you our phone numbers so you can call anytime you want to drink. Or talk. Or have coffee."

Carol smiled. "Or get a burger."

"Maybe I'd better get a phone," Manda mumbled. But she probably couldn't go for burgers and fries every week without blowing her budget and gaining a ton of weight.

Manda still had no phone a week later. After supper—a quick salad— she headed to the library and spread out her books, notes, and review sheets on a table. She had been using this quiet area of the library lately because it was in view of the checkout desk. She set her "creeper beeper"—

STEPPING UP TO LOVE | 53

the name students had for the electronic escort device issued to them by campus security—close at hand. She opened her laptop, and immersed herself in review for her Senior Accounting exam.

When she heard the fifteen-minute warning just before closing time at midnight, she packed up her materials. She slung her tote bag over her shoulder and felt it bump against someone before settling on her shoulder. Hands gripped the straps of the tote and pulled it backwards and Manda with it. Instinctively, she activated her creeper beeper. Two alarms shrieked, one overhead and another at the entrance just beyond the checkout desk.

"They won't be here in time, Manda baby," Kristof snarled. "I'll have your face sliced and be out of here before they even get out of their chairs."

Manda wasn't listening. She managed to shrug out of her tote, and she slipped out of his grasp, throwing him off balance. As she twisted away from him, she felt a searing pain in her shoulder. She made a break for the checkout desk but first caught a glimpse of a small knife—or maybe it was a straight-edge razor—in his hand. One student worker gaped at her. Another said helpfully, "Miss, you left your tote bag and laptop behind."

Manda took a steadying breath. "Call nine-one-one," she ordered them, her voice hard.

A librarian came out of her office, phone in hand.

When she hesitated with her finger on the Send button, Manda yelled, "Now!"

The call went through, and Manda took the phone to explain the problem. Just as she finished, two campus security officers burst into the library.

One officer went after Kristof, who was exiting through an emergency door at the end of the darkened reading room. The other officer planted himself at Manda's side. He told her, "Tony Pinelli told me to yell at you for not registering your cell phone number with security. He's on his way in, and he's steamed."

Manda groaned, "Wait until he finds out I don't own a cell phone."

"Ma'am, no offense, but you have to be insane to be a victim of stalking and not own a cell phone."

"That would be correct, yes," Manda said humbly. If she could spend money on olives and burgers and fries, she could spend money on a cheap cell phone. What was she thinking? That was one more piece of evidence that alcohol had crippled her commonsense. Maybe she could still work an accounting problem at competitive speed, but her judgment was faulty.

"Are you aware you're bleeding?" the security officer asked her.

Manda noticed the students had backed away from her. The librarian pointed to the shoulder of her fleece jacket. The light blue fleece was sliced through and stained with her blood.

Manda investigated her skin under the three layers of clothing and registered the searing pain where the knife had penetrated all three layers and broken the skin on her shoulder. She felt the blood drain from her face and told herself to sit on the floor.

The officer yakked, "It's probably a superficial cut, but it's going to bleed until we can get something on it, and we need to keep you here until the police arrive."

Sitting wasn't working. Manda felt like she was going to pass out. She lay flat on her back on the floor to stop the dizziness.

The officer rambled on, "They'll take your statement and then we'll get you some treatment."

Manda watched everything around her blur. Voices faded. Someone crouched down beside her, and she heard Tony say, "I've got her. Wake up, honey."

She looked up at him gratefully.

Tony told his colleague, "Your partner has Kristof in custody for assault and for violating the Order of Protection. Kristof took a header off the stairs in the dark and sprained an ankle. He's out of commission at least for tonight, but we can expect him to talk his way out of custody before noon tomorrow."

Tony shook his head and told Manda, "The guy is connected. Let's see that cut."

Manda opened her jacket and showed him the slice on her shoulder. The wad of tissues the librarian had given her was soaked with blood.

Tony pressed a clean handkerchief to the wound and made a call to the nearest Urgent Care facility. "Put some pressure on that for me, honey. The police just came. I need you to give them a very brief statement. Then I'm going to carry you out to the truck, and we're going for a ride."

She nodded and did as he said. While she was telling the police her side of what happened, she could hear the two students giving two entirely different stories. One said Kristof was a student offering to help carry her books. The other knew it was Kristof but insisted he had been helping Manda with her work when she freaked and started yelling at him.

If she were paranoid, Manda would say Kristof knew her habits, had planned the attack, and had chosen a night these two students were on duty and would mislead the authorities and discredit her. But that was insane, wasn't it?

The librarian had only seen a bleeding, wild-eyed Manda descend on the front desk and did not know what incident had transpired between Manda and her alleged attacker. And so the authorities had contradictory information about the incident. Even though Manda was bleeding, her story seemed not to be credible in some eyes. But she was sober, and she was clear about what happened.

Help had arrived in time. This time. What about next time? She gave into tears. *God, I did my best, and so did the police, but I couldn't keep myself safe. I don't know what to do now.*

The ride to Urgent Care with Tony was frightening. Manda could not hold on tight enough to keep her shoulder from bleeding, and she felt nauseated. She did not remember being carried into an examining room, but the sting of anesthetic brought her fully awake. She tolerated a shot of Procaine and felt a tugging on the shoulder. She turned her head to watch someone's hands draw three stitches through her skin and carefully tie them off. Next came Steri-Strips on the more shallow sections of the cut.

After the young physician applied a bandage over his handiwork, he gave her two Tylenol and told her to go home and rest.

Tony accepted a sheet of wound care instructions on her behalf.

"Can you walk?" Tony asked her.

Manda shook her head. "Too dizzy."

Tony scooped her up, deposited her in the truck, and slammed the door. He headed the truck back to her campus apartment and lectured her, "You cannot—I repeat cannot—operate without a cell phone programmed with campus security, my number, and Joel's. Do you hear me?"

"I do. I will take care of that first thing tomorrow," she said meekly.

"And how will you pay for it?"

Manda confessed, "I don't get paid until next week."

"So how are you going to do this tomorrow?"

"I don't know, Tony. What do you recommend?"

"Good answer. I recommend I pick you up at your door—not the outside door; your apartment door—and we go shopping together. I can convince Joel to run a tab for you, but you and I first have to determine everything you need to save your butt until you are no longer the responsibility of this campus and its security force. Be ready with a list at eight o'clock sharp. And be ready with a repayment plan to your boss."

He helped her up the stairs, double-checked the locks on the apartment door and her bedroom door, and asked her, "Quick quiz: when am I picking you up?"

"Eight tomorrow morning."

"Where?"

"Here at my apartment door, not outside."

Tony gave her a gentle hug without putting pressure on her wounded shoulder. "You sleep with your creeper beeper next to your pillow and take it into the shower with you. Promise?"

"I promise. Thank you, Tony."

"And don't forget to tape plastic over the bandage when you shower."

"I will. I promise."

"Get some sleep."

"Joel, she is not playing with a full deck," Tony ranted into his cell phone on the way home from campus. He had just explained the situation, including Manda's visit to Urgent Care and Kristof's arrest.

Joel pretended to be calm and rational. "She's less than a month sober, and she's doing well in some areas of her life. She's got a lot of clearing up to do."

"She is not protecting herself," Tony complained. "She was at a table in the least populated part of the library at midnight."

"In full view of the main desk, with her beeper, which she had ready."

"How did you know that?"

He knew because he and Manda had strategized a few

days ago. "I have spies."

"Do you want me to be her bodyguard or don't you?" Tony yelled.

Now that his heart rate had returned to normal, Joel could tune into Tony's anxiety. He realized Tony felt solely and personally responsible for Manda's safety.

"No one's asking you to be her solo bodyguard, man. This is a team effort. And you went above and beyond tonight. Thank you for all that you did. I owe you."

Tony grumbled, "No problemo. I'm taking her shopping in the morning unless you want to."

"Shopping? For what?"

"A cell phone."

Joel groaned in disbelief.

"See what I mean, she's not playing with a full deck. What girl is without a cell phone in this world? She's got a stalker who has beaten her in the past and has now sliced her shoulder. She claims he was going for her face. And she's got no cell phone."

Joel hadn't heard about the attack on her face. He tried to get his breathing under control. He had to get her off campus, out of Kristof's reach entirely. "Do me a favor," Joel said to his friend. "I'll pick her up instead. I will read her the riot act about the cell phone."

"Well, okay, but I told her she's going to pay you back for the phone and whatever else she needs."

"I'm with you, buddy," Joel pacified.

Joel hung up before Tony could get on another roll. The last thing he worried about was getting paid back.

He paced his apartment to slow his heart rate. When that failed, he went out on his porch for some serious think time. He came out here any time quiet eluded him, and the answer always came, out here in the fresh air overlooking the beautiful lake. Tonight there was not a ripple of a breeze, and no stars were visible. The lake and sky were so dark nothing caught his eye.

He searched the lake for some glimmer of serenity. There it was, a faint light flickering on one of the islands. He could not fathom how a light came to be on the island in the frigid lake this time of night, this time of year. No one used the islands in winter. In the summer, campers might set up a primitive campsite or local kids might dare one another to sleep over, but not in the dead of winter.

He remembered, back in his wild-child days, taking a girl out to one of the islands one warm summer night. He was probably fourteen, and she was sixteen. Drunk and stoned out of their minds, they'd used her father's boat, and Joel had thrown up all the way out to the island. He never could control his motion sickness when it came to boats.

The girl left him on the island, if he remembered right. Humiliated, he slept it off, swam back to the closest shore at the crack of dawn—at least half a mile—and walked several miles home.

He felt just as inept now. Kristof was out of control. Since they could not secure Manda's safety on campus, he would need to argue for some alternative. He knew he had a solution to her housing problem, and he would talk her into it in the morning. However, to exempt her from being on campus until graduation, he'd need her buy-in and that of many others. He'd call the provost in the morning at a decent hour and set the ball in motion.

For now, though, he needed the quiet and bracing cold of his porch high above the frigid lake. The light continued to burn on the island, and he stared at it, not questioning it or analyzing it any further. He found himself thinking about his Irish grandmother Bridey, his mother's mother, the architect of Lakeside Terrace.

Bridey read tealeaves when she cared to, and he always suspected she worked a little magic from time to time. He wished she were still alive to give him a glimpse of the future or maybe work a little magic on Manda's behalf. When the cold got to him, he went back inside, took a hot shower, and tumbled into bed.

Chapter 3

Manda peered through the side panel of the downstairs door and saw that it really was Joel waiting for her. She gave him a big smile, went out to greet him, and explained, "Tony said he'd meet me At My Apartment Door!" She was trying to make light of it, but Joel felt her nervousness. "Are you filling in for him?"

"We're double-teaming you on the cell phone issue. I understand you have a list—things you need that will carry you through to the end of the semester."

Manda shook her head. "I apologize about the phone thing. And there really isn't anything else I need."

Joel put his hand on her back and steered her to her car. "We'll talk about it over breakfast, which is going on your tab." He did his best to sound stern, but he could tell from the way she rolled her eyes that Manda saw through it. "Seriously, I want to hear about this injury."

"It just needed a couple of stitches and mostly Steri-Strips, which will fall off in about a week."

Joel's eyes looked gravely into hers. "The way I heard it, you are lucky that's all it was. And you were smart to have the beeper ready. Do you feel safe?"

Manda wet her lips. "No. Not on campus. Not with him on the loose."

Joel took a walk around Manda's car, knelt to check the undercarriage, and asked her to pop the hood. Satisfied there were no booby traps—which he doubted was Kristof's style—he gave her a thumbs-up.

She laughed when he deposited himself in her front passenger seat. "I cannot believe you are riding in this clunker."

"Makes two of us."

While they waited for their breakfast, Joel poured each of them a second cup of coffee and proposed, "I have a situation you can help with, and it could solve your housing problem."

Manda held her breath. She'd prayed all night for a way to live off campus. "I'd love to hear it. It would feel good to help you for a change."

Joel beamed. "Thank you. I don't know if you're aware I manage some rental properties along the lake at the south edge of the city."

Manda shook her head. "So, south of the marina. I'm trying to place what's there. Overlook Park?"

Joel nodded. "Adjacent to the park, going north. Lakeside Terrace."

Manda's eyes lit up. "You mean those ginger-bread-y row houses that curve up from the beach and climb the bluff?"

"Exactly. I live in one and manage the rest."

"In your spare time, after putting in a full day at the Manse?"

"Don't go there." Joel sat back as the waitress set down platters of eggs and home fries.

"You're going to eat that?"

"Half. You?"

"I am hungry enough to eat the half you leave."

"No dinner again?"

"Never got to it." Yesterday when she came home to fix supper, Stacey was on the couch, entwined with a tattooed biker. Manda had backed out and gone directly to the library.

She did not bother Joel with that part of the story. He knew what happened in the library after that.

The eggs and potatoes were delicious, but she gave up two-thirds of the way through.

Joel had stopped at half and was watching her.

She felt herself blush. "The only reason I haven't gained weight is that I've missed so many meals. You are so disciplined."

"It helps. Had enough?" At Manda's nod, he signaled the waitress to take away their plates and returned to his original topic. "The dorm situation is not good, is it?"

"No."

"Here's an alternative. I used to have a part-time bookkeeper who collected all the rents and tracked the repairs and expenses to the units. She got married about six months ago and left me in the lurch last month when she moved with her husband to the west coast. I need someone to do that job.

"It's not a big time commitment, but it requires someone with a head for details and good customer and supplier relations. I think you could manage it easily, even with your work at the Manse and your end-of-semester course work. Sound okay so far?"

Manda nodded.

"There's a furnished studio apartment that could go with the job in lieu of a paycheck. Nothing fancy, but it's clean, safe, and comfortable."

"That's pretty generous, and I'm betting that wasn't the arrangement with the old bookkeeper."

"Does that matter?" Joel said brusquely.

Manda knew he was trying to manipulate her. She smiled at him. "It doesn't tally with running a tab."

Joel grinned, "Busted."

"I've got your number, Cushman."

"But you'll consider it?"

"I will do it if we can make it a business arrangement."

"It is a business arrangement. I'm not looking to put you in a compromising position."

Manda heard the anger in his voice and said quickly, "No, I know that. I wasn't questioning your intentions."

"So what's the problem?"

Manda was determined not to give in to the pressure she felt. She squared her shoulders, drew in a very slow breath, and let it out just as slowly. "For my self-esteem, I need to pay some nominal rent. Let me give the amount some thought after seeing how much this cell phone is going to cost me every month. Fair enough?"

Joel nodded. "You can get anything from a no-frills phone with a year's worth of calling time to a sophisticated smartphone with video, texting, international calling, and apps to the max. The no-frills option will run about a hundred dollars a year." He started to ask, "Do you—?" and stopped.

"What? Out with it."

"It's my understanding that most college grads are twenty-to-forty thousand dollars in debt, between college loans, car loans, and credit card balances. Do you even have a credit card?"

"I paid cash for my car four years ago. I have no college loans. Although I have a credit card, I only use it to establish a credit history."

"Satisfy my curiosity. Do you ever actually use the card?"

Manda nodded. "For car repairs, gas and groceries. I pay it off every month."

"You're telling me you have no debt?"

"I have no debt."

Joel sat back and folded his arms.

"What? You're looking at me like I'm an alien species."

"I'm torn between admiring your frugality and wanting to choke you for being cheap with yourself. What drives that?"

Manda took a swallow of coffee. "Fear."

"Of?"

"Not having enough to take care of myself. It's on my fourth-step inventory as both an asset and a liability," she admitted, referring to the effort alcoholics made to examine their character strengths and failings.

Joel was quiet, thinking. She noticed he didn't need an explanation of "fourth step inventory."

"So tell me how you see me being cheap with myself."

"Not having a phone, for one thing. Not eating meals when it means paying outside of what you've budgeted. Not having clothes that fit. Am I offending you?"

Manda had looked away in embarrassment. "No, it's just humbling to hear how other people see you."

Joel reached for her hand. "I see you as bright, beautiful, and way too worried."

Manda stared at him, not believing what she'd heard. Beautiful? Her?

"You are about to graduate with a solid business degree that is very marketable, and I think you're planning to go on to grad school, which will instantly increase your earning power. You can afford to make some small investments in your future by being safe, comfortable, fed, clothed and even happy."

"Good to hear, because I'm buying breakfast." She plucked the bill out from under his credit card and beat him to the register.

An hour later, they sat with their heads together on a bench in Overlook Park, programming Manda's no-frills cell phone. "You've got Campus Security, me, Tony, nine-one-one and the local AA number on speed dial. You know your voicemail password?"

"Eleven-eleven."

Joel laughed. "You're not supposed to tell me!"

"I trust you. You know all my secrets."

"So what's eleven-eleven? Just something easy to remember?"

"No, it's the day of surrender—the eleventh hour of the eleventh day."

"Got it."

"A constant reminder that I have surrendered to my alcoholism and am changing almost everything about the way I live and think."

"Do you really have to do all that to stay sober?"

Manda nodded. "People in the AA program tell me that's the way to do it, and I believe it's true for me."

He let her be quiet with her thoughts. They sat looking out through the bare trees to the lake, brilliant blue on this sunny day. Joel was thinking the lake was exactly the color of Manda's eyes.

Manda said quietly, "I am so grateful you gave me a chance and sent me in the right direction."

"I'm glad it's working out."

"I would be dead by now. I realized that last night."

Joel shivered to hear her say it. "I agree. Listen, let's take a look at the studio apartment I had in mind for you." He pointed through the trees to a row of white houses that marched up the hill on their own little street.

"Which house?"

"The last one, at the top of the bluff. I live on the lakeside on the third floor. The studio is on the first floor in front."

Her smile warmed his heart. He offered his hand and pulled her to her feet.

Manda relaxed the moment she walked through the door. "Sweet," she pronounced. The space was small, but the high ceiling and tall windows made it feel more spacious.

"Will it work for you?"

"The kitchen will be a challenge, but I can make it work." She pointed to the half-height shutters at the windows. "As long as we never have a thunder storm, I'll be fine."

"Why do you say that?"

"I'm terrified of lightning."

"We'll add shades or something before storm season." He watched her opening drawers and cabinets. "Furniture looks reasonable? You can sleep on a futon?"

"It's really great, Joel." She turned to him and gave him a hug that took his breath away.

He pulled her tight and enjoyed the feel of her in his arms. What he wouldn't give for more of that.

"Thirty-five dollars a week," Manda proposed.

Joel let go of her as if she were too hot to handle. "What?"

"My rent. What else? And don't object."

Joel let out his breath in a laugh. He tried and failed to recover his equilibrium. "I'm not objecting, but I want to know how you came up with that figure."

"That's what I can afford now that I'm not drinking anymore. It's how much I save every week being sober, minus the weekly cost of the cell phone."

Joel was speechless.

"What, you think it should be more?"

"No. When do you want to move in?"

"Like right away, this morning?"

Joel reached for her hand and deposited a key in her palm. "This is house number fourteen, unit one. Your parking space is fourteen dash one, around the back," he explained. "Tony will be by later this morning to install a deadbolt and to check the window locks. You probably know he does carpentry and repairs on the side."

Manda nodded. "And you and I will get together to go over the books?"

He'd forgotten about that. He nodded. "Tomorrow afternoon is best for me." He ruffled her curls. "It's good to see you smiling."

"I am hugely relieved."

That was music to Joel's ears. It would make it easier to persuade her not to set foot on campus again until graduation. He still had some politicking to do on campus before he proposed it to her.

Manda dropped Joel at the visitor lot to collect his car and raced across campus to pack. She wanted to get everything out of the campus apartment and into the studio before noon so she could show up for work at the Manse by one o'clock.

She pounded up the stairs, burst through the door of the apartment, and walked in on Stacey and her biker friend inhaling lines of white powder at the kitchen counter. Her first thought was to go around them, but some invisible hand made her step back into the hallway and think about it.

If it were just Stacey, she would walk right by, pack her things, and get out. But two of them—high—posed a risk she was unwilling to take. The biker was well over six feet and muscular. Tony would kill her if anything happened to her through her own carelessness. She walked back down the stairs holding her cell phone, debating which number to call. Because the situation had gone beyond unpleasant to illegal, she opted for campus security.

In less than a minute, Stacey and the biker rushed by Manda, out of the building, and jumped on the motorcycle. Both gave her the finger as they sped away.

It took another minute for two burly officers to arrive. Manda explained the situation as they climbed back up to the apartment. She packed her things while they investigated the powder residue on the counter and found drug paraphernalia stuffed behind the cushions of the sofa.

Manda lined up her packed duffle and boxes, double-checked the kitchen and bathroom, and appropriated the ice cube trays to keep her food from spoiling on the drive.

Seeing that, the taller officer told her, "No need for you to make a statement right now, but we do need to know how to reach you."

Manda gave them her new cell phone number and new address. She loved the way it sounded when she said, "Fourteen dash one Lakeside Terrace."

When her face lit with a smile, the stress vanished for all of them. Manda gratefully accepted their help hauling everything down to her car.

She smiled all the way across town, up the hill, into her parking space, and into her little apartment. "Home," she said.

She stood in the center of the space for a moment, thinking about her prayer in the car the night she left Kristof's. *You were paying attention, weren't you, God? Thank you. I could never have imagined living in a place like this.*

Halfway through organizing her kitchen, she heard Tony arrive with tools in hand.

"You beat me," he teased.

Manda described the scene that greeted her on campus after her shopping trip with Joel.

"Doing lines on the counter? Hey, if that was the last straw, what else went on before that?"

Manda laughed. "Last night it was a snake dance on the sofa. That's why I didn't get supper."

"Do I want to know what you mean by a snake dance on the sofa?"

"Stacey has a snake tattoo on her belly, and the guy has one—well, let's leave it at that."

"Other highlights we should know about?" Tony went on.

"Nothing else illegal. I'm sure security will be asking for a statement from me, and I'll fill them in. Hey, I need to lighten up right now."

Manda was busy stocking the tall cupboards and hadn't heard Joel come into the apartment. He came up behind her and put his hands on her shoulders. "You okay?"

She turned and welcomed his hug of reassurance. "I'm good. I'm where I'm supposed to be, and I'm really grateful that Tony is getting those locks in place today."

"Did Kristof do something after I left you?"

"No, I walked in on my roommate and her biker buddy doing drugs. I called security, and they helped me vacate. I hope it's okay that I'm here this early?"

"Of course it's okay. How can I help?"

Manda was aware of Tony's eyes ping-ponging back and forth between the two of them, taking note of Joel's hands stroking her arms. She was suddenly self-conscious and wondered when she had become so comfortable with Joel's touch. She felt her face flame.

She announced, "I…actually need a break. I'm going to walk down Lakeside Terrace and see what's at the other end. Catch you later."

Tony grunted a reply that sounded like, "A little family beach. Not much action there!"

Manda flew past him so fast he dropped the drill.

"Hey! Take it easy, girl!"

In rhythm with her walk—left foot, right foot—she recited, "I am off men for life! I am off men for life!" all the way down Lakeside Terrace, around the curve, and onto the beach. She sat down hard on the sand, locked her arms around her knees, and glared at the dark blue of the lake. White caps were building, and two foolhardy sailboats bent into the wind as they raced to their moorings.

Manda had never felt so at home in her life or so happy with her choices. But was she crazy living in the same building as Joel Cushman? The last thing she needed was to fall for a man who was way too sexy, who—if the rumor mill had any credibility—charmed every woman that came onto his radar. If only she didn't love his touch and admire practically everything else about him. She really needed to be off men for life—at least right now. Feeling this way about Joel was way too confusing.

She hated that she'd dared to give him a hug this morning when he'd first showed her the apartment. And he'd hugged her back for a second and then let her go like she was off-limits or something; what was that about? Her Grandma Doughty would say, "Joel Cushman's not interested in the likes of you. He'll be wanting someone sophisticated and high-class for a serious relationship."

Manda didn't think Joel was looking to seduce her. Or was he? Her experience with Kristof had really messed with her head. She needed to get a grip.

She dug her cell phone out of her pocket and speed-dialed AA. "Hi, I need a meeting tonight. What's scheduled in Tompkins Falls or nearby?" She had a choice of a big open meeting at the Lutheran church at seven or a women's meeting at six o'clock in Clifton Springs. She'd find her way to the women's meeting right after work, even if it meant she wouldn't know a soul.

She closed her eyes until a phone number came to mind, the one for Janine the therapist she'd been seeing since she got sober. Manda really needed to talk about the violence last night and Kristof's mind games and the way it was messing with her head even now. She hated that she doubted Joel's generosity and concern. She punched in the therapist's number and left a voicemail requesting an appointment.

As it turned out, the women's meeting was eighty percent of what she needed.

"I bounced from one empty relationship to another for a long time around these rooms," the guest speaker told the women, "until I did a thorough fourth-step inventory and really cleaned house. Once I did, I learned how to be friends with a man, not jump into bed with him."

Manda laughed and heard several women around her do the same.

"Sounds like a few of you identify with that!" the speaker chuckled.

Manda thought the woman's name was Gwen, and she'd seen her once or twice at the Tuesday night women's meeting in Tompkins Falls. She really should get back to that meeting now that the semester was winding down. She could get a meal at home and study a couple of hours at the desk in her studio apartment before going to the meeting.

Her whole routine could change now that she had her own place. She could put her meetings first since she wasn't scheduling her movements to avoid contact with Stacey or with Kristof.

But how could she possibly avoid Kristof if he was stalking her? *Stop. You can't solve that right now.* Manda wasn't sure where that thought came from, but it felt exactly right. For now, with help from Joel, she had a safe place to live and freedom to rethink her schedule.

On the drive home she found herself thinking about other things that needed a fresh look. Had she made a mistake asking Barb to be her sponsor? She didn't feel very supported in her efforts to work on the twelve steps, and she didn't feel comfortable talking with Barb about the situation with Kristof.

Her foot hit the brake before she realized there were deer on the road. Somehow she navigated through them and pulled onto the shoulder shaking. *God, I'm glad you're paying attention. All these obstacles. I need your help in so many ways.* She rested her forehead on the steering wheel for a moment until her shaking subsided. At last she let out a long, cleansing breath, put the Beetle into gear, and continued on her way to her new little home.

Joel arranged to meet with Manda the next afternoon at a coffee shop downtown. It was time to hand over the books that had been driving him insane for too long.

He appropriated a meeting room off to one side of the coffee bar, opened his laptop, and smiled at the sound of Manda's laughter. She was ordering the largest size coffee and joking with the barista about the stuffed Easter Bunnies that overflowed the display cases.

When Manda found him, she teased, "Is this your office away from the office? You work too much, Boss."

"You have no idea how glad I'll be to turn this work over to you." Joel patted the chair beside him. "Sit here so we can look at this monstrosity together."

Manda raised her eyebrows. "How bad can a spreadsheet be?"

"I'll let you be the judge. Denise was conscientious, I'll give her that, but I wouldn't call her logical. I have doubts about the accuracy of this thing."

Manda tucked her tote under the chair and slid onto the seat. Wordlessly, she studied what was on his screen.

Joel nudged the laptop closer so she could reach the trackpad and keyboard. He took the opportunity put his arm along the back of her chair and lean over her shoulder. "I don't mean to crowd you," he fibbed.

"You're not," she told him absently. He sighed and gave up all hope of this being a romantic exchange.

Fascinated by her digital dexterity, he watched her navigate back and forth through several worksheets, jot questions on an electronic notepad, expose formulas, and double-check the most complex calculations by doing unexplainable things with the calculator accessory.

In less than ten minutes she concluded, "No problem. I wouldn't have done it this way, but it works just fine. I'd give it, like, zero points for design, but it is accurate."

Joel was speechless.

Manda turned to his silence. "What? Again, you're looking at me like I'm an alien species."

He held up his hands and shook his head in surrender. "I am humbled to my core."

"Get out," she told him playfully. "It's a spreadsheet. I'm an accountant. I can see where this—okay, this thing is a monstrosity, let's face it."

Joel was laughing out loud at her monologue.

Manda forged ahead. "But it does work. Hey, I can see where it would give you nightmares if you weren't a numbers guy. You had me really concerned she'd created something unmanageable or logically flawed, but that's not the case."

She stopped talking, and Joel did his best to sober up.

"What's next, Boss?"

Joel clicked on a tab to bring up her notepad full of questions. "Let's start with these."

Halfway through her jumbo coffee, Joel was sure Manda had learned the inner workings of the properties he managed. He employed a small army of contractors to keep them in top condition, plus grounds keepers, a paving company, and a decorator. Rents came in monthly with few defaults or delays.

"I'll handle any defaults," he assured her. "Just give me a statement each month highlighting the overdues."

Together they reviewed the procedures Denise had put in place and the forms and standard phrases she used to communicate.

"What do you think?" Joel asked after Manda had run out of questions.

"I think it will keep me out of trouble."

"Too much work?"

"If I weren't nearly finished with the semester's assignments, I'd be worried."

"You say that as if you're ahead of schedule in your classes." So far she was saying everything he wanted to hear. She was making it easy for him to make his pitch.

She nodded. "I am. I have a project due in a couple of weeks that just has to be polished and packaged and submitted. And I have a huge, semester-long spreadsheet assignment that still needs a day or two of concentrated work. And that's it. Then, please God, I can graduate."

Joel double-checked the DVD he had just burned for her with all the files, forms, and procedures.

"Sorry if that sounded snarky," Manda said to his silence.

"Snarky?"

"I have a bad attitude about school right now."

"What's driving that?" he asked casually.

"Fear."

He slipped the disk into a protective sleeve and handed it to her.

Manda put it in her pocket. Her eyes swept the table, and he guessed she didn't know how to have this conversation with him.

"Fear, like you don't want to get your face slashed when you're studying in the library?"

Manda physically shrank at the question and her hands started to tremble.

Joel reached for her hands and looked into her eyes. "Even with the police and campus security doing everything by the book, you are in danger," he affirmed, "and the way I see it you should not be on that campus—ever—with the exception of your graduation day."

A few tears escaped. Manda could only nod her agreement.

"I want you to talk with your professors—by phone, by email, however—and ask to be excused from classes from this point forward. Here's why they will agree. Campus security has been acting as the collection point for all the reports pertaining to the danger you are in and the impact on your health. They have privately alerted each of your professors that you cannot attend classes without putting yourself in jeopardy.

"Manda, I have every confidence your professors will excuse you from classes, if you have that conversation with them, and if you agree to submit all the assigned work on or before the scheduled due dates. Will you do that, please?"

Manda was sobbing with relief by the time he finished his speech.

He drew her gently to him and let her cry her heart out on his shoulder. He didn't care who witnessed this exchange or what they thought about it. She was a young woman whose need for safety could not be guaranteed by the college she had faithfully attended for four years. A gentle hug was the least its officers could do to demonstrate their humanity and their concern.

"It's going to be all right," he whispered and felt her nod her head against his shoulder. He had never thought himself capable of tenderness, but he believed that's what his heart radiated at this moment.

The storm struck two weeks later on Friday. Manda came home from her women's meeting in Clifton Springs, saw no deer on the journey, changed into her only pair of clean pajamas, and fell into bed at eight o'clock. She was totally exhausted from a week of overwork. Three areas of responsibility were a little overwhelming right now. She still worked part time four days a week at the Manse, and Dan was pushing her to do a little more, giving her new tasks to challenge her. She was pushing herself to finish her schoolwork and submit it as soon as possible. And she was busier than she thought she would be with the bookkeeping job for Joel's properties.

She knew the new job would get easier as she became more conversant with the tenants and the properties and the suppliers and the contractors who kept the properties in shape. Her initial look at Denise's spreadsheet and her working session with Joel had not given her a true appreciation for the size of the job. Joel managed all the units in the Lakeside Terrace row houses—several dozen—and another thirty rentals scattered around the marina and along the lakeshore. All were well maintained.

Some of the rents were below market value. Manda was sure there was a reason for that, but she was not yet comfortable asking Joel to explain his business practices. Her boss at the Manse Dan would cheerfully explain things in detail, but Joel was much more guarded, even defensive with her. It was really none of her business, but his business sense and his management style interested her, and she wished she could pump him with questions.

Manda wondered some days how he had ever managed to keep the books, on top of all the work he did at the Manse and his constant interactions with people in the business community.

Anyone who believed the rumors about his being rich had to be ignorant of the workload he carried. Anyway, he didn't live in a mansion. Sure, Lakeside Terrace was beautiful, perched right by a private beach on a bluff overlooking the lake, but a wealthy bachelor's preferred residence? No way.

Manda had to wonder who owned all these prime rental properties and why Joel had taken on responsibility for managing them when he already had heavy responsibility at the Manse.

The Manse, she knew, was not a moneymaker; nor was it in the red. It operated more like a not-for-profit, although it did not have that status. Salaries at the Manse were higher than average for the type of business; she knew everyone on staff was hand picked and had impressive credentials. Although the facilities were luxurious and the grounds were meticulously groomed, even those expenses were closely watched.

There was no waste anywhere. There was no "lateral passing" of goods; Manda still chuckled when she heard that old football term used to describe employees walking off with property and supplies. It was common knowledge that if someone tried to sneak a spa-sized shampoo out the door—let alone a lobster tail or an antique desk—that person would be terminated without recourse and without so much as a polite letter of reference. Someday she would ask Joel how to make up for the spa supplies she had consumed without authorization that fateful morning in March when he'd walked in on her in the shower.

She wished she could continue her job at the Manse after graduation, but she suspected it was more of a good-will position that supported a worthy Tompkins College student. She would wait to talk to Joel about that when she finally had the answers to her questions about grad school scholarships.

It bothered her that "ask Joel" seemed to be her quick solution to most of her problems. She worried that she was not gaining much independence. That was another thing she wanted to talk over with the substance abuse counselor and with an AA sponsor. And Joel was definitely not her AA sponsor. How many times had she heard "Men for men; women for women"? It was a golden rule that made sense. He was her friend and her mentor but not her sponsor.

So where was she going to find a good AA sponsor? Barb was a nice person, but they weren't doing well as sponsor-sponsee. Barb was not willing to work with her on the twelve steps, and Manda had heard over and over that the steps were the heart of the program.

Part of her wanted to become more self-sufficient. Maybe she should accept the full scholarship to University of Texas at Austin she had been offered, where Lyssa was studying for her doctorate. But another part of her knew she did not want to be any closer to her sister's "marijuana maintenance plan" while she was still so new in sobriety.

Besides, the graduate business program that most interested her was at a private college forty or so miles away in Rochester. St. Basil's program emphasized not-for-profit business models and ethical workplaces. She knew a scholarship from St. Basil's was a long shot. Still, if she could work something out, it would give her the opportunity to stay in Tompkins Falls, a place that felt like home and where she had bonds with sober people. Maybe she should take out a loan for St. Basil's.

All of this whirled in Manda's head as she tossed and turned on the futon and finally fell into an uneasy slumber just after ten o'clock.

Two floors above her, Joel heard the rumbles around midnight and knew they were in for a doozey of a storm. The damage reported west and south of them had caused him to alert Tony and a few other contractors that the properties might be damaged. All of them told him to relax, that the odds were in their favor. The forecast was saying "twenty percent chance."

Joel stepped out on the porch off his bedroom and watched the storm approaching. Lightning illuminated the clouds—towering gray masses tinged with green. He saw a bolt of lightning strike the communications tower north of town and seconds later heard the crack. They would lose power soon. He headed back inside, flipped on the light, and hunted for a flashlight. Another lightning flash lit up the French doors to the porch. "Manda," he breathed. They'd never fixed her windows.

At first, the rumbles sounded like a motorcycle cruising the street, but Manda knew she'd left Stacey and the biker behind weeks ago. She turned over and settled back into a fitful sleep. A loud crack and a lightning flash brought her fully awake. She sat up with her heart pounding and her head throbbing.

She'd always been terrified of thunderstorms, and she'd never been through one sober. She tried to steady her breathing, but it was no good. She tried praying. She tried covering her eyes and ears at the same time. Finally she fell apart in panic. She didn't remember wrapping herself in the futon cover like a cocoon.

Joel knocked at her door, called her name, and pounded the door before using his master key. He flipped the light switch, but by then the power was gone. He stood his flashlight on the table by the futon and followed her sobs to find her buried in the futon cover.

"It's okay, Manda," he told her, pulling the covers away from her head. He wedged himself onto the futon beside her and pulled her against his chest.

Manda clutched at his bare shoulder and buried her face in his neck.

"It's okay. It's just a bad storm. We're going to be just fine."

Her trembling brought him close to panic, too.

"Talk to me, Manda," he said sternly, but he could not seem to reach her.

He let out a steadying breath and remembered that was her way of calming herself when she was under pressure. "Manda, take a big, deep breath with me."

Joel heard her pull in a breath and let it out in a shaky sob.

"That a girl," he encouraged. "Five more just like that. You can do it. Breath with me."

With each breath, Manda became calmer and more present. Joel said a silent prayer of thanks and stretched out more comfortably beside her. "You're doing great," he cheered.

"I feel like a two-year-old."

Joel ran his hands down her back. "Trust me, you do not feel like a two-year-old."

She laughed. "Thank you." She propped herself up a little and brushed at his shoulder. "I have soaked your neck."

"It's not fatal." He smoothed the hair off her forehead. "I am sorry for not getting to those windows before this happened."

"I totally forgot. Or maybe I thought I was going to grow up before it stormed."

Joel shifted his weight and arranged her body more comfortably against his. "Tomorrow we'll check the attic and see what's there that might work. Or I'll make an emergency call to my decorator."

"You have an attic?"

"A very cool space. My grandmother's things completely fill it. The decorator raids it whenever she needs anything for one of the units. I'm pretty sure there are curtains or whatever you call that stuff that people put on windows." He was being silly, and it was exactly what she needed.

"You don't believe in window treatments?" she teased.

"Only my decorator knows the answer. I may have vetoed something you call window treatments, but I don't pretend to know."

"What have you ever vetoed?"

"Let's see, a chartreuse ottoman comes to mind. Made me want to throw up." He twisted his head to look at her. "You're not—?"

"Going to throw up? No." Manda ran her hand over his chest and did a little swirl with his chest hair. "I wouldn't ruin a perfectly good cuddle."

Joel chuckled. "It is that," he agreed. It was also way too tempting. "However, there is another round of lightning not far off."

Manda tensed.

"I have a very comfortable sofa in a very dark living room that is yours for the rest of the night. And if you'd prefer, we can trade, and I'll sleep down here."

"Don't be ridiculous. I'll take your sofa. If you're worried about me jumping your bones, it's frowned upon in early sobriety," she said solemnly.

He grinned. Maybe the "frowned upon" was only a suggestion, but AA his sponsor Phil treated it like a rule, and Joel had, too, until right now. *Damn.* "Then I won't feel insulted. Anyway, I'll be on the phone and out checking on the properties. I'll try not to disturb your sleep."

"Don't worry about it." She yawned dramatically.

"Grab some clothes for morning and your toothbrush."

"Good idea."

"Self-preservation," he corrected. "It will not look good for you to sneak down the stairs in your pajamas tomorrow morning."

Manda gathered her things. She smiled saucily and told him, "Lead me to your man cave."

Joel let out a laugh and shook his head. "One of us is in trouble here," he predicted.

Manda awoke mid-morning with a killer headache and a satisfied smile on her face. She'd dreamed of steamy sex with Joel all night long.

"Manda Doughty, you wicked woman," she said out loud and then covered her mouth. She glanced around to see if Joel had heard her. His apartment was silent except for the ticking of an imposing grandfather clock. She squinted at its face and made out nine fifteen. It must be the real thing, the kind of clock he wound periodically that ran without power. The squint told her she'd forgotten to bring her glasses with her. She didn't dare run downstairs without putting on clothes.

Joel's guest bathroom was immaculate, fully supplied, and very masculine. She brushed her teeth and downed two of his Tylenol before helping herself to shampoo and spicy scented soap. She turned on the shower, and multiple jets assaulted her. Squealing and dodging, she finally found the combination that gave her soothing rainwater from the ceiling.

Wide-awake and clean all over, she reached for two thick brown towels to dry her hair and body. Her final discovery—silky, spicy body lotion—really needed to be on her grocery list from now on.

Dressed in blue jeans and a t-shirt, but barefoot—another thing she'd forgotten—she started for the front door only to see that it was pinned with a note for her. She plucked off the note, walked across the carpeted living room with it, and drew back the draperies. Sunlight sparkled on the dark blue lake for miles and miles to the south, interrupted only by a dozen evergreen-covered islands. *I'd like to start every day this way.*

Manda wondered if the lake had a different mood every morning. Today it shouted with joy.

She peered at Joel's note. The gold, block-letter heading read "Joel T. Cushman." *Thomas, probably.* She'd never seen his handwriting. It was bold and slanted, every letter at the same angle. "Water damage to your kitchen," it said. "Tony is on it. Your laptop and glasses are on the island. Help yourself to coffee and breakfast. I'll be home before 10. Joel."

She looked skeptically at the lake. *On the island?* When she realized what he meant, she burst out laughing. She set the note on the kitchen island beside her laptop, grabbed her glasses, and went in search of coffee supplies. "A real kitchen," she said out loud as she spied the sophisticated coffee maker, filters, three choices of beans, grinder, and carafe.

She was sitting cross-legged on a kitchen stool with her laptop open when Joel returned.

"That sigh tells me you're exhausted," she told him. "Coffee is hot. Want some?"

He nodded wordlessly and stood looking out at the lake.

When she carried a full mug to him, she smelled smoke on his clothes and saw smudges on his face. "One of the units burned?"

He nodded and gratefully accepted the mug. "House near the marina. Total loss. Kid broke an arm from jumping from an upstairs window, but that was the worst of it. No one else hurt, no one burned. I hate fire," he said.

"Why don't you grab a shower, and I'll fix us something to eat?" She'd seen eggs in the refrigerator and assorted fresh vegetables that would make a tasty frittata.

"I'll take the world's fastest shower and—if you don't mind—I'll fix us a mushroom omelet. I really need to do something creative right now."

"You cook?" she said to his back.

"I do. On weekends. Would you mind drying off the chairs on the porch?" His bedroom door closed before she could reply.

Guessing he'd rather slice the mushrooms himself, she ventured onto a small balcony off the dining room, armed with one of the brown towels. She could see why he called it a porch; it felt like a sheltered, old-fashioned outdoor living space. She tipped the chairs and table to let most of the water drain and drip, before returning to the first chair to buff it dry. It took a few minutes to work her way around. Joel was thick-slicing the mushrooms when she came in. "Thanks for not using a whole roll of paper towels to dry off the furniture," he said.

"I couldn't find any white linen napkins," she told him and was glad to see a smile curve on his mouth.

"I will need more coffee. That was a great pot, thank you."

Manda worked around him easily. "We're a good team," he observed.

She smiled, thinking about how well they had fit together on her futon during the storm. And then there was the wild sex of her dreams.

"What's that smile?" Joel teased.

"A girl needs her secrets," she insisted and changed the subject. "You really know how to handle that omelet pan."

He nodded. "If it weren't so important for me to use the community, I would cook all my meals."

"What do you mean 'use the community'?"

"At one time, I didn't know my way around a kitchen at all, and I ate every meal at one restaurant or another, either alone or with friends. That really put on the pounds. I cut down on restaurants and started cooking for health. That had consequences. The local businesses worried that I didn't like their food or had another favorite restaurant, or yada yada. I realized then it was important to keep good relations with local food service providers. So I continued to eat around town, but in self-defense enlisted their help with a healthy food plan. It has all worked out well."

Joel cut the omelet in two and slid each half onto a plate. "If the coffee's ready, I'll take a carafe out to the balcony. Will you grab the plates and the forks?"

Moments later, seated on the porch overlooking the lake, Manda moaned with pleasure at the taste of the omelet. "What is that herb?" she asked.

"Cilantro. While the eggs are setting up in the bigger pan, I use a small pan to sauté the mushrooms in olive oil with a little fresh ground pepper and cilantro. I do need to take these calls," he apologized when the phone buzzed in his pocket. "And you can't leave until Tony gives the all-clear."

Manda was in no hurry to leave. She tipped back her chair and propped her bare feet on the porch railing. Joel, she noticed, followed her example, all the while carrying on a conversation with one of the contractors.

The sun warmed them. Manda sipped her coffee and listened with half an ear as he fielded phone calls from the work crews and the insurance company and the displaced family. After a while his voice got testy, and she knew he was past his limit. She checked the carafe, poured the remaining coffee in his mug, and took the dishes inside. She decided not to start a fresh pot and, instead, washed her way through the plates and pans, and found where they belonged. Joel came inside, mug in hand, looking for more coffee.

He scowled at her just as she reached to put the larger pan on the rack over the stove. It fumbled in her hand, and she caught it just as Joel grabbed it away from her.

"Let me do that," he snapped. "Make another pot, will you?"

Manda backed away and let him see the fear in her eyes. Her voice trembled when she said, "You are no good to anyone right now; you need sleep."

Joel looked like he wanted to say, "How dare you!" but he held his tongue.

"I came inside when you started snapping, and it did not get better." She kept her gaze steady when she told him, "You're way more effective when you're rested." She watched his jaw harden, but she stood her ground.

Slowly, Joel's face changed as he realized how badly he'd treated her and how much he'd frightened her. His voice was deep and dark when he told her, "You are right. I can't tell you how sorry I am."

Wordlessly, he handed his smartphone to her. He walked into his bedroom and closed the door, leaving her standing with her mouth open, cradling his phone in her hands.

Manda quieted her breathing until all she heard was the ticking of the grandfather clock and the pounding of her own heart.

Chapter 4

Had Joel surrendered his smartphone to her, or did he want her to take messages? With a shrug, she set the phone to vibrate, set up her laptop on the island, and angled the stool for a view of the lake. With her fair skin, she'd had enough sun, but she could never have enough of the dazzling view.

Manda wiggled her fingers and immersed herself in the massive semester-long spreadsheet assignment. When Joel's phone vibrated, she picked it up without thinking, punched the green-phone button, and said, "Hello?"

One of Joel's contractors was checking in to say his job was finished. Manda noted his name, the address where the work was done, and a summary of his message while she introduced herself and chatted for a bit. During the three hours that Joel slept, she logged thirty-eight messages and watched the count of voicemail increase by fifteen.

The calls she answered were intriguing. Two callers were women making personal calls. Joelle with the syrupy Southern accent, wanted to know "when Joely will be coming to Atlanta?" Manda confessed she had no idea. She could hear the pout in Joelle's voice when she said goodbye. Manda noted in her log, "left no phone number and did not ask for a callback." She might get some good teasing out of that, if Joel's mood improved. And, okay, she was a little jealous.

Rachel was a different story. Manda took down the message verbatim and did not ask for any clarification. "Let him know my brother Randy really valued everything he did. The family is grateful." Rachel left a phone number but did not ask Joel to follow up.

The call piqued Manda's curiosity, but she knew it was private and she would not ask Joel about it. Her therapist had been helping her understand boundaries—her own and other people's. Boundaries were a foreign concept to her before she got sober, so every week at her regular therapy appointment, Manda had abundant material to sift through.

Every time one of Joel's contractors called they asked who she was. Manda simply introduced herself as the new bookkeeper. Even though they were under pressure with long lists of repairs after the storm, all of them were calm and professional and glad to meet her, even if quickly over the phone. She could not imagine a faster way to get to know so many of them.

Her favorite caller was Phil with the gravelly voice. Phil challenged her, "Joel doesn't let anyone take his calls. Who are you really?"

"Manda. I really am the bookkeeper." She gave him a cheery voice. "I'll just tell him you called."

"Hold on there. How'd you get him to hand over his phone?"

"I'm not at liberty to say," Manda simpered.

"When's he coming back? He'd better be picking me up at seven. We're solo for Corrections tonight." *Whatever that means.* Phil was obviously not one of the contractors. Manda liked this character.

"I'm sure he knows that and he'll be there on time." Hey, she was getting good at this boundary stuff.

"I don't suppose he's developed the good sense to get some sleep, has he? Was he up all night checking on those properties of his?"

Manda chuckled, "He was up all night checking the properties, and—while I'm not sure good sense was the motivator—yes, he is sleeping."

"Well done, Manda," he said graciously.

"Okay, thanks. And I'll remind him he's picking you up at seven."

"Tell him he'll need to explain what you did to get him to hand over his phone and get some sleep."

"You know, Phil, I'm not going to put that in the message."

He barked a laugh. "I can see your point, Manda." He hung up on that note.

Manda noticed the last missed call was Tony's number. She still had no idea what had happened to her apartment that needed his attention. She wished she could just let the rest of the calls go to voicemail and head back to her apartment to see if the work was finished.

Well, why couldn't she? No one had told her she needed to plant herself on this kitchen stool and take messages. She issued the Print command for her log of messages before realizing Joel's Wi-Fi network was pass-worded. "Bother," she muttered. She couldn't print or email the log to him.

While she debated leaving her laptop open on the island and slipping downstairs, Joel's bedroom door opened a crack and the phone buzzed again. Manda gestured with the phone to ask if he wanted to take the call himself. He shook his head. Manda's eyes followed him across the kitchen as she listened and typed. He was bare chested, and those biceps and shoulders were even more impressive in daylight than they had been last night by flashlight.

Joel came up behind her and rested one hand gently on her back. The heat of his touch made her breath quicken and her heart dance. Joel read the screen over her shoulder. "Thank you," he said quietly when she stopped typing. "I am mortified for yelling at you and scaring you."

Manda turned sideway to look at him. "You really were over the edge. That wasn't doing anyone any good. And you're right, I was scared when you dove for that pan." She knew her therapist would shout, "Hooray! You told him your truth!"

"I apologize. I need to pay attention to how I'm acting and how it affects other people."

Manda nodded her agreement. "You missed a bunch of contractor check-ins," she told him, her voice light. "No crises, unless there are some in voicemail. And some personal calls, everyone from Joelle to Phil."

He laughed softly. "God help us."

"I'd like to print this out for you, but I don't know your password."

"Actually you do. Try yours, but add the year at the end."

Manda pulled up the Wi-Fi setting again and typed the password eleven-eleven-eleven. The printer stirred and quietly issued her call log.

"That is seriously spooky. Or did you just reset your password when I told you mine for voicemail?"

"No, I've been using that password for years. I agree it's spooky."

Manda wished she had the courage to tell him what she'd been thinking during the three hours she fielded his calls. Was this violating a boundary? She didn't know. Probably. She opened her mouth and closed it again at least twice.

Joel made no move to retrieve the printout or to reach for his cell phone. The suspense got old. "Just say it, whatever it is."

Manda took measure of his face and told him, "I've been thinking, you can't be any more than thirty, and you carry a heavy load. I think too heavy, too much work and responsibility. And I don't see someone sharing your life or your work."

He started to object.

"I know," she held up her hand, "You've got lots of people working with you and for you. Good people, competent people. But I don't see someone you love."

Joel looked away awkwardly.

"Someone who warms your heart every day and who shares the day with you. And the night."

His eyes were slits.

She started to apologize but knew she meant every word. "I just... wanted to say that." And she kind of thought she'd earned the right after he'd treated her so badly a few hours ago.

"And you want that for me?" He nailed her with his hawk look.

This time she didn't feel like a helpless little song bird. She nodded calmly.

"I... will take that under advisement," he said seriously, "and point out that's probably a good description of what you want for yourself."

Manda felt her eyes open wide.

Joel laughed. "What, you never thought about finding your soul mate, getting married, the whole package?"

Manda realized her mouth was open. She laughed at herself.

"Well, duh, Manda."

"Duh," she agreed.

On his way to the printer, Joel mumbled, "Couple of orphan loners."

Manda barely heard him. She was busy contemplating the notion of a soul mate. She liked the idea.

Joel listened to his voicemail messages while reading through the log. "Tony is done with the repairs," he told Manda. "He left some clean-up for us." At the next message, he looked quickly at Manda and scanned the rest of the printed log. Relief flooded his face.

When he offered no explanation, Manda shrugged and busied herself shutting down her computer and gathering her things. She told Joel, "I can take care of whatever clean-up needs to be done downstairs. You've got other things to worry about."

Joel shook his head. "Turns out you can't take care of it by yourself. I'll explain when we get there. Let me grab a sweatshirt."

"Darn," Manda said to herself.

"What?" he called from the bedroom.

"Nothing," she said with a saucy smile.

Inside Manda's studio, they found a pile of twigs, leaves, and household trash in the kitchen. Puddles of water stood on the tile. Joel pointed to the window in the kitchen area. "They had to replace that. Something came through it, probably a projectile blown by the wind. Tony'd like you to look around, sort through the rubble and identify anything that would not normally be here."

Manda was on red alert. Had Kristof discovered where she lived and come after her last night? He'd have to be insane to come out in a storm like that, but then he was insane. Anyone who wielded a razor in a college library was insane.

"You're worried Kristof broke in, aren't you?"

"You read my mind." Manda poked through the pile in the kitchen and looked around for anything else that might have caused the broken window. She spotted a metal watering can that definitely was not hers lying on its side near the bathroom.

"I think that's it. It's not mine. A strong wind could pick it up and slam it into anything in its path. Either the spout or the handle could have broken the window. What do you think?"

Joel nodded. "The spout is bent but not rusty, as though it just happened. It's unusable this way, and someone would have thrown it out before this. You don't recognize it as yours or as something from Cady's Point?"

"No, it probably lived on someone's porch nearby. I can't see Kristof using it as a weapon."

"Problem solved." Joel put in a call to Tony while Manda went to work scooping leaves and debris into a trash bag and straightening up the mess in the kitchen. Joel's call to Tony was followed by one to the insurance adjuster concerning the property that burned.

Manda listened to Joel's voice get tighter and more anxious, even though the discussion was amicable and business-like. When he finished the call, Manda was uneasy with his level of agitation.

He snapped, "You're looking at me like I'm doing it again."

"I'm hearing how frustrated and upset you are about the fire, and I didn't make the connection before. That was subject of the phone call earlier that sent you off the deep end."

Joel would not meet her eyes, but he nodded his understanding. "Thank you for making that connection. Now I get it."

"Want to talk about it?"

"I'll talk with Phil about it tonight, but thanks for the offer." He added, "And I would appreciate a kick in the butt anytime I am out of line like that."

Manda moved around him with a smile and told him, "It's such a cute butt, I don't know."

Joel grinned and made a grab for her.

Manda dodged him.

"You are good for me. Seriously, I want you to know I didn't intend to take advantage of your good nature to field phone calls like you did today. That was a big help, but—"

"Listen, it was a good chance for me to meet the contractors, and it will make it easier when the data starts coming in for all the repairs they're working on. So it worked out okay."

"You had to sit indoors on a beautiful day."

"I had committed to studying this morning, which I did between phone calls. I actually finished the killer spreadsheet assignment that's due at the end of the semester, so I came out ahead. I'm not saying I want to be your answering service. I'm just saying it worked out okay this time, so don't worry about it. And it's still a nice day outside."

"Let's postpone the visit to the attic and get this place in shape. Rain check tomorrow morning?"

"Only if you promise it's not going to storm again tonight."

"If it does, you're welcome to crash on my sofa again." He wiggled his eyebrows. "If you dare."

She teased, "I have come to the conclusion you're not sneaky about sex."

Joel frowned. "And that's a good thing?"

"It's a very good thing." She gave him a peck on the cheek and went looking for a sponge and pail to clean up the kitchen floor.

Phil was less willing to give Joel an endorsement for his sexual conduct when Joel picked him that evening. After a bone-crushing hug, Phil settled himself in Joel's passenger seat, buckled his seatbelt, and settled back for the ride. He gave Joel a few minutes to catch him up on mutual friends.

When Joel did not bring up the subject himself, Phil growled, "So who's this fair maiden that knows how to get you into bed when you need it. And are you taking her to bed with you?"

"Manda is my bookkeeper for the properties and my junior accountant at the Manse, and she's newly sober. No, I am not sleeping with her, although it's in my plan after an appropriate period of sobriety and persuasive courtship and marriage."

Phil said grudgingly, "I'm glad to hear you're exercising restraint. You'd lose my respect and that of everyone in the program if you put the moves on a newcomer. I don't care how long you've known her or how well you know her outside of the program, she needs time to clear up and get a foundation with the twelve steps—would you agree?"

"I'm on board with that. And I don't pretend it's easy holding back, but I have every intention of waiting at least a year and letting her get a strong foundation in the twelve steps before we take it any further."

Phil looked at him sideways, and Joel saw the skepticism on his face. "How long do you suppose you'll hold out?"

Joel let out a laugh, then apologized. "Sorry, I do take this seriously. Do you mean my resolve to keep my hands off her, or are you thinking my interest in her will fade away?"

"Thank you for the apology. Both good questions."

"Assuming she stays sober and works a good recovery program, I don't plan to lose interest in her ever."

Phil's head swiveled in surprise. "Back up. When did you meet this object of desire, and exactly why do you think she's worthy of a lifelong commitment?"

"You went away for a month in the sun." Joel lifted his hands from the wheel in mock dismissal, his mouth curving with a smile. "And life happened."

"Details," Phil ordered with a laugh. "I need details. We have an hour's ride to this meeting. I'll navigate while you spill the whole story. Do I need to remind you that AA is a program of rigorous honesty? And I am your sponsor, so don't give me any guff. I will know it if you try it."

"Yes, you will, and that's why you're my sponsor. I have seriously missed these long talks."

Phil's chest puffed up. "That has the ring of truth. I've missed you too, boy."

Joel smiled affectionately at the old man. It was hard for him not having a brother or father. His only relative—his Uncle Justin—was always on the move and frequently out of range of internet or cell phone coverage; it was always a struggle to track him down and carry on a conversation. Phil had taken on a lot when he agreed to sponsor Joel in recovery.

Joel told Phil about his encounter with Manda Doughty in the shower at the spa.

"Manda the Brave," Phil commented.

"What?"

"Her name. Doughty is Irish. I believe it means plucky and courageous. And anyone contemplating involvement with you needs courage. Manda the Brave," he repeated.

"Her name made me think of 'Dowdy,' because she was a frump. Who knew what she was hiding?"

"And what exactly was she hiding?"

"A spectacular body and a lot of bruises." Joel filled him in on the abusive situation with Kristof and the fiasco at the college with the Presidential Scholars.

"Leave the college side of the story for later. I can tell there is a lot to say about that. What's her status with Kristof, and have you told Manda your history with the Kristofs of Cady's Point?"

Joel drove silently for a minute.

"I'll take that as a No, you haven't made her aware of your history there."

"Do I need to?"

Phil let out his breath in frustration. "Only if you want to have an honest relationship with this woman."

"I'm afraid she'll freak."

"Imagine how she'll freak when she finds out from the rumor mill, and realizes you've been keeping it from her."

Joel swore under his breath.

"No kidding. Put that on your list of discuss-with-Manda topics. Probably at the top of the list, but let's hear the rest."

Joel ran through the follow-on attacks by Kristof, along with Manda's move to the dorm and subsequent move to

Lakeside Terrace. Finally he explained the situation with the storm and the clean-up at Manda's place.

Phil twisted in his seat. "And you expect me to believe this object of your desire slept undisturbed on your sofa all night while you rescued all of your tenants?"

Joel took his eyes off the road long enough to make eye contact with Phil.

"Yeah, okay, it does sound like something the new, improved Joel Cushman would do. How long have you been in this self-imposed moratorium on dating every beauty that comes along?"

"Coming up on two years, and I think you imposed it first."

"Two years? Hard to believe."

"Tell me about it."

He was glad to get a laugh out of Phil. They were finally back in synch after a month apart.

"I need to tell you what happened between Manda and me that got me to hand over my phone and hit the sack for a few hours."

"I've been waiting for this. Let's hear it."

When Joel finished telling him the story and added Manda's perception of the fire as a trigger for Joel's anger and irritability, Phil pressed Joel's arm. "Let me give this some thought."

A few miles passed before he said, "I don't think either of us realized your post-traumatic stress about your sister Christie dying in the fire could impact a relationship that way."

Joel nodded his agreement and swallowed with discomfort, remembering the fear on Manda's face.

"It speaks well of her and of you that she could push past being afraid and call you on your behavior. Sounds like she's got some good sobriety and good counseling already."

Joel nodded his agreement.

"Has anybody ever confronted you that way? Besides me, I mean."

"Certainly no woman has. Tony's been in my face a few times. Uncle Justin, of course."

"Well, I'm impressed that you let the criticism penetrate and are using it as a stepping stone for more growth. Do you feel you need more therapy?"

"I don't think so, but I am open to it."

Phil sat back. "I'll say this: your moratorium has paid off, but I have to say I'm still very uneasy about the fact this woman is so young and so new to sobriety." He raised his voice, "I mean it when I say you need to let her work intensely with a sponsor for as long as it takes her to move through the steps. That's the way she'll develop healthy relationship skills and maturity."

"I get it, and I agree."

"So you haven't told her your history with Lorraine Kristof. I take issue with that. What other secrets are you keeping from her?"

"What do you mean?"

"We've talked about the way you keep secrets. I understand you come from a family that hid its dirty laundry, and I commend you for working hard to be up front and honest in your professional role. But I'm concerned you're back to keeping secrets, and that's no way to have an honest relationship with a woman."

Joel felt puzzled. "For example?"

"Does she know you lost your family?"

"No."

"Why not?"

"We talked about her losing her parents. I wasn't going to lay my stuff on her."

"You don't think she'll understand?"

Joel waved it aside. "I think she's got enough to think about."

"Then, does she know you have a fortune and a charitable foundation?"

"Probably."

"Probably?" Phil pressed. "She who has been struggling to put food in her mouth might or might not happen to know you're filthy rich? And you're certain she's not playing you for Prince Charming?"

Joel yelled back at him, "I don't know. I never know what to do with that. You know there's only ever been one woman who didn't have money as her motive with me. I want this to be an honest relationship, and I guess I'm too conflicted about the money to test her knowledge or her understanding."

"Good that you can admit that to yourself and to me," Phil prefaced and thought about what he wanted to say. He checked the passing signs and waved at the traffic signal up ahead. "Don't miss our turn up here. We've talked about that conflict, and I understand your hesitation, but it has to be put on the table. The real test comes when you have a conversation with her about it."

"So, okay, that's on my discussion list," Joel snapped. "Above or below the Kristofs?"

"I don't know, but you'd better make it soon. If you put off discussing those hard truths, they're likely to come out unedited under stress, and that could destroy any trust you've built to that point. Get your ID out for the guard before he turns that machine gun on us."

Joel nodded, half his attention focused on the security check-in at the tollgate.

Phil assured him, "I will always pick up the pieces—you know that. And you don't have to drink."

Joel kept his hand at Phil's elbow as they walked from the parking lot. He went ahead of Phil through the familiar, but never comfortable protocol, of signing into the prison, relinquishing their possessions, walking through the screening devices, navigating a series of electronically controlled portals, and finally arriving at the room where they would put on an AA meeting for half a dozen inmates at various stages of sobriety.

Joel would never have volunteered for this form of AA service, but he was grateful to Phil for involving him in the Corrections meetings two years ago. He was at a point in sobriety where he needed to make fundamental changes—even more than he had when he first got sober.

Learning the inmates' stories, while having the freedom to leave the prison at the end of the meeting, had convinced him he had nothing to feel sorry about in his own life. The saying, "There, but for the grace of God, go I," played in his head all through the prison meetings and every time he thought of them during the month between.

"All right," Phil commanded, settling in his seat as they made their way on dry roads back to Tompkins Falls. "Let's hear about the college situation—the lothario professor as you call him, the scholarship program, and whatever else is related." He shook a finger at Joel. "And I'll tell you right now, I don't want to hear that you're being overly responsible. I realize the college carries your mother's name, but you're not solely responsible for making it successful or for cleaning up the mess caused by criminals."

"I get that," Joel said with more confidence that he felt. "However, the students need to be protected, and, to the extent the criminal activity affects admissions and development dollars, we've got to clean it up."

"I like the sound of '*we* have to clean it up'. Proceed." Phil shifted in his seat so he could see the expression on Joel's face.

"For one thing, the whole mess with Kristof goes way beyond the demise of his marriage and the abuse toward

Manda. I'll give you details in a minute—but first I want to say it's been tricky having contact with Manda while we investigate." Joel lifted first one hand from the wheel, then the other, as he told Phil, "I'm in a delicate situation as her boss, landlord, and friend on the one hand, and trustee of the college on the other."

Phil's eyes narrowed in concentration. "So, how have you been handling this particular trickiness?"

"Probably not the best way. After the attack on her in the library, I took her shopping for a cell phone."

"Took her shopping because she has no money?"

"I had to be sure she would actually get one and use it."

Phil motioned with his hand for Joel to answer his question. "Did you pay for it?"

Joel chuckled. "No. Turns out she has a credit card and enforces very strict rules for her spending. She used the card to buy the phone." Joel swallowed his pride and added, "Then she picked up the tab for breakfast."

Phil hooted with laughter. "Good for her."

Joel rushed on, "The point is, I picked her up at her campus apartment for this excursion."

"Risky," Phil agreed, "in the middle of an investigation, for the chair of the board of trustees to be seen at a complainant's dorm." He shook his head.

"I know, even though I parked in one of the visitor lots, and I was lucky no one was stirring at eight in the morning. I buzzed her apartment from the main door and asked her to come down. Afterwards she dropped me at the visitor lot to get my car. The campus was still basically deserted. It is simpler to have her off campus now."

"Except," Phil shook a finger, "she's living two floors away from you now. Have you thought about how that looks?"

"She's legitimately doing a job for me and paying a nominal rent for her apartment."

"Was that your good thinking?"

"The job definitely was. I was going crazy trying to handle the rent checks, the contractors, and the lunatic spreadsheet Denise set up."

"And Manda's rent?"

"Her idea. She was very sensitized by the financial threat Kristof made. He threatened to have her scholarship revoked if she didn't put out for him. And as it turns out, her spring tuition had still not been paid at the point we started investigating. Someone had blocked the system from automatically applying her scholarship benefit to the tuition bill, so as far as Manda knew, she was still on the hook for a little more than fifteen thousand."

"Piece of—" Phil muttered and moved his right foot on the floor mat as if moving aside a smelly pile.

"So she's paying in rent what she saves each week by not drinking after work at the Vintner's Lounge."

"How does that compare with what you would normally get for that apartment?"

"A small fraction, but I'm not concerned about the money."

"Of course not. And I'd say that was a smart move on her part, insisting on some kind of rent. It protects you as much as it protects her."

Joel turned his head and made eye contact with Phil for a second. "Good point. I missed that completely."

"Your ego got in the way. I'm hearing your obsessive need to rescue all through this story," Phil pointed out with a shake of his head. "I hope she's graduating soon?"

"In May. I'll be glad to have that complication behind us."

"Well, be careful in the meantime. You don't want to compromise your position or your investigation." Phil powered down his window and took a few deep breaths of fresh air before powering it up again. "There, I think I'm ready to hear what's happening with the Kristof side of the investigation."

"It's ugly. What we know so far is that this guy has been preying on students for a while, possibly years. We have no shortage of academically weak students, and many of them think it's okay to sleep with the professor to get decent grades. There's nothing new about that. We have a strong sexual harassment policy and workshops for faculty, staff, and students. To find out we have violations going on of this magnitude and this duration, without anyone's awareness, is alarming."

Phil gave him an incisive look. "There are probably complaints being issued, but they're going nowhere or being misdirected or mishandled, don't you think?"

"I agree. What's unbelievable is that we handpicked the people who act as point persons for students with concerns and allegations. We've followed up with those people, and they say complaints were filed and forwarded to the officers and to the authorities. But there's no record anywhere that complaints were ever filed."

Phil opened his hands and offered his explanation. "That tells me Kristof has a student hacker at his disposal altering the systems, besides having connections inside and outside the college."

Joel nodded, his mouth set in a grim line. "Exactly. He's been very well-protected by persons still unknown. He probably has the goods on one or more college officers who look perfectly respectable. And I'm sure from what the police said he has connections in the community."

"And in law enforcement?"

"Almost certainly. I've talked a few times now with the police chief, and I know he's digging within his organization."

"This is a serious investigation then?" Phil asked for confirmation.

Joel nodded and took a deep breath to calm the turmoil in his stomach.

"Does that mean Manda's name has been on the table as one of the victims?"

Joel breathed quietly for a minute, trying to keep his emotions under control.

"Joel, I'm waiting for an answer."

"Yes, it does mean her situation is known to the president and other administrators, as well as the police, campus security, counseling services, and residential services."

"And does she realize this?"

"Not about the administrators, no."

"Are you going to tell her?"

Joel snapped, "How can I? Without destroying her self-esteem, which is pretty fragile at this stage." He shook his head. "I'm sorry I snapped at you."

It was Phil's turn to be quiet. He responded with another question. "Is she a good student?"

"Nearly first in her class. All her professors vouch for her genuine talent and intelligence and diligence."

"So there's no question. She was not looking for a kinky kind of grade inflation."

"Not at all."

Phil pressed Joel's arm to offer support. "I don't know how to advise you about what you say to her and when. But I do know if it comes out publicly, she's going to have a very bad time with it."

"I know. But I couldn't keep her name out of it and also conduct the thorough investigation we needed."

Phil nodded his agreement. "I'm sure that was a very difficult decision for you. It shows a lot of integrity, Joel. Think anything will come of it?"

"The investigation? The police are handling things from the criminal side. At the college, I think we've built a solid case for blackballing Kristof in higher education in this area. But I don't see any way for the college to prosecute without dragging at least a dozen students' names into the media at a time when they're trying to move on with their lives, get into grad school, get jobs and start careers."

"Is Manda the only one among them that was not looking for grade inflation?"

"Not at all. We've heard some serious accusations by very strong students. I wasn't kidding when I said it was ugly and alarming both."

"Anyone else threatened with loss of scholarship or other funding?"

Joel opened his window a crack. "Not that we've heard yet. We will continue to investigate, but the more we dig, the more we're in danger of exposure to the media. If the alumni hear about this, our development dollars are impacted. If parents and high school counselors get wind of it, our applications and admissions will suffer."

Phil flipped his hand over and back as he concluded, "So potentially, doing the right thing could sink your college, the one your forefathers' founded in what year?"

Joel shrugged, "I don't know. Eighteen something."

"Sucks."

Joel let out his breath in a laugh and nodded his agreement.

"Joel, I admire you for having the courage to go forward with the investigation. I wish I'd been here for you."

Joel gave him a warm smile. "Thank you. Because you were away, I tried to get hold of Justin to—"

Phil squinted. "Your uncle? Who is a Cushman but not a Tompkins?"

"Family just the same. With a right to know and to weigh in."

"Did you get him?"

"I did. I don't know what's up with him. But he did get back to me and gave me his blessing."

Phil's voice cracked in surprise. "But not anything more?"

"Some good advice. What were you thinking?"

"I'm just thinking he's been very hands-on in the past when you've called upon him."

Joel shrugged. "Like I said I don't know what's up with him. He didn't sound well."

"Physically?"

"Yeah."

"Is he one of us?"

"I've never known Justin to over-indulge in anything, including alcohol."

Phil's eyebrows arched. "Not even women? What is he, a saint?"

Joel laughed. "Can't be a saint. He likes money too much."

"More than women?"

Joel tipped his head from side to side as he thought about it. "Could be."

Phil sighed and sat back against the seat. "Doesn't sound a bit healthy to me."

They drove in silence for another mile before Phil asked, "What happened with the scholarship program Manda was on?"

Joel shook his head in frustration. "That's looking like a corruption case—embezzlement."

"You can't be serious?" Phil sat forward again and turned for a better look at Joel's face.

Joel was wearing a grim smile. "A few years back, someone made a stellar case for having the Presidential Scholars give up their room, board, and living allowance to engage in community service. They would be guided to other funding to make up the shortfall as needed. The pitch was linked to the new college initiative for civic engagement.

"However, no one followed through with the scholars about their unmet financial need. All the scholars were left stranded with just tuition reimbursement. Most had to leave the college entirely. Or go part time, which jeopardized their standing as Presidential Scholars; their scholarships were demoted to part-time. Manda is one of the few that toughed it out and found a way to finance the missing pieces as well as graduate in four years." Joel smacked his hand on the steering wheel. "Why would anyone target the top students? Or was it just a handy source of money for someone?"

Phil's face filled with disbelief. "And no one realized all this?"

"I didn't. None of the trustees did. The president had no clue."

Phil waved his hand. "No one realized the best and brightest students were disappearing in large numbers?"

Joel shook his head. "Possibly the people who had set up the situation to siphon off the money — room, board, and living allowances — for their own purposes."

"You can't be serious?"

Joel nodded. "We can identify one individual who retired very recently —February of this year, to be specific— who apparently master-minded the scheme."

Phil waved his hand back and forth. "And no one knew? No one stopped him? Or her?"

Joel shook his head. "We're pretty sure a few others knew about it and were paid to let it happen without opposition."

"How much money are we talking?"

"At least half a million."

Phil jumped in his seat. "What! What's going on at that college?"

Joel sighed heavily. "There have been more than a few people shocked by both situations—Kristof's long-term harassment and the embezzlement on the backs of our brightest students. Myself included. And I think I can identify a few bad actors at pretty high levels of administration who must have known all about it. I'm committed to cleaning it up and keeping it out of the media as much as possible."

Phil directed his finger back at Joel and shook it at him. "I didn't hear 'we' this time. You cannot take full responsibility for this. You do know that?"

Joel nodded. "I do know that. I threatened to resign from the board and withdraw the Tompkins name and backing from the college if the trustees don't receive a full accounting for the Presidential Scholars embezzlement and recommendations with an action plan, and the same for fixing the holes in the reporting system for sexual harassment. No later than the end of June. This June."

Phil dropped his gaze for a moment and then raised his eyes to Joel. "Good use of your power, Joel."

Joel blinked and then met Phil's gaze. "Thank you. I needed to hear that. I am probably the least popular figure at the college at this moment. Even Kristof is coming off as a harmless lecher in comparison."

"I doubt that. And I'm sure people are aware that without your backing the college is history. Are you prepared to follow through?"

"Pull out my support and financial backing? I believe I am. Not as early as June, perhaps, but by the end of the calendar year."

Phil folded his arms and heaved a sigh. "That would be a sad day for the town and the college."

"I am not insensitive to either. At the same time, the college is struggling like all small liberal arts institutions, and there are plenty of other colleges nearby to serve the students. I'm sure that scares anyone who's hearing rumors about the investigations even if they're not involved in the corruption or the harassment."

"Good point. And related to that…" Phil sat up straighter and uncrossed his arms.

"What?"

"Rumors. I'm sure people are seeing you with Manda and speculating about your relationship. Maybe no one spotted you on campus picking her up for your phone date, but I know you. You've probably been walking with her at work and around Lakeside Terrace. Tony certainly knows about you, and he's not the soul of discretion."

"Tony's been warned to keep it quiet," Joel defended his friend.

"Tony's got a lot of friends who know how to get little tidbits out of him and turn them into juicy stories."

Joel rolled his eyes.

"Am I right?"

"You're right, but he is not malicious, and I am a big boy."

"But Manda is not."

Joel thought a moment and let out a frustrated breath. "You're right. I'm not used to thinking that way."

Phil exhaled loudly. "Start thinking that way. And, realistically, Manda may have to face that one way or another."

"What are you saying?"

"I'm saying you are doing all in your professional power to protect her and to protect the college, but she's vulnerable all the same. In a way that can affect her sobriety. Does she have a strong sponsor?"

"She's asked Barb, but I don't think—"

Phil twisted in his seat. "Barb with the 'bad picker, good picker' story?"

Joel nodded.

"That's a mistake."

"I know. What can I do?"

Phil opened his hands and offered, "Everything you can—as her employer and her friend—to strengthen and support her program. Including giving her a wide berth at her meetings."

"I don't go to her meetings."

"Good."

"In fact, I haven't told her I'm in the program."

Phil studied Joel's profile, the firm jaw and patrician nose. "What's up with that?"

"Honestly, I'm not sure. I guess I want her to find her own way with the support of others in the program and not rely on me."

Wondering about his silence, Joel looked over at Phil.

"You think I'm wrong?"

"No, I'm just surprised. But I think it's going to come up soon, and I'm hoping you're not uneasy or ashamed in any way."

"I'm not. I half suspect she's already figured it out."

"How?"

Joel shrugged. "We in AA have our own vocabulary sometimes, and I'm sure I use it when we talk about her sobriety."

Joel dropped Phil at his house on the lake, returned to Lakeside Terrace before midnight, and slept like the dead. He had desperately missed his sponsor and their long, candid talks each week. It felt good to unburden the way he had.

When the sun rose outside his French doors, he drifted awake and ran through his litany of morning prayers. Usually his first thought was coffee. Today it was Manda.

He stumbled half asleep onto his porch and breathed in the fresh morning air. Pockets of mist clung to the islands this morning; an orange sun blazed a trail across the lake toward him; a flock of geese honked to his left as they rose from the water. His eyes followed their flight until a movement on the beach caught his attention. An early-morning walker was stretching, warming up for the trek. He saw it was Manda in blue jeans and a hoodie.

Joel pulled on blue jeans and a sweatshirt, laced up his sneakers, and pounded down the stairs. He called to her from the parking lot to wait for him.

She waved happily and gave him a thumbs up. When he caught up with her, she asked, "Were you going to yell at me for walking alone?"

"That was going to be my excuse," Joel said, his eyes sparkling in the sunrise. "Truth is I wanted to walk with you. But," he emphasized, "Kristof is a free man and a danger to you. You've got your cell phone?"

Manda whipped it out of her pocket and showed him it was already programmed to autodial 911 with a single press of a button in an emergency. "I know you wanted me to have GPS or whatever that's called. We've already had that argument, and I'm not a sore winner."

Joel ruffled her hair.

"Any hope he'll ever be detained for more than the hour it takes him to summon his lawyer each time he's arrested?"

Joel exhaled in frustration. "I can't speak for the police. I know they're committed to this case, and they can do more than the college to put him out of action. If he's not behind bars by the end of the semester, I think the college will make him an offer her can't refuse to take an extended sabbatical. Far away."

Manda gave him a searching look.

"I can't tell you any more than that, and I'm sorry it's not more reassuring," he closed the discussion. "Where are you heading? Want company?"

"I'd love company. I'm glad you're rested and relaxed this morning."

"An improvement over yesterday. I apologize again. I appreciate your willingness to forgive me."

Manda shrugged. "You know, I was thinking how freaked out I was by the lightning, and it kind of seemed like you were having a hard time just like that."

"Lakeshore?"

She nodded.

Joel put his hands in his pockets as they walked. He wanted to talk with Manda about some of the topics Phil had identified last night, but he wasn't sure if he had the courage.

Their route covered half a mile of residential streets to the lakefront park and a mile of gravel path along the lakeshore to a big public parking lot. One more mile of gravel path stretched beyond the parking lot, along the shore, but Joel knew from experience it was soggy with slush and mud.

He gathered courage as they walked and talked. Finally, Joel slowed his steps. "Do you know the term PTSD?"

"I've heard it at least a dozen times lately from everybody—my therapist, people in AA, and even Tony. I guess I have it, but they suggested I focus on the alcoholism for now. I'm mostly confused about what PTSD is."

"Post-traumatic stress disorder is a response some people have to a traumatic or life-threatening situation, whether it's a big one-time event or a series of threatening encounters or a chronic living situation like growing up in the middle of gang wars. You and I have both experienced trauma in one of those ways.

"The way I understand it, one of the symptoms is reliving the situation when something triggers a reminder. For me, dealing with fire triggers it, which I didn't fully understand until you pointed it out to me."

Manda's eyes were wide. "You were feeling like I do sometimes; powerless, anxious, maybe angry, too?"

"Exactly. Lightning is a trigger for you, maybe for the ordeal at Kristof's, but I think you said you've always been afraid of it. I'm not trying to pry."

"That's okay. With two alcoholic parents, our house could get pretty violent. It seems like the noise of the thunder should be the trigger, but lightning is what does it."

"Your dad was the violent one?"

Manda nodded.

"I'm sorry you went through that."

She shrugged. "I know I picked up attitudes and behaviors watching my mother, who just stayed in the marriage and took the abuse and drank right along with him. It probably sounds familiar."

Joel face creased in a smile. "Like you did with Kristof."

"Got it in one."

"Manda, can I ask how your parents died?"

"Drunk driving accident. Lyssa was a senior in high school, and I was a junior. Our parents went out to a movie, stopped afterwards 'for a couple' and never made it home. When they still weren't home in the morning, Lyssa and I called the hospitals and finally the police. They searched for a day before they found the car. The sheriff told us the car had gone off the road for no reason—no sign of braking or hazards—just went off the road and dropped through the trees into a ravine. They both died right away, and I'm grateful for that."

Joel put his arm across her shoulders.

She gave him a smile. "And I like feeling your arm around me."

He gave her a squeeze and let go. He really shouldn't do that in public. Yet.

"I don't think it would freak me out if you told me about your fire, but I understand if you don't want to."

Joel's heart pounded. He took a deep breath. "Actually it might freak me out." He laughed at himself. "I do want to tell you." He felt Phil urging him on.

When he was quiet a while longer, Manda told him, "I'm a pretty good listener."

"I know that." He reached for her hand and gave it a quick squeeze. "My sister Christie was killed in a crash. I was thirteen; she was sixteen."

"That's horrible, Joel. I'm so sorry."

"She was great. I am grateful we were always friends." He took another deep breath and hoped he could tell her the rest.

Manda was quiet, listening.

"It was an accident in a heavy snowstorm. Our SUV flipped and rolled. I was thrown clear of the wreckage; no one knows how. Christie was trapped. She was conscious, calling out for help—even before the fire started—and I couldn't do anything. Both my legs were broken. I kept yelling to her that I loved her and it would be all right, but it wasn't all right. A fire started. She screamed, and it just killed me to be so powerless.

"When the whole car exploded, I knew it was finally over for her." His heart was racing, and he felt tears fall from his eyes.

"Joel, I don't know what to say. How horrible."

He choked on a sob and, when he felt Manda's arms come around him, he buried his face in her hair. He let her hold him and listened to her soothing voice.

"You're okay. All of that happened a long time ago."

Manda's hands stroked his back, and he felt himself growing calmer. The trembling stopped at last. His head ached but no longer throbbed. He loosened his hold on her and wondered if he dared look her in the eye.

Manda's hand brushed across his shoulder and came to rest on his cheek. The palm of her hand was soft and cool.

"I'm glad you told me, Joel. I understand better why you were so freaked yesterday."

Joel took a steadying breath. "I will hopefully be able to see it coming if I get freaked about fire again, instead of taking it out on you or someone else."

"I'm sure you hated that, when you realized the impact on me. And I'm fine now. We're fine, Joel."

"Even with a lot of therapy, this is one thing that has never gotten better," he told her. "I guess there are some things you just never get over."

"Right now the Kristof nightmare seems like a minor detail compared with losing your sister that way, but I hope I get over it."

"You will." Joel felt his whole body shudder in the aftermath of his adrenaline rush.

Manda put her arms around his waist and pressed her cool cheek against his until he stopped shaking. "I can't imagine how you survived that mentally," she whispered.

"I need to leave that chapter for another time," he decided. "But the end point is—and this is probably no surprise to you—it eventually led me to AA."

Manda loosened her arms and smiled at him. "I wondered about that."

They walked silently, arms brushing, and finally turned and started back the way they came. "I've been avoiding your meetings just to give you space, but I wanted you to know."

"Would you mind if I showed up at a meeting you're at?"

"I don't think so. I know you like that women's meeting on Fridays, but there's also a good meeting in town Fridays at seven."

"What other meetings do you go to? Or is that it?"

"I'm an Early Riser."

Manda waited a beat and then chuckled, "Is that the name of a meeting?"

He laughed. "Sorry, yes. Seven o'clock every morning, 365 days a year, at the bagel place downtown. There's a back room, and about twenty of us show up most mornings."

She checked her watch. "You would normally be there now." She teased, "Let me guess—black coffee, whole-grain bagel dry."

"Close. Sesame seed or sun-dried tomato. Occasionally yogurt with fresh fruit instead of the bagel." He pointed to a little coffee shop across from the park. "I am suddenly craving coffee."

"Sounds good to me."

In the afternoon, Joel delivered on his promised trip to the attic to scrounge window treatments for Manda's apartment. "You'd have liked my grandmother. This is her stash we're raiding."

"Your father's mother or your mother's mother?"

"Mother's. She was Irish. O'Donohue by birth, from the old country, and it was said she was fey."

Manda grinned. "I haven't heard that term in years. It means she could see the future?"

Joel nodded. "I figured a Doughty might know what it meant."

"And what did she read in your tea leaves?" Manda teased.

"She said I would kiss many women before I found the one."

"Oh, I totally believe that."

Joel reached around her to unlock the attic door.

Manda stepped through the doorway ahead of him. "Un—" she started to say and paused to run her hands across the bolts of fabric piled on shelves. "—believable," she finished. "It's like an upholstery shop."

Joel laughed. "Grandmother Bridey was a fanatic decorator."

"This fabric! I already see three bolts that are perfect for the studio."

"How do you know about this stuff?" Joel wondered.

"My mother was really good with a sewing machine. She made all our clothes and curtains and slipcovers and yada yada. She taught us a lot. I wonder if there are supplies up here, too? It would be really easy to make Roman shades."

Joel pointed diagonally across the space. "Check by the dormer where the sun's coming in."

Manda picked her way through tables, lamps, lamp shades, pillow forms, braids and trims, tassels, ottomans, and foot stools. "What did your grandmother do? Was she actually a decorator?"

"No way. She just loved changing the way things looked every couple of years. She had great taste, and my grandfather indulged her. She knew a very talented seamstress and decorator. In fact, her decorator's daughter is the person I use for my place and for the other apartments when anything needs to be done."

"Did your decorator set up my studio?"

Joel nodded. "So I'm not surprised you're seeing things that will coordinate. I don't pretend to know anything about this stuff."

"I doubt that. You have very good taste."

"I completely depend on people who know what they're doing," he confessed.

"For clothes and everything?"

"For clothes and everything. I did not inherit my grandmother's fine taste. I'm a basic blue jeans kind of guy when I have a choice."

Manda wondered aloud, "Then why do you have the kind of day job where you need to wear cashmere jackets and fine tailored suits?"

Joel looked across the space at her wide eyes and open face. She really didn't know, he realized. "We'll talk about that soon," he promised. Manda scrunched her face in puzzlement. "I know that sounds cryptic. It's kind of a long story," he added as she shrugged and smiled.

They went in different directions—Joel to check for leaks from the storm, Manda to explore. The silence was broken only by Manda's exclamations and the clinks and bumps as boxes, rods, and brackets yielded to her probing. "Yahoo!"

Manda dropped two oblong boxes on the floor and pulled a scrap of paper from her pocket. She compared her measurements with those on the packages. "Yes!"

"What's all this?"

"I measured my four windows. These two kits will work. I need two more just like them. Can you help me look?" She pointed to the numbers on the boxes that identified the winning combination. "If I can find them, it will be a snap to make shades. Everything I need is in the kit, except the fabric."

Joel dug through boxes and found one.

Manda found another. "Yes!" she cheered. "High five!"

She reached across the intervening boxes to meet Joel's raised hand.

"Let's check out fabric." She stood up and gasped.

"What?"

She pointed. "A sewing machine. Does it work?"

"Where?" Sure enough, there was a spool of thread standing on top of a shiny black old-fashioned sewing machine. "I never noticed that."

"It's an old Singer Featherweight," Manda marveled.

"Is that good?"

"They are indestructible. Can we try it out up here?"

Joel found an outlet and lugged the machine to it.

Manda folded onto her knees, fed in a scrap of fabric and worked the foot pedal with her other hand. The fabric fed through with no hesitation. The stitches were even and straight.

"Joel, it's perfect. May I use it for a while?"

"You can have it."

"That's not necessary, but I'd love to use it to make the shades."

"It has been gathering dust in this attic for more than a decade. I think." There was no actual dust on it. "You found it. It's yours."

"Joel, really, I can't just take it. But will you help me move it down to my place for now?"

"Sure. Where will you set it up?"

"Good point. Maybe there's a little table." She looked around her from her spot on the floor. Seeing none, she stood up and searched the perimeter of the attic.

Joel waded into the jumble of furniture, lamps, and lampshades in the middle.

"What about this?" he called to her.

He had uncovered what looked like the original stand for the sewing machine.

"You're brilliant. It will fit just inside my door, won't it? There's a little straight chair there right now that I can use with it. You really don't mind?"

"Mind?" Joel came up to her and touched her cheek.

Manda's eyes sparkled with joy.

Everything else shifted into soft focus for Joel.

Without a moment's thought, his mouth was on hers, and her lips parted. The kiss deepened.

Manda's hands traveled across his shoulders and up to his silky hair. She guided his mouth to her ear, her neck, her throat.

Joel's hands explored her body, stroked her back, cupped her buns and pulled her against him.

Manda parted her legs and lifted just enough for his hard bulge to press against her sweet spot. When she squeezed, his breath came out in a burst of pleasure. That woke her up. "Geez, Joel, are we out of our minds?"

Joel's head came up in shock. He pulled back too quickly and moaned with the discomfort of it. "I am sorry. This is my fault. I'm supposed to be the mature one here."

Manda laughed and gave him a playful punch on the arm. "Well, thanks!"

Joel ran a finger down her cheek and looked into her eyes. "Mature in terms of sobriety, I mean. Obviously, I have no brain."

"Me, too," Manda breathed and felt her face flame.

Joel leaned against the sewing table, and it held his weight. "I like making you blush," he teased.

Manda moved closer, and he pulled her to him. She rested her head in the curve of his neck.

He told her, "I may be old-fashioned, but I am trying very hard to keep my hands off you until you're in a position to decide if I'm someone you want to be dating, which should come before groping in the attic. The way I see it, you're someone that's meant for a loving, committed relationship."

"I can't tell you how good it is to hear that." Manda eased back with a happy smile.

Joel reluctantly let her go. "Got an idea," he proposed. "I'll take the sewing machine and this very sturdy table down to your place, while you hunt for fabric. And I'll get my act together as a mature, sober alcoholic who happens to think your body is spectacular." He gave one last longing look at the curvy beauty standing a foot in front of him. "And I have never enjoyed a kiss so much in my life."

"Thank you," Manda grinned.

Joel nodded. "My pleasure."

Manda straightened her sweatshirt and looked around to get her bearings. She turned back to him with a saucy smile. "For the record, I enjoyed that hugely."

"Really? I had no idea," he quipped.

She tossed a lampshade at him.

Chapter 5

Manda realized she'd been burying her head in the bottle and her nose in her books for four years. As a student she'd rarely set foot in the city of Tompkins Falls. Most of her time was divided between the campus on the southwest corner of the city, the Manse southeast of the city, and Cady's Point several miles farther south along the lake.

Now her route to and from AA meetings took her through old residential streets, past half a dozen elegant homes, through middle class neighborhoods, and even into a few pockets of poverty. She saw some small industries, but Manda was willing to bet the economy was mostly fueled by tourism.

Tourists flocked to Tompkins Falls and Chestnut Lake, just as they did to all of the Finger Lakes. Camping, boating, and swimming were popular half the year. Motorists enjoyed drives through the countryside dotted with vineyards and picturesque Mennonite farms, complete with horse-drawn buggies. Limos took tourists on wine tasting tours year-round.

The name of the lake made no sense her until an AA old timer heard her ask, "Why is our lake Chestnut Lake and not Willow Lake or some Indian name?"

He told her about the American Chestnut trees that had been plentiful in the area more than a century ago. They'd been the tallest trees on the east coast, growing to more than a hundred feet; they had all but disappeared, destroyed by the chestnut blight.

The name of the city still eluded her. In all her routes through Tompkins Falls, she had still not found a waterfall. Nor did she know if a Tompkins family had founded the city and the college or if the city derived its name from the college or the other way around. Either way, they seemed to be long gone like the American Chestnut. All Manda knew for sure was that—with a population of about twenty thousand, plus one thousand college students—Tompkins Falls was on old U.S. Route 20, just a few miles south of the New York State Thruway, making it easily accessible for tourists from Canada, New York City, and anywhere else. And it was becoming home for her, now that she was sober.

For Manda, living on Lakeside Terrace meant she could walk along the lakeshore anytime she wanted. From her perch at the top of the bluff, she walked downhill and around a large marina to the public park. There a two-mile, willow-bordered bike and walking path stretched along the north end of Chestnut Lake.

While it was not the largest or the prettiest of the Finger Lakes, Chestnut Lake was magical in Manda's eyes. The color of the water constantly changed, the winds and breezes blew as they pleased, and the quality of the light sparked her imagination. It was dramatic like her recovery —always fresh, always revealing new truths and possibilities.

Her personal recovery might be constantly changing, but her AA program was a rock-solid foundation, like the rocky bluff that Lakeside Terrace was built on. One Friday in April, Manda worked too late to drive to the women's meeting in Clifton Springs. She grabbed a salad instead and made her way to the Friday night meeting at the Lutheran church.

Joel watched her walk into the fellowship hall, looking a little unsure. One of the old timers yelled across the room, "Hey, Mandy, where ya been?" He could see her blush all the way across the room. Friends from another meeting spotted her and drew her into their conversation. Joel started toward her but was pulled aside.

Barb dug her fingers into his arm and whispered loudly in his ear. He listened, smiled politely, and continued his path to Manda.

Manda saw him coming and gave him a big smile.

Joel asked her, casually, "First time at this meeting?"

"Someone I know suggested it."

He held her eyes and once again everything blurred for him into happy swirl of movement and conversation.

"Are you okay talking to me at a meeting?"

She nodded.

He touched her elbow. "I just learned something new about you," he said and raised one eyebrow.

She raised both eyebrows, "I can't wait to hear this!"

He chuckled. "Barb just told me, and I quote, 'She's my sponsee, she's new, she's off men for life, and in case you didn't get the message she's off limits'."

Manda's face got red, this time from anger, he thought.

"So is it true you're off men for life?"

"I can't believe she repeated that. To answer your question, since other women suggested I keep an open mind about men, I'm thinking of it as 'not interested for a good long time.' Present company excepted, since you know all of my secrets."

Joel grinned, "We have, after all, shared your bed."

Manda punched his arm playfully. "That is so wicked!"

He leaned closer and lowered his voice "For all of fifteen minutes during a storm. And you've slept under my roof as well."

"You didn't tell that to Barb?" she implored.

"Young lady," a gravelly voice intruded, "it won't do for you to keep secrets from your sponsor."

Manda's eyes widened. She turned to see an older man with twinkling eyes. "I know that voice," she realized. "You're—"

He grinned. "I'm Joel's sponsor Phil, and I've been wanting to meet you."

Manda held out her hand. "Manda. So you're the one that keeps him in line."

"From what I've heard, you do a better job of that than I do. Catch you later." With a wink at her, he disappeared into the mix of meeting-goers.

Manda turned to Joel, puzzled by Phil's statement.

Joel was looking into his empty coffee cup. "I told him about you calling me on my behavior and making me get some sleep. Remember?"

Manda nodded.

"He commended me for apologizing to you and for taking your good advice. Apparently I don't do enough of either, and he's been trying to point that out to me for a long time. Somehow you got through."

"I do remember talking to him while you were sleeping. That's how I knew his voice. I should have known from what he said that he was your sponsor."

"Why, what did he say? I don't remember."

"He wanted me to remind you to pick him up for the corrections committee or meeting or something like that. I don't know what that means."

Joel explained. "We take a meeting into the prison every other week."

Manda put a few more pieces together. "You've been sober a while?"

"Coming up on fourteen years."

"Seriously? How old are you?"

"Thirty exactly. I got clean and sober when I was sixteen."

"Holy moly. That must have been hard."

"In the beginning, yes, but being miserable made me ready to do the work."

"You mean to get into the twelve steps, do the personal inventory, clean up your act?"

"Exactly. I hope Barb is giving you good support with that."

Manda rolled her eyes.

Joel simply said, "Phil is a tremendous support to me. I can talk to him about anything, and we're totally open and honest with each other. I can't imagine going it alone without a good sponsor, even after fourteen years."

From the quiet nod and the serious look in those big blue eyes, he could see that she got his message.

He wished he could talk with her all night, but he noticed a migration to the folding chairs set up in the middle of the hall. The meeting was starting. "Listen, I celebrate my anniversary here next month, if you want to hear my story."

"I do, yes."

"And some of us are going out for coffee and decadent desserts after, if you'd like to join us. It's an annual celebration."

"Does that mean I get to see the guy that eats dry toast dig into a no-kidding dessert?"

He laughed and nodded. "Once a year."

"I wouldn't miss it." She gave him a wave and headed to the beginner's meeting in the back room. Joel watched her walk through the crowd, greeting people by name, exchanging hugs with men and women who had supported him for many years.

A voice said in his ear, "Off. Limits. Joel."

"You do know she works for me," he told Barb.

Barb fixed him with a look. "Cassie has the men watching her back. You wouldn't know anything about that?"

"Yes, I'm the guy that told her to go to Cassie."

Barb cocked her head.

"I'm not the bad guy, Barb. Manda's story is for her to tell you." Joel stopped short of saying that, if Manda had not told Barb where she worked, let alone opened up with Barb about the sick situation with Kristof, she and Barb were not a good match for working through the steps.

Barb narrowed her eyes, pushed past him, and found a seat in the third row.

Joel poured another coffee and made his way to the chair Phil was holding for him. Phil—not Barb—was the one to hold him accountable, and he was doing his level best not to rush his relationship with Manda. He had something lasting in mind, and Phil was right that Manda needed time to get a foundation in recovery.

Manda persisted with "her step work" as the women called it, but she was struggling without the guidance of a good sponsor.

Joel was away the next two Fridays, but Phil made it a point to talk with Manda at the Friday meeting and to ask how it was going with her sponsor.

She dodged the question.

At the first dodge, he emphasized that the sponsor's main focus for the newcomer was working together through the steps.

Manda mumbled something like, "Yeah, I know, thanks."

The next week, he posed the same question, got the same dodge, and repeated his caution, but this time he also invited her to join him at a Wednesday evening Big Book meeting. "Plenty of newcomers and old timers. You'll feel right at home."

Manda took him up on it, and after just two Big Book meetings she began to see how drunks had used the steps to clean up their "wreckage" and live well without dependence on alcohol and without returning to their old dysfunctional behavior and self-centered thinking. She went back to her fourth-step inventory with renewed dedication, but still wished she had a sponsor's help.

The first nice day in April, Manda abandoned her desk for a walk in the sunshine.

"Want company?" Manda turned to see Joel catching up to her on the path. "Hope I didn't scare you," he apologized.

She shook her head. "I was aware you were back there; I just figured you were doing the same thing I was—getting some fresh air to clear my mind."

"Hey, if you need some space?" he tested.

"No, I'm over-thinking my fourth-step inventory. Glad to have a break from it. I really like walking on these paths," she told him. The Manse had added fitness trails to the property last fall, just before the winter weather closed in. Neither Joel nor Manda had used them until the snow melted a few weeks ago. They were quickly becoming favorites with the guests and with the staff.

He fell into step with her and they walked in silence for twenty yards. He was obviously uncomfortable about something. "So what's up?" Manda asked him.

"Something's been on my mind, and I wanted to mention it to you. When I saw you at the meeting a few weeks ago on Friday night, it was obvious Barb didn't know anything about your…"

"History with Kristof?" Manda supplied. "Is that why she asked me after about the guys watching my back at meetings?"

"Guilty. She was concerned that I was hitting on you and she wanted to know if I was the reason the guys were watching your back."

Manda laughed. "That's ridiculous!"

"Thank you. And I didn't tell her your story."

"I haven't talked with her about it yet. She mostly wants to talk about her history with men, and I'm really discouraged trying to bring it around to the inventory I'm working on and how to use the steps in my life.

"But at Phil's Big Book meeting, the experienced men and women are always saying we have to be honest about our own issues instead of always focusing on the other guy, 'the bad guy.' Help me understand about acknowledging my part. I feel like my part was I drank to cope. I don't feel like I'm responsible for what happened."

"I agree, you're not responsible. I tell my sponsees, when they do their inventory, to look for any take-aways that can make their life better. Usually it's something they can practice or be aware of going forward."

"I'm definitely planning not to drink to cope from now on. And I want to be on guard about getting isolated."

Joel stood still on the path, hands in his pockets. "Good. There's a reason we're given the herd instinct. Those both sound like good take-aways."

Manda let out a big breath of relief. "Thanks, that really helped."

Joel continued, "And I know I'm jumping the gun, but I think your experience puts you in a good position to reach out to other women who come into the program with abuse in their experience."

Manda's face showed the dawn of a new understanding. "Wow. Is that what they mean when they say our experience can help others?"

"Yes, that's what they mean." Joel prompted, "So, how are you exercising the herd instinct lately?"

"By getting connected in the program," she said automatically.

"That's exactly what I see you doing. When we finished our conversation at the Friday meeting, I watched you cross the room and give at least a dozen people hugs, and you knew their names and they knew yours. Good people. People you can trust and count on."

"So I am getting better; I'm not just kidding myself?" she said with a bright, beautiful smile.

Joel's throat tightened and his eyes watered.

Manda reached up to kiss his cheek and told him, "I'm so numb most of the time, but when I'm with you, I can feel a little. It feels like the ice cube trays in my heart are melting. It gives me hope."

Joel drew her close. When he could trust his voice again, he told her, "It means a lot to me that you're getting better."

"Don't think I don't know how much you're helping me."

He held her as long as he dared, desire flooding through him. It was not time. Not yet. He felt her shiver. "Let's get back," he proposed. "I'm chilled, and I bet you are, too."

Manda nodded, turned back toward the Manse and linked her arm with his for a minute, while they were still out of sight of watching eyes. "I have always liked walking with you," she told him. "I hope we'll do it again."

"I'd like nothing better," he agreed.

The following weeks were a blur as Manda worked at her two part-time jobs and attended to the endless paperwork for loans for grad school, her backup plan if a scholarship did not come through. She found a cryptic note from Joel on her door one morning, "Please save graduation afternoon and evening for a small gathering." She had no idea what to make of that. She wanted to ask him, but he was scarce at work as well as around the house on Lakeside Terrace. She tucked the note on her tiny desk, and it was soon buried.

Evenings during the week, she went to her Tuesday women's meeting and the Wednesday Big Book meeting. She and her AA friend Melissa tried one new meeting each week. Manda felt like they were sharing an adventure every time they headed to a new meeting.

Any free time went into sewing for her apartment. By the time her decorating project was finished, she had expertly tailored Roman shades that, except during thunderstorms, remained open, with ten inches of subtle blue and gray striped fabric showing at the top of each window. *I should make a shirt out of that fabric.*

Another bolt from the attic—blue and gray paisley—had been fashioned into a futon cover. Scraps covered an assortment of throw pillows in bright blue and white designs, and one girly pink pillow made her think of Lyssa. She loved the look.

She wished she could live here a while, but everything in her life seemed to be in transition right now. The one stable piece was her AA program; she knew AA was everywhere, and she could stay sober wherever she lived. She also knew that, in spite of the ordeal of her last year and a half at Tompkins College, she liked living in Tompkins Falls, liked the people she worked with, loved her new friends in AA. And, she could not deny it, she was fatally attracted to Joel Cushman.

When she finally admitted that to her therapist Janine, the response was, "From everything you've said, I can see why you're attracted to this man. Let's talk a bit about your choice of words. Why do you say 'fatally' attracted? Is he dangerous?"

Manda laughed. "He's totally un-dangerous. He's actually been a life saver."

"Literally?" her therapist said skeptically.

"You could say that. He got me into AA, into therapy, into a safe apartment. He helped me in a lot of ways that have kept me safe and healthy and moving forward with my goals."

"So he's a hero to you?"

"Well, partly, I guess. But he's human." She spoke about the confrontation in Joel's kitchen, but she left out the part about Joel crying in her arms the next morning. That was just too personal about Joel.

"So, how would you describe your relationship with him?"

Manda talked about the easy friendship she had with Joel. It was a relationship unlike any she'd had before. She could be honest with him, tell him anything about herself and what she thought of him. She knew she could talk over any issue with him and she valued his ideas, even when she didn't like what he had to say. She smiled when she thought of the many roles he played, not just in her life, and how easily he slipped in and out of them. He seemed always to be comfortable and confident. "How do people get that self-assured?" she asked her therapist.

"Well, for many of us, it starts with that technique you hear around AA, 'act as if.' And, gradually, acting self-assured becomes a habit and eventually becomes a way of thinking about yourself. But let's talk more about your relationship with Joel. You don't talk about him as a father figure." Manda blushed at that, and they both laughed.

They talked about the feeling of closeness she had with Joel, which she'd never had with a man before. She skipped over the incredible necking session in the attic, which still gave her a rush when she thought of it. She did say, "I felt close to him—on the same wavelength—from that first morning in his office when he slid off his monster desk and came beside me to listen to my problem and work with me on a solution." She admitted wanting their relationship—which had begun when she was at her lowest point—to continue to grow, just as she continued to grow.

Her therapist speculated, "Maybe you aren't 'off men for life,' so much as needing to do experience a relationship differently?"

Manda acknowledged that she needed and wanted to have an honest, open, respectful relationship, instead of—well, at best drinking buddies and at worst being in the sordid hostage situation she'd played out with Kristof. She shuddered. "No wonder I decided I was off men for life."

"Think you have the courage to change your mind about that?"

Manda didn't know. "Right now it feels way scary."

"Give it some time," Janine suggested. "Our time is up for today. Just a reminder we have only one more session together. If you want to continue after graduation, I'd be very pleased, but it would be at your expense then."

The second Saturday in May was Manda's long-awaited graduation day, and it was anti-climatic at best. She tried to work up some enthusiasm during a short morning walk along the shore. She fixed toast with peanut butter and her favorite blackberry jam. Dressed in her only skirt and blouse, she grabbed her rented cap and gown and drove to the appointed parking lot.

There were plenty of people milling around and no one that looked like Kristof, so she made her way with the crowd to the chapel. She was moved by the Baccalaureate ceremony, even though it seemed to take hours. At the honors brunch she bypassed the made-from-powder eggs and sampled every fresh-baked pastry and every kind of cheese.

At last, she lined up with her class under a big white tent for the ritual of walking across the stage, shaking the hand of a vice president she had never seen, and receiving her diploma. Halfway across the stage, her sense of anti-climax turned to self-pity; no one was on hand to cheer for her.

Lyssa had sent her a silly card from Texas, with a handwritten note "Welcome to the club, little sis! Come on out to TX for your Ph.D."

Manda realized with a sigh she'd not told any of her AA friends she was graduating, even though they'd helped her stay sober and work through her challenges so she could complete her degree. And Joel. He had gone out of his way to make it possible, and she hadn't thanked him either.

This really was everyone's victory, and she had been selfish not to share it. She resolved to get to her Happy Hour meeting tonight and let them know how much their support and friendship meant to her.

The thought cheered her, and she found herself smiling at the vice president and smiling as she made her way through the throng of parents and graduates to hand over her rented cap and gown at the back of the tent. "Manda Doughty," she announced herself and watched carefully as a harried helper checked off her name. "Thank you," she told the woman with a big smile.

The woman looked stunned, as though Manda was the first student to thank her for doing this thankless job. "Good luck to you, honey," the woman said.

Manda walked thoughtfully to her car, diploma in hand, and felt a hand on her shoulder. She knew it was Joel before she turned around. What was he doing here?

"Congratulations," he told her.

She felt her smile brighten a few notches and told him honestly, "This would not have happened without your intervention."

He waved it away. "Listen, I'm having a cookout on the patio for a few graduates, including you. I hope you got my note and you'll come."

Manda hated herself for forgetting. She stammered, "I was just thinking I needed to get to Happy Hour to thank everyone for their support these last few months. Oh," she realized, "today is Saturday. No Happy Hour. This is perfect! And I am babbling." She laughed at herself and felt tears well up. "I guess my emotions are all over the place."

Joel fought his desire to give her a hug, and simply moved closer to give them some privacy. "The Happy Hour crew knows, believe me. In fact, a few of them were here today for their own families, and I heard them shout when you walked across the stage."

"Really?" She confessed, "I was so busy feeling sorry for myself and trying not to trip, I didn't realize."

Joel raised an eyebrow. "Well, that's honest anyway. Three of you in the program graduated today, and I have planned a cookout to get us together for some good food and sober fun. You'll come, won't you?"

"I will. Thank you, Joel." She brushed away the pesky tears. "I'm sorry; I don't know where this came from. Why am I crying?"

"Maybe you're crying because the ordeal is over. And, by the way, Kristof is officially history at this college. We have many good things to celebrate." He ruffled her hair. "Did you think you would get away with not telling the world you graduated third in your class?"

"Yes, I thought I would get away with it." She hated being the center of attention, but she was touched that he knew. How did he know that anyway? Instead she asked, "What are people wearing?"

"To the cookout? You decide. This is my favorite kind of party. It's just about relaxing and enjoying the people and the occasion and the food."

"What a concept," Manda quipped.

Joel touched her elbow, his face serious. "The past is past," he said quietly, "and I want you to be happy now. I care about you and I'm proud of what you've done."

Manda felt her heart dance with happiness. She kissed Joel's cheek, and his eyes went from serious to sparkling. "Thanks for salvaging my degree, and for having a party."

He grinned. "Go get your party clothes. I'll come by to pick you up at five."

"Cool!" She waved with her diploma and sauntered to her car.

Joel watched her go and had a memory of her walking into the spa at the Manse after their breakfast that first morning. She had come a long way. He wanted so much for them, and he knew better than to rush her. He said a silent prayer to give her time, to give their relationship time. She was just a few months sober, twenty-two years old, and he didn't even know her plans. For all he knew, she was planning to move to the other side of the country and put her experience in Tompkins Falls behind her. Well, not if he could help it.

Manda turned back to him when she reached her car and gave him a salute with her diploma. He waved. With a jolt, he realized he no longer needed to keep his distance from her in public. She was a graduate of this institution now, not one of its students. The investigations had moved beyond her particular case. He would not compromise anything by seeing her openly. If she would have him.

Manda tossed her diploma on the front seat of the old VW Beetle. She had just achieved her biggest goal, and the only problem in her life right now was she had nothing to wear to the celebration. She remembered Joel chiding her not to be cheap with herself. She had a credit card, she had an occasion to dress up, and she had two hours to get a party dress.

She knew nothing about fashion, but she knew there were two boutiques on the main street with women's clothing in the windows. She hoped one of them would have something for a festive cookout on a patio on a sunny evening in May.

When she walked into the chic boutique La Bella, she saw clothes that she could wear to work at a place like the Manse. She wasn't sure anything would work for an outdoor party.

"May I help you?" the salesperson asked, her voice high-pitched with doubt.

Manda saw her evaluating her baggy skirt and blouse. She laughed at herself and told the woman, "As you can see,

I have no idea what size I wear or how to buy clothes. I am going to a graduation party on a patio in a couple of hours." She flashed her Visa. "I need serious help."

The young woman winked at her and held out her hand for a ladylike handshake. "I'm Anita. Let's have you take the first fitting room and—not to be indelicate—get out of everything except your underwear. I'll measure you so we know your size, and I'll bring in a few possibilities." The measurements taken, Anita brought in two sleek black dresses and a pencil skirt paired with a bright blue sequined top.

Manda loved all the outfits, but none would work for a cookout on the patio.

"See, you do know something about clothes," Anita told her with a big smile. "I'm going to call down to the Lemon Tree, which has more trendy clothes. Carolee will take good care of you. But, before you go, keep in mind—when you get asked out to dinner by that special guy— this is the place for that perfect little black dress. And, between you and me, the second dress you tried—the one that showed off your legs—will be on sale June first. Now, you get dressed and I'll make that phone call."

When Manda arrived at the Lemon Tree a few doors away, Carolee greeted her. "Anita said you're looking for a great outfit for a special cookout. Sounds like fun! Let me show a few things to get a handle on your taste."

Manda laughed out loud. "Carolee, if I have any taste at five o'clock tonight it will be what you teach me in the next hour."

"Listen, to start, we know from Anita that you're a size eight with long legs."

"That's good?"

"Honey, that's something most women would die for. Get your clothes off, and we'll get to work."

Manda worked her way through sundresses, flouncy skirts and peasant blouses, capris and skimpy tops, and something called a salsa dress. "I love the way the salsa dress moves, but I'm not a ruffle person," she confessed. "When I came in the store, I saw a dress that reminded me of a sports bra on top. Do you know what I mean?"

"Sure, the racerback. That will show off your shoulders and you'll love the way the skirt moves." Carolee was back in no time with three new possibilities.

Manda loved the deep blue dress with the racerback top.

"The built-in bra makes it so simple for a party. The skirt length is very sexy on you, but you could still get away with it for work if you added a little sweater. Let me show you." She came back with what she called a "classic shrug" in filmy, light gray cashmere.

Manda tried it on. "That's the kind of classy outfit people wear at the Manse where I work."

"Exactly, and the shrug is on sale. You should take it to your party, too, in case it gets cooler after sunset. Shoes? Purse?"

"I don't think I need a purse, but all I own are sneakers."

Carolee smothered a laugh and came back with "ballet flats" and "slides." Manda went with the silvery slides, which she knew she could wear to work. "You are so ready for this party, girl," Carolee cheered her.

Manda handed over her credit card and did not even flinch when she looked at the total on the slip she was signing. She was relieved to see it was not as much as a semester's worth of textbooks for even one course.

"You and Anita are my heroes, Carolee." She bounced out of the Lemon Tree and headed home to Lakeside Terrace to get ready.

When she opened the door to Joel's knock, his eyes did a lingering pass from head to toe. She felt her nipples grow hard and a warm stirring between her legs. Joel took notice of her reaction, closed the door with his foot, and moved in. The first kiss was deep and hungry. Manda's skin thrilled to his touch, and his kisses drove her to the edge.

"We really need to stop," she breathed. *I wish we didn't.* "Everyone's waiting for you."

"For both of us." Joel stepped away and gave her an apologetic smile. "I've destroyed your lipstick."

"Your anatomy needs a little adjusting, too," Manda teased on her way to the bathroom for a makeup repair.

Joel had arranged for the party to be held on a large patio that sat on the bluff between Number 7 and Number 9 Lakeside Terrace. Manda had never noticed it. "There is no Number 8?" she asked Joel and they strolled down the hill.

"Seven and eight are corner lots, and neither was large enough for a house. Eight became a driveway to the parking area behind the units. The patio was put in a few years ago for use by everyone that lives on the Terrace."

Manda saw that it was large enough for the dozen partygoers, plus a grill, two tubs of cold drinks, and a long table laden with food.

"Graduate number three is here!" Joel announced. Faces turned their way, and glasses were raised. "And I'm serious about number three—she graduated third in her class." Manda was treated to cheers. She blushed and set about hugging the people she knew from meetings, who in turn introduced her to their spouses and dates.

The two other graduates being honored at the party were Jerry, who had finally finished his degree in information technology after seven years in the program. "One semester at a time, I made it," he told Manda. The other graduate being honored was a woman named Marie, who had completed her bachelor's degree in nursing, with honors. Manda had not met Marie, but knew her husband Les from Happy Hour.

Manda expected to be shy at her first sober party, but she was at ease. She moved from group to group, engaged in a little light flirting with the men she knew, and pumped the women about their work. Half the group were assembled in a loose circle when one of the women asked Manda, "What are your plans now that you have your degree? Grad school? A job?"

Manda saw Joel's head swivel in her direction. "Both, I hope." She wished she had talked with Joel about this earlier. "I've been accepted to three schools, and I'm waiting to hear about scholarships."

"What would be your first choice school, if you didn't have to think about the money?"

"That's a big 'if,' Jerry," she reminded him, which brought a laugh from all the grads and their spouses. "St. Basil's in Rochester is my favorite," she told them. "They have strength in not-for-profit business models and in business ethics, both of which are important to me."

Jerry challenged, "You're not looking to make a bundle?"

Manda shook her head. "It's never been a goal. I do want to get my CPA, though, and—"

"Your who? What's a CPA?" Jerry's wife Suzanne asked.

Jerry guessed, "Certified Private Accountant?"

"Close! It's a Certified Public Accountant. Many of the masters-level accounting programs qualify as preparation for the CPA exam, if you've had the requisite undergrad courses. Tompkins College's program allowed me to get all but two of those required courses, and I picked up the other two online last summer. I sound like a nerd."

"We're both nerds." Jerry laughed. "Keep talking."

"So, if I go fulltime for my masters, I can be done in a year and then sit for the exam. With the masters and the CPA, I can comfortably support myself."

Jerry teased, "Unless you go broke paying for your education."

STEPPING UP TO LOVE | 139

Manda laughed. "That's why I'm waiting to hear about scholarships. I have a full ride at UT Austin if I want it."

She noticed Joel tense.

"I'd rather be here, though."

"Well," Jerry observed, "we gotta do what we gotta do. I wish you luck."

"When will you hear?" Suzanne asked.

"Normally, schools have made their decisions by now, so I don't know what to think."

"They may have been delayed," Joel contributed. "A lot of the smaller schools are struggling to make their enrollment quotas, and they don't want to commit scholarship funds until they have a handle on how many new students will be starting in the fall. I wouldn't rule out St. Basil's at this point."

How did he know these things?

"What's the third school, Manda?" Les asked her.

"Syracuse."

"Great program," Les observed, "and great basketball."

"So let's say Syracuse comes through," Jerry said, "and St. Basil's does not, would you pick Syracuse?"

"A couple months ago, I'd have said yes, but I would consider taking out a loan, especially if St. Basil's could meet me partway. I used to think 'all or nothing,' but I'm not as worried about it now."

Jerry raised a glass to her. "You've got one degree in the bag. That makes it easier to lighten up."

"Amen."

"So you don't need to make a bundle. What's important in a job?" Jerry persisted.

Manda said without hesitation, "I want to work in an ethical workplace."

Jerry's wife snickered. "That sure narrows it down." Several of them got into a debate about an area industry that had just made the news for unethical hiring practices.

Manda felt Joel come close behind her. "You'll let me know when you hear from St. Basil's?"

"Of course I'll let you know."

"I do want to talk more about your plans soon. But for today, I want to share something my Uncle Justin told me when I graduated from college."

Manda's face warmed with a smile. "I hear affection for this Uncle Justin."

"He's been a major influence in my life. I'll tell you more about him sometime."

When the debate about the local industry quieted down, Joel raised his voice so all the grads could hear him. "I'd like Jerry, Marie, and Manda all to hear this."

They paused to give Joel their attention.

"When I got my degree, my Uncle Justin took me out for lobster—" he gestured to the catered buffet table, now picked clean of lobster, steaks, salads, and rolls— "and said to me, 'Joel you've arrived at a place you've never been. Imagine you're halfway up a mountain at a scenic overlook. Just for today, enjoy the view. Spend some time looking at the world from this new perspective. Let go of the struggle that's behind you. And dream—don't worry—about what's to come.'" Joel raised his glass of iced coffee to the three of them, "To the present," he toasted, "and to those who helped you make it here tonight."

Manda raised her glass of iced tea and clinked with the others. She felt Joel's hand come to rest on her waist. She liked it there. "To the present," she agreed, thinking she had never been so happy. Three months earlier she could not have imagined a sober celebration like this, a sunny patio overlooking the lake, caring friends who shared their struggles and accomplishments. And Joel, who brought out the best in her. At this present moment, he felt like her best friend and maybe something more. At this moment, she had nothing to worry about and some things to dream about.

Chapter 6

"Most of you know my story," Joel prefaced, "but I only tell it once a year, and there are some new people since the last time."

He noticed Barb's mouth was tight, probably expecting him to sugarcoat the past and glorify the present, working on the lecture she was going to give him later or the retelling she would do for Manda.

He needed Manda's sponsor on his side, if at all possible, so he looked her in the eye and said, "So I'll keep it short, and I'll tell it straight."

Barb was startled enough to unfold her arms.

Joel looked over at Phil and spotted Manda next to him. "Besides I know my sponsor will bust me if I'm not honest."

Phil's shoulders moved with a silent laugh. He saw Phil give Manda's hand a squeeze. What was he up to?

"I grew up in a loving family. No alcoholics that I'm aware of. A few crackpots."

He heard a few chuckles.

"No crackheads, except me." He stole a look at Manda and saw her surprise. "I started drinking when my family was killed. I was thirteen, and I couldn't handle it. Everyone I loved and counted on was gone. I inherited a fortune and a legacy that was staggering.

"My Uncle Justin was appointed my guardian, and he had all the right qualifications. But to be honest, he knew more about the world economy than supervising a traumatized teenager. I got a DWI at fourteen, and he made me spend a few days in jail, which was the right thing to do. I can't imagine how hard that must have been for him." Joel made eye contact with a friend in the program who was dealing with a similar nightmare with his daughter; he saw the man nod and Joel gave him a nod of support in return.

"Shortly after the DWI, I was introduced to crack cocaine and became addicted. I overdosed at fifteen and nearly died. I would not be alive today if my uncle hadn't dedicated himself to finding a solution. If he had let me die, he'd have had the fortune to himself and not a single responsibility, but that's not what he wanted. We were the only family either of us had left, and that meant more to him than anything else." Joel shook his head remembering how pivotal the realization had been for him as a teenager. "I was sick and stupid and traumatized, but I knew for sure I wanted to grow up to be that kind of man, and I knew I couldn't do it if I kept on the path of self-destruction.

"My Uncle Justin made one decision I hated, but it was my salvation: he sent me away. He enrolled me in a prep school in New Hampshire that was academically rigorous and that had zero tolerance for drug or alcohol use by students, faculty, or staff. There were many recovering addicts and alcoholics among the adults; I was definitely in the right place.

"It took more than a semester for me to get with the program. Even though I wasn't drinking or using, believe me when I tell you I was a nasty, foul-mouthed, defiant little twit the whole time." He took a swallow of his coffee. It still bothered him to remember what he'd been like in those days. "The person that finally got through to me was one of the Humanities professors who was very active in AA. He had a spirituality I could not denigrate. That really intrigued me.

"I started asking questions and listening to what he had to say. He took me along to his meetings and hooked me up with a young guy named Manuel—Manny—who'd gotten sober at my age. Manny took me through the steps.

I also attended another twelve-step program, Narcotics Anonymous, but I settled on AA for long-term recovery.

I needed and was fortunate to have a lot of help outside of AA. A psychiatrist helped me recover from the trauma of losing my family. And there were other professionals working with my Uncle Justin and me to settle the estate and help me prepare to do something responsible with it.

"Those years at school were probably the hardest years of my life, but I had support every step of the way. The miracle is, I was open to it." He stole a look at Manda, and they exchanged a smile.

"By the time I finished college and graduate school, I was a whole human being with some direction. I chose to settle here, which has always been home, and I found a very strong AA program here, which has helped me make a happy, useful life. There are men and women of integrity everywhere, and I am very fortunate to work with some of the finest right here in the Finger Lakes.

"Because of you people and these meetings, I've been able to stay sober through every adversity and every celebration, for fourteen years now. You kept me on the right path when my fiancé and I broke up five years ago; I didn't have to drink, but I did have to get honest about my feelings and my motives.

"I've always found it very hard to honor that saying on our coins, 'To thine own self be true.' In the beginning it was hard because I had no idea what I was meant to do or who I was meant to be. And now as I get clearer about those things, I find that being true to myself and my beliefs is pretty unpopular and very uncomfortable sometimes." Joel surveyed the room, making eye contact with a few people he knew blamed him for the tension at the college and one who supported what he was trying to do. "But I know it's what I need to do—to be sober and sane and useful and happy in this life." He drained his coffee mug.

"Enough about me. It's the speaker's prerogative to pick a topic. There are some here tonight who are just getting into AA's Twelve Steps. Let's talk about how the steps have changed our lives for the better. In particular, how the fourth-step inventory has benefited us going forward."

It was customary for the group simply to pass the basket at the end of a speaker's story, without applause or other acknowledgement. Tonight, though, the group clapped; Joel knew from experience that this group usually reserved applause for those stories that demonstrated honesty and that emphasized how the twelve steps made it possible for alcoholics to move beyond their often wretched histories to become happy, useful, caring people. As the applause ended and the basket circulated, members of the group spoke in turn, most of them making an effort to stick to the topic Joel suggested

Joel looked down and saw his white knuckles gripping his coffee mug. He made an effort to relax before looking at Manda. She seemed intent on the discussion. Phil had his arm along the back of her chair.

Joel was sure Manda had not known half of what his story had revealed tonight. Phil was right. He really should have told her about his engagement and had that discussion in private. He drew in a deep breath and let it out slowly. If someone blurted out Lorraine's name during the meeting, or later over coffee, she would never forgive him.

Someone offered to refill his coffee, and he said automatically, "Thanks, no cream or sugar."

He looked at Manda again; she was looking at him, not smiling, not glaring, just a quizzical gaze. She turned back to the meeting, and Phil looked at him, glared, shook his head, and shrugged. Joel got the message: he had blown it, and Phil had expected as much and was being protective of Manda. Joel let out a heavy sigh just as his coffee arrived. He smiled his thanks to the coffee-bearer.

After the closing prayer, the room erupted with conversation, the clatter of chairs being stacked, windows slammed shut, coffee pots dismantled, and serving tables put away. Joel shook hands with half the people in the room, reminded several others about coffee and dessert, and wondered if Manda would still join them.

He turned to look for her, and saw her eyeing him as she made her way through the crowd. Then he was face to face with her, and he was speechless. She was wearing that blue dress the exact color of her eyes, the one that left her shoulders almost bare.

Manda asked, "I'm hoping I can ride with you?"

He nodded dumbly.

"I came with Phil and his driver, and Phil decided not to come to the party, so I'm—"

"Of course we'll go together," Joel said in relief.

"I know there are some things we need to talk about, and maybe we can get a start on that in the car."

"So Phil took off already?" *Duh, Cushman.*

Manda nodded.

"He's not sick?"

Manda shook her head and smiled. "I think he's throwing us together to make sure we have that conversation."

Joel laughed.

"He had me sit with him, because Barb was, well…"

"Barb's not one of my fans, and I'm not a saint. Let's head out."

Joel put an arm around her shoulders as they walked. He beeped the Passat awake, held the door for her, and settled himself in the driver's seat before either of them spoke again.

"Gentleman's treatment," she said with a smile. "I like it a lot."

He smiled over at her and squeezed her hand. "You're trying to make this easier, aren't you?"

"Phil said I was not going to like what you have to say. And I told Phil that I am trying to be a big girl and to accept that we've all got our secrets." She gave him a dazzling smile. "And anyway I want to see you eat that decadent dessert, so if we're not speaking to each other after tonight at least I'll have that memory."

Joel let out his breath in a laugh and backed out of the parking space. "I was wrong, you're not going to make it easier. You're going to torment me."

"I've got your number, Cushman," she teased.

"Yes, you do." He smiled then teased her right back as he reminded her, "and I know how to make you blush."

When all the festivities were done, Manda was exhausted, but she knew they were both on edge, and she would not sleep a wink until they'd made a start on the two thousand questions she had for him.

"I figured you for French Silk Pie to go with your cashmere persona," she said to break the silence on the drive back to Lakeside Terrace. "How was the Turtle Cheesecake?"

"Pure decadence, as always. How was your Chocolate Oblivion?"

"Incredible. This was a really fun evening, and I got to know some people I hadn't talked to until now."

"Good, I'm glad you had fun. Manda, I know I should have talked to you about my story before this, just us. I was just being stupid, and I apologize for that. So what surprised you?"

"Everything. First, I'm very sorry about your family. I didn't realize you'd lost all of them in that accident. And finding out that the Joel Cushman on the list of the Board of Trustees for the college wasn't your father. That added a whole new dimension to the Kristof situation. And then finding out you have a fortune."

"I had meant to tell you about the money, if you didn't already know," Joel interrupted and then realized how lame that was.

"I'm probably the only person in the room that didn't know," she said testily, "but how would I know, Joel? You work. You work hard. I see you at work everyday, and you go home and take care of the details of a whole bunch of rental properties, and you're capable of keeping the books on those properties. I don't think of people with fortunes working like you do. So it didn't occur to me you're rich." She ran out of steam.

He honored the silence this time; he did not have long to wait.

"So, do you own those properties?"

"I do."

She raised her eyebrows. "And do you own the Manse?"

"I do." This was not the part of his story he thought would upset her. He tested, "I get that you're angry, and I want to know why."

She burst out, "I just have to wonder where my brain has been the last two years. I'm probably the only person at the Manse who didn't get it that you were not only the boss but the owner. And probably creator of the whole concept and—"

"Yes, I am. But I don't go around telling people that. And someday I'd like to have a conversation about the business plan for the Manse and for the rental properties and a few other things, assuming you'd like to know."

"I would very much, but—you're right—we have other things to talk about tonight, and I'm avoiding them. I didn't want to ask anything hard while we were in a moving vehicle."

Joel reached for her hand. "Thank you."

He headed up Lakeside Terrace to the last house on the left and pulled into his parking spot. "My place or yours?"

"Yours."

That surprised him.

"I'm not going to jump your bones. I just need to put some things together, and I think it will be easier in your space."

"Okay, and I understand that gives you the option to storm out of my house and slam the door on your way out."

She smiled. "It's that bad, huh? Do I know this person you were engaged to?"

He nodded. They climbed the stairs side-by-side, Joel's arm tight around her shoulders.

Manda shed her jacket and fixed a pot of tea for them. "Green?" Joel took it as a good sign that they were settling into their usual routine whenever Manda came up to his apartment for a talk.

"Green is good." Joel tuned the sound system to a satellite station. "You okay with classical?"

"Sounds good."

Joel set two mugs on a tray, added the steaming pot, and carried it to the living room. Manda curled her legs under her and raised an eyebrow when he handed her a half-full mug of tea.

"I still haven't guessed about the fiancé," she told him with a curious look at the level of liquid in her mug.

He sat as close to her as he thought advisable. "Lorraine."

He watched the mug jerk and the hot tea slosh close to the rim. She was upset but apparently not homicidal.

"Thank you for not throwing that at me."

Manda seemed not to hear him. He could see her recalculating many things.

She was quiet long enough for the tea to cool.

He took a sip and told her, "The children are not mine."

"No, I knew that," she said. "They both look totally like Kristof, not you and not even Lorraine." Manda looked to Joel to continue.

"Our involvement ended when I broke off the engagement. We did continue to be in touch."

Manda registered the statement about the continuing contact and let out a long, slow breath as if she was trying to release some of the pressure building up in her. "You know I admired Lorraine, and I can see that you and she were an obvious match."

"Everyone thought so. It was always assumed that we would marry, even when we were growing up. By the time we reached adulthood, we were the only remaining children of wealthy families in Tompkins Falls. I moved back here and planned to make it my home. Lorraine had not found anyone she wanted to marry, and we just went along with what everyone expected. She was a good sport, but she was not happy or in love. Neither was I." He waited for Manda to meet his eyes, wanting her to see that he was being honest.

When she did look at him, she searched his eyes and gave a nod.

"We both deserved better than a marriage of convenience. Phil walked through that whole period with me, and he stayed out of it unless I asked for his advice, which I mostly didn't. My Uncle Justin came for a visit, saw Lorraine and me together, and asked me what the hell I thought I was doing. When the dust settled from that argument, I knew the answer was: I was doing what was expected of me. Justin suggested I grow up and get a life. I disrespectfully disagreed, which was just old behavior." Joel shook his head, remembering the look of disgust on Justin's face.

"Then Lorraine brought up a subject we'd never talked about: children. She wanted a bunch. Right away. I had no idea if I wanted children. That woke me up. I got the courage to call off the wedding." He looked at Manda and wished he could restart this whole conversation. Her eyebrows were set in an angry vee.

"That conversation didn't go well either," he admitted. "I have a talent for poor communication with the people who mean the most to me."

"You think?" Manda glared at him.

"I have done it again." He knew was just making things worse, and it was time to give up the lead. He fidgeted with his mug while Manda gathered her thoughts.

"Joel, there's no reason in the world I would be upset that you'd been engaged. But finding out it was Lorraine, after all this time..."

Joel wisely did not interrupt.

Manda continued, "So Lorraine married Kristof on the rebound, and the marriage failed because he's incapable of marriage."

Joel nodded.

"But you continued a relationship with her. Why would you keep that a secret?"

Joel was studying the tea in his mug. "I do not have a relationship with Lorraine. We talk from time to time. Amicably."

The silence lengthened. Manda demanded, "Joel, I need you to tell me what's going on between you and Lorraine in the present. And look me in the eye."

"You're not going to like any of it."

"I already don't, so just tell me."

He took a swallow of tea, set down the mug and met her eyes. "Lorraine and I got back in touch when our relationship—yours and mine—started. When you told me about Kristof, I had to know the truth of your role in the breakup of Lorraine's marriage."

"My role?"

"Until you told me your side of what happened, I wondered if you were the co-ed Kristof was having the affair with that led to the breakup of their marriage."

Manda was aghast. "Why would you think that?"

"Why wouldn't I? At some point after Lorraine left the country, there were rumors all over here—I mean, the Manse and the college—about you living at Cady's Point. Lorraine never named the student, and I was unaware she'd hired you."

Manda dissolved in tears. Joel kicked himself for not editing his honesty. Phil had warned him about blurting out too much when he was under pressure instead of having a well-times conversation, sooner rather than later.

"Manda, when I saw you in the shower and saw the bruises, I knew I was wrong and I knew you were in trouble and I had to understand where the truth lay. And when I heard your story I instinctively believed you. But there was too much at stake to…"

"To trust the word of drunk, I get it." Her voice trembled, and her hands shook.

He reached for her, but she stood up and moved away from him.

"Don't. Just keep going. What was at stake? Explain that."

"Three things. One, I'm a trustee of the college, and you had just told me about a violation of a female student—you—by a tenured faculty member—Kristof—and also about a serious consequence of the Board's decision to take away promised financial support to our Presidential Scholars. I needed to know the truth around both those things. Not just your truth, but who dropped the ball at the college after that decision was made. And who knew what about Kristof. And who the co-ed or co-eds were that he was involved with before the breakup, and after."

Manda tapped her foot and breathed heavily. "And did you find out?"

"Pretty much, yes. We're still looking into the whole mess."

"'We' meaning all the important people at the Tompkins College?"

Joel heard the embarrassment in her voice, and it killed him to know how much this was hurting her—how much he was hurting her by the way he was handling it.

"Yes," he confirmed. "And I wasn't able to keep your name out of it." He went into the bathroom for a box of tissues and handed it to her.

"Thank you," she said. Six tissues later, she prompted, "That's one. You said there were three things."

Joel wished he could start over, leave out the numbers, and edit out every hurtful thing. "Two, you were my employee, very close to graduation and soon needing a letter of recommendation. I needed to know if you were trustworthy."

"And three?"

Joel stood, put his hands in his pockets, and moved as close as he could without violating the keep-away force field surrounding Manda. "Three, somewhere between the white linen napkin you dipped in your ice water to make an eye compress and the laughter we shared before your departure with Tony in his truck, I fell in love with you. And now I know it's real, and you're the woman I want to share my life with. But at the time I needed to be really careful."

Manda's eyes seemed to study the floor and she looked confused. She held onto her elbows as if trying to keep herself together.

Joel felt his heart breaking, and he was pretty sure he'd just broken Manda's heart, too. "Manda, please say something."

Manda rubbed her arms as if she were cold. He moved toward her, but she held up a hand to stop him. "I need to ask some questions," she said quietly. "When did you call Lorraine about me?"

"I was waiting for her call-back when Tony picked you up in front of the Manse that first morning."

"That was your crisis?"

"Yes."

"And when did she call you back?"

"A few minutes after you left in Tony's truck."

Manda drilled him with a look. "And what did she say—that's relevant to this conversation?"

"That," he filtered the one-hour conversation and all the subsequent conversations. "She verified your story up to the point when she left the country. And she was cool with you having the bike."

Manda stared at him in disbelief. She shook her head as if she'd given up trying to make sense of what was happening.

Joel was sure he'd blown it and that, right now, she couldn't handle any more.

In the second he looked away, Manda snagged her keys and opened his front door.

Joel came up behind her and gripped her shoulders. "Manda, please don't go like this."

Without turning around, she warned him, her voice low and angry, "You knew I would be upset. I am upset. And I need you to give me time with this." She was out the door and down the stairs—barefoot—without a backward glance.

Joel listened until she made it safely inside her apartment, and he held his breath until she slammed home the dead bolt. He had never wanted to drink so badly in his life.

He closed his door, reached for the phone, and speed-dialed Phil.

Manda glared at the morning sun. She did not feel sunny. She was numb and sad and— okay, seething. She stood in the shower until the numbness wore off, until she could feel the warm water hitting her shoulders and sluicing down her body.

As she spooned coffee into the pot, she said her usual morning prayer, but it was half-hearted. *God, don't let me waste this sunny day. Help me to enjoy what you've given me.*

The aroma of the coffee and the feel of the hot liquid sliding down her throat helped her realize she could do whatever she felt like today. Why not? She'd take Lorraine's bike—her bike now—for a tune-up. It was about time she rode it instead of just chaining it to the banister outside her apartment.

When Joel had given her the bike she found a magnetized business card for the bike shop Lorraine used in the pouch behind the bicycle seat, and the card was on her refrigerator door. Manda called the shop and asked if they could schedule her soon. "Get here in the next half hour, and we'll get right on it," was the answer.

She pulled on blue jeans and a T-shirt, cotton socks, sneakers, and a hoodie, grabbed her purse, and slammed out the door. And trampled a pair of silver slides someone had placed on her welcome mat. Her silver slides. She must have left them at Joel, and he'd come down to return them. And there was her jacket draped over the banister.

Manda debated for a second—should she break down in tears again, leave them where they were, what? If she left them, she'd have to deal with them later, and she really hoped to be over this in a couple of hours. She tucked the shoes under her sewing table, hung her jacket on the peg behind her door, and left with a little more composure this time. *I can do this.*

"I warned you," Phil said for the sixth time. He and Joel had taken their coffee to the lakeshore after the Early Risers meeting. "You have done serious damage to your relationship, and you'd better hope Manda is out getting the support she needs rather than drinking."

"How can I make it right?"

Phil snorted. "I'd say 'tell her the truth,' but you've already bombarded her with more detail than she could possibly handle."

"I have no idea what to do."

"So, for now you do nothing. Tell me, what are the points that especially upset her?"

"She kept asking about my relationship with Lorraine."

"And do you have a relationship with Lorraine?"

"No."

"Joel?"

"Not a personal one."

"Then what?"

"It's business."

Phil shoved at Joel's arm and glowered at him. "If you don't come clean with me in the next sixty seconds about what's going on, you can find a new sponsor."

Joel swallowed hard. "Lorraine has asked me to help her create a gated community at Cady's Point. She proposed it when I called to ask her what she knew about Manda and her ex-husband, and we've been working on a business plan since then."

"Are you insane?"

"It's a business matter and she asked my advice. I think it's the least I can do for her after I screwed up her life."

"When did you screw up her life?"

"I broke off the engagement practically on the eve of the wedding of the decade."

"Oh, boo hoo. You think Lorraine hasn't recovered from that? She married and had children in the meantime, didn't she?"

"Yes, and the marriage was a nightmare, as you know."

"And that's your fault?"

"Isn't it?"

"No, it isn't. Maybe you do need to see a therapist again for a while, Joel. Your guilt is clouding your judgment, and it sounds to me like Lorraine is leading you around by the nose ring again."

Joel turned away and swore loudly.

"Look at me," Phil growled. When Joel turned back and met his sharp-eyed look, he continued, "I kept my mouth shut about the way you behaved with Lorraine once, and I'm not going to do it again. You have a chance at a long, happy, loving relationship with a beautiful, smart woman. I mean Manda, by the way, not the queen of Cady's Point."

Joel nodded curtly and felt his face flame.

"And you're letting your guilt about Lorraine's failed marriage—misplaced guilt—blind you to what Lorraine is doing, and blind you to how it's affecting your relationship with Manda."

"What? You think Lorraine is deliberately interfering in my relationship with Manda?"

Phil spread his hands wide apart. "Hello."

Joel insisted, "She wants to unload Cady's Point, and she wants top dollar. It's business. It's not a relationship."

"Oh, and is there any reason in the world you need to be involved in that particular business? Which just happened to materialize when you called Lorraine about Manda, probably sounding very concerned about and very interested in the beautiful young lady who used to make supper for Lorraine and clean up her mess every night?"

"You—you're making this up." Joel's face showed torturous confusion.

"Joel, I am begging you and warning you. Let Lorraine find someone else to do her bidding. You've got a relationship to mend, unless you're planning to give up altogether on Manda, who I happen to think is the woman of your dreams." Phil turned around and headed back toward the parking lot. He muttered, "But what do I know?"

"I always liked this one," the mechanic told her. "I fitted it for Lorraine five or six years ago. She didn't use it much. I wondered what happened to it when she left for England." He stood waiting for an explanation.

Manda hadn't stopped to think the shop would know it was Lorraine's bike. She said simply, "I was working for Lorraine when she left and also working for the guy she was engaged to when she got the bike. They wanted me to have it, and I'm really excited about it. I've never had anything like this in my life." She laughed, "As you can see, I drive a beat-up Beetle, so buying a bike like this is way out of reach for me."

He nodded, "I always thought she should marry Joel, but my opinion didn't count for much."

Desperate to change the subject, Manda asked, "How much will it cost to tune it up?"

The mechanic stroked the handlebars. "Joel bought a lifetime service plan for it, so it'll only cost you if we have to replace a part, which I don't expect. We should have it ready for you in a couple of hours."

Manda had guessed right about the bike being a gift from Joel to Lorraine. And apparently now a gift to her, brokered by Tony when he was sent with her to Kristof's to get her things. This was way too complicated. She wondered if she should just walk away from the bike and the tangled relationships it represented.

The mechanic misunderstood her frown. "Look I know there's no place to wait here, but there's a nice coffee shop in town, just past the traffic light on the right. In fact, you'll probably find some people waiting for their bikes. If you give me your cell number, I'll give you a call when it's done."

Manda agreed. She could at least walk to the coffee shop, have a bagel, and think it over.

She took a table by a window, nibbled at a bagel with peanut butter, and looked idly through a local newspaper someone had left behind.

"Manda?" a familiar voice asked.

She looked up to see one of the women who had been at Joel's dessert party the night before.

"Gwen, isn't it? Hi."

"I'm having my bike serviced and thought I'd grab a coffee. Can I join you?"

"Sure." Manda wasn't sure if this was a bad dream or an answer to her prayers.

Gwen pulled off her hoodie, tossed it on an empty chair, and took the chair opposite Manda. "No offense, but you look like you had a bad night," she ventured.

Manda felt her eyes fill up. "Sorry, I may not be very good company."

"What, don't tell me you drank last night?"

"No."

"So how bad could it be?"

Manda gave a weak laugh. "Thank you for that."

"I found early sobriety to be very difficult. I was confronted with every failing I had and every mistake I made during my drinking."

Manda nodded. She could identify with that.

"I imagine it's hard, too, being in a relationship with someone like Joel."

Manda was sure her bafflement showed on her face.

"I'm sure I'm not mistaken that you came and left with Joel, and I'm even more sure the look on Joel's face was one many women have longed to see."

"Joel and I are just friends, although it's a little complicated by..." She shook her head. "It's a little complicated."

"I wasn't trying to be catty," Gwen apologized. "Really, I was just offering support."

"God knows I need support right now."

"You can tell me as much or as little as you want."

"You and Joel are friends?" Manda tested.

"We've known each other all our lives. We even dated back in our wild-child days, and we dated a little after he and Lorraine broke up." Gwen laughed, "Actually, for a while after they broke up Joel dated every woman in Tompkins Falls and any available woman guest at the Manse."

Manda glared at her.

"I'm not helping, am I?"

Manda rolled her eyes. "Sorry, I am, like, totally over my head."

"What do you mean?"

"I'm trying to do this sobriety thing and take the next steps with my education and career. And Joel's really supportive, but—"

"What do you think of Joel?"

Manda remembered Gwen was a psychologist. Maybe Gwen could help her sort it all out. "That's a hard question, actually."

"Why?"

"He's my boss, my friend, my landlord, provider of many things that make my life easier. And I think he might be in love with me, which blows my mind."

"How so?"

Manda laughed. "Well, I'm just this screw-up. And I'm totally off men for life."

"You are, or you were a few months ago?"

Manda thought about what she had just said. After all the conversations with her therapist about this, she knew she had moved past her self-image as a screw-up. She thought she had said it just now because it was really tempting to go back in time to the issues she had already dealt with, instead of struggling with the jumble of issues and confusion she felt now. "I definitely was a few months ago. And I'm not anymore. I'm just extremely confused and upset."

"You know," Gwen said gently, "I've seen some people come into the program and just get it, just start using the fellowship and the steps and turn their lives around. You're one that has done that, really quickly. I don't think you've caught up with yourself."

Manda was quiet, listening.

"And I've watched Joel keep a respectful distance at any meetings you've both attended, because he wants you to focus on recovery. But he's very definitely in love with you, and I've never seen him in love with anyone in all the years I've known him, which is three decades."

"Why me?" Manda wondered out loud.

"You're beautiful, you're smart, you're on his wavelength. You know, a few weeks ago I saw you two talking at the Friday meeting, and Joel was so relaxed. I think you punched him in the arm or something, and he was eating it right up. He's never playful like that with anyone. He hasn't been playful or happy since he lost his family."

"Not even with Lorraine?" Manda ventured.

Gwen shook her head, took a swallow of coffee, and added more sugar. "Look, I'm not trying to sell you on Joel, and I apologize if this is coming across as pressure."

Manda was tired of having agendas pushed on her. She needed insight and guidance, and if she didn't take charge, this was a wasted opportunity at best. "Did you know Lorraine?" Manda asked.

Gwen sat back and wondered aloud, "Why do you ask?"

Manda answered, "When I said it was complicated, I meant that Joel is still in a relationship with Lorraine, and I feel like I stepped in the middle of whatever's going on between them. And I have a history with Lorraine and her ex-husband who made my life a nightmare."

"Have you talked this over with your sponsor?"

"Temporary sponsor. And no, I haven't felt I could share any of it with her."

"Then ditch the temporary." Gwen was stern. "You need a woman in the program you can talk with. Or possibly a therapist who can help you sort through it and who'll treat the information confidentially."

"I saw a therapist, provided by the college, through graduation. I couldn't afford to see her on my own. She helped a lot with—well, she called it trauma. She was really good, and I learned a lot about how a perpetrator sucks in a victim. But she's not in AA, and I know from everything I've seen around the rooms that the twelve steps are what I need. There are a lot of women with worse experiences than mine, and they are in healthy relationships now, with loving partners, and they say it's because they use the steps all the time to make their lives work. I need help with the steps and with using them in my life."

Gwen gave her an encouraging smile. "Manda, there are several women like me that focus on the steps with their sponsees. You probably know Marsha C. and Marilyn W. I would recommend either of them."

Manda nodded tentatively; their names were familiar, but she couldn't put faces to them. "Thank you."

"Listen, we've got at least an hour before our bikes are ready. How about a walk in the sunshine? If you're comfortable talking, great; if not at least we'll stretch our legs."

Two hours later, they had talked through many of the tangled details that were troubling Manda. Gwen had surprised her by starting with, "What do you think of Lorraine?"

Manda said readily, "I admired her style. I admired the way she nurtured the children and provided the best for them."

"Were you friends?"

"No, I worked for her as a live-in housekeeper—just keeping the day-to-day clutter picked up and fixing evening meals for her. She was committed to eating well and being surrounded by quiet and beauty."

Gwen smiled. "Cady's Point is certainly quiet and beautiful. Some say it was Indian land that had healing properties. There was some claim dispute—back in the seventies, I think—and a lot of money changed hands before it was settled. Lorraine inherited it outright and claim-free."

"The whole Point?"

Gwen nodded.

"I loved biking and walking and swimming there. It was really good for me when Lorraine was still around."

"Probably that was true for her as well, and that may be why she had the house built on that land. It was intended for her and Joel when they married."

Manda's head whipped around.

"And we know how that worked out," Gwen concluded.

"No wonder Joel has an edge in his voice when he says 'Cady's Point'."

Gwen observed, "I know Joel despises the way Kristof treated Lorraine, but if Joel has resentment there, he needs to look at that. Resentments will take us right back to a drink; I'm sure you've heard that. Personally, I think in this case it's just a cover for his guilt, but what do I know? Tell me more; did you and Lorraine walk and swim and bike together?"

"No, never. She was strictly an employer. The most contact we had was a weekly review of what she needed and any adjustments to the quality of the work I was doing."

"Did she pay you?"

"She provided a place to live, use of the kitchen and grounds, and a food budget."

"You did the grocery shopping for the family?"

"Just for the evening meal for her and Kristof, and for myself, although I ate in the kitchen, not with them. Kristof was rarely there for a meal. She wanted a salad made up and fresh dressing ready, for two, each evening. Lots of fresh produce, lean meat, edamame, nuts, things like that. I began doing the same for myself. I had never eaten that way, and it was really, really good for me."

"So you were healthy, and it sounds like you were fit when she was still living at Cady's Point."

Manda nodded. "Definitely an important change in my life. I'd always been chunky and didn't pay attention to exercise."

"Tell me about your drinking. When do you think you crossed the line into alcoholism?"

"After Lorraine left and Kristof started pressuring me. Before that- like in high school and freshman year at Tompkins—I'd go out for beer with friends; sometimes we'd get drunk, sometimes not. When the Presidential Scholars—who were most of my friends—lost half of the scholarship commitment, most had to quit, or they went part-time and worked, so our group broke up. Then in the spring of sophomore year, when I was working for Lorraine, I got an internship at the Manse, too. I'd drink beer for happy hour after work with some of the staff at the Manse, but that was only if I knew Lorraine would not be home waiting for her meal. I drove home drunk sometimes, and it scared me."

"You didn't drink at Lorraine's house?"

"No, not until after she'd gone to England, and Kristof introduced me to fine scotch. Then I started drinking alcoholically pretty quickly. I drank more and more all the time, and toward the end I was getting drunk any time he was in the house at night because I just couldn't stand it."

"You drank to cope?"

"Yes."

"And how did it help you cope?"

"I kind of numbed out, and the next day I could forget what had happened and just focus on my work."

"So things happened that you wanted to forget. Tell about that, if you're willing."

Manda went through the history with Kristof and her

early days in AA. When she'd run through the whole saga, she and Gwen turned back the way they came.

"It sounds like you're placing the responsibility on Kristof appropriately. I think you've done a good inventory around that, and you've seen some important truths about yourself. That was hard work. Do you believe Joel that Kristof is out of the picture now and won't be a danger to you after this?"

"I don't think Joel would give me false hope around that. While I don't know the details of what was said and done, I think Joel believes he's gone and won't be returning as a threat."

Gwen didn't look so sure. "With your permission, I'll do some probing around that."

Manda hesitated, and Gwen let her think about it.

Manda decided, "I don't think it will do any harm. Joel told me that there's an investigation in progress, and my name is…"

"Your name is being talked about by people like the college administrators?" Gwen guessed.

"Was, actually. I think they're on to other people and other issues now."

"I'm sorry that happened. That's a lot to deal with."

"Joel just told me last night. That's half of why I feel so slammed today."

"It hadn't occurred to you that could happen?"

Manda laughed at herself. "I guess I was in denial. I just focused on my safety and my sobriety."

"That's not a bad thing. Weren't there any rumors you picked up on?"

"I knew there were rumors, and I tried not to let them bother me because I knew my truth. But I never imagined the officials at the college were openly discussing me by name and talking about what happened. I worked so hard to

STEPPING UP TO LOVE | 165

maintain my grades and graduate with honors. Gwen, I'm so ashamed and humiliated."

"I can see they'd have to know and have to look into it objectively. You know, Manda, we talk about 'the wreckage of the past,' meaning the mess we find ourselves in when we get sober, and any damage we did to ourselves and to others while we were drinking alcoholically. This is your wreckage, and you are facing it in a mature way, I believe. And I think you are facing it with dignity and honor."

Manda sighed deeply. "It would be really helpful to talk things over with you or someone in AA."

"I'm willing. We probably won't have time today, but we can plan it for another day." Gwen checked her watch. "I'm expecting a phone call soon about my bike. I've got a bunch more questions for you. How would you like to proceed?"

Manda gave her a hopeful smile. "Can we keep going with your questions?"

"Good. My original question to you was 'What do you think of Lorraine?' You told me what you used to think of her. Let's come to the present day and have you tell me what you're thinking about Lorraine since you joined AA and since you learned about Joel's former engagement and his ongoing relationship, whatever that's about."

Manda let out her breath. "Wow, tall order. When you asked me before, I wasn't even thinking about her in the present."

"So, tell me how you feel about her now."

"Well, for sure, it's not what I used to feel. I mean I still admire her for the way she was and for what she made possible for me then, but I am really angry about what happened after she left."

"Angry with her, in addition to Kristof?" Gwen clarified.

"Yes. She left me in the lurch, and the consequences were terrible."

"She didn't give you any warning about her departure or the divorce?"

"No, there was nothing that clued me in. She was obviously unhappy, but I had no reason to think she was pulling out of the marriage or leaving the country."

"It's not something she would have shared with you," Gwen pointed out.

Manda let out her breath in exasperation. "Except, I was dependent on her for a place to live and couldn't afford to just find another place to stay for the remaining year and a half, or even for one semester."

"In dollars and cents, what would it have taken for you to live on campus—room and board—for three semesters?"

Manda did a quick calculation, "Around fifteen thousand, roughly."

"That was a real burden to you," Gwen acknowledged, "and you deserved a heads-up at the very least. To say nothing of the courtesy of an employer's thank you and letter of reference."

"That helps me put it in perspective. Thank you. I don't think I could have sorted that out for myself."

Gwen made her voice light when she told Manda, "Hey, I know people who would tell you to sue her for the fifteen thousand."

Manda laughed. "That's not a bad idea. If I weren't in a good place, and I didn't have the degree now, I'd probably do something like that."

"Yet you're still angry?"

Manda nodded. "I guess for two reasons. One, it's probably stupid, but I'd appreciate an apology or an acknowledgement. And compensation. And a letter of reference. By leaving me in the lurch, she put me in a difficult spot financially, and she treated me like my needs were of no interest or consequence. I deserved better."

"I agree. On the one hand, I have to say, as someone who has known Lorraine all her life, that is the way she thinks. She's always had more money than she knows what to do with, and she has no concept that other people struggle financially or that her actions affect their struggle for better or worse. So, frankly, any apology from her would be pro forma, without meaning. On the other hand, I think you're the one that brought the yellow bike into the shop, and I think it was Lorraine's, and Joel arranged for you to have it. Am I right?"

Manda nodded. "It's a complicated story, but, yes, Joel arranged for me to have the bike."

"I used to bike with Lorraine, and I can tell you that bike—which is custom, with a lifetime service contract—is worth roughly one semester's room and board. Could that ever equate to an apology or an acknowledgement or compensation from Lorraine?"

Manda stared in disbelief. "In dollars and cents, I can see where you're going with that. It doesn't make me any less angry. Maybe that's why Joel arranged it. And Joel arranged for me to live in campus housing this semester, even though it didn't work out. He wouldn't tell me who was paying for it."

"That is something Joel would do, and he had the influence to do it. I need to add that Lorraine's apparent act of compensation to you—the bike—is not something she's capable of without Joel's influence. As an aside, they were both kids who grew up with unlimited funds, but Joel developed compassion and a big heart, while Lorraine has a void in that area. Whose phone is ringing?"

"Yours. My bike probably won't be much longer."

Gwen added, "By the way, Mother Hen Gwen has to point out that you need a helmet, chickie, and a better lock to go with your bike. We're still a few minutes from the shop. If you're still sane, I'd like to hear the other reason you're angry at Lorraine."

Manda was not sure. "I did say there were two reasons, didn't I?"

Gwen nodded. "We were talking about how you feel about her since coming into AA and since finding out about her past involvement with Joel."

"I think it goes back to what I first said—that my relationship with Joel is just too complicated, because he's still in a relationship with Lorraine. It's too hard for me to deal with right now. My focus needs to be on sobriety and education and career." That last sentence sounded false to Manda. She laughed at herself. "Listen to me, Goody Two Shoes. To be honest, I think Lorraine is putting the moves on Joel, and I'm just afraid I can't compete with Lorraine."

Gwen looked intrigued. "Is she really? Actually, I have no doubt you can compete with Lorraine, but I think you're wise to back off from the relationship with Joel for now. You have so much going on in your life right now. If you were farther along with your career plans and had a stronger foundation in sobriety, you could pick this battle and fight for your man."

Gwen made a fist and punched the air. They both laughed.

"But the better course of action is to detach and let Joel come to his senses. And honestly I don't believe for a minute Joel is involved with Lorraine in any kind of romantic relationship. He's clearly in love with you."

Manda had another question. "So, taking the full scholarship for the doctorate in Texas is probably 'running away'? I've been kicking that around since I woke up this morning. I almost called my sister to tell her I was going to do it."

"Is the doctorate from Texas a reasonable path to what you want for your education and career?"

"Honestly, no. I applied when I didn't know what I wanted, and my sister is there. But now I know what I want, and that's not it."

"Would it work, with what you're thinking you want to do?"

Manda thought about it from that perspective. "I think it would work if I wanted to be in academia and consulting. But it would make people question my sincerity in the work environments I have in mind. So, no, it would not serve me well."

They rounded the corner to the bike shop, and Gwen suggested, "We'll do more career discussion another time. Under the circumstances, though, my take is that Texas is probably running away." She grinned. "On the other hand, a visit to your sister might be a provocative move."

Manda smiled at the thought.

"Feel better?" Gwen asked.

"A lot, thank you, Gwen. Will you work with me on the steps?"

"You're a hard worker, Manda. It would be a privilege and a pleasure."

Gwen paid for her bike while Manda perused the helmets and locks. She asked the shop owner for advice, and he helped her find a yellow helmet in her size and an intimidating lock. "Rack for your car?" he queried.

She shook her head. For now, she would ride from home. When she needed to transport it, as she did this morning, she could fold down the seats of the Beetle and carefully fit it inside.

"And I just got the signal your bike is all set. Enjoy!"

She thanked him for his help and paid for her items.

"I'm thinking," she said to Gwen, "I want to ride to the coffee shop for lunch and then ride back here to my car. Want to join me?"

Gwen gave her a smile. "Absolutely. I'm starved."

As they worked their way through harvest salads and hunks of multigrain bread, the conversation moved back to Manda's inventory of moral strengths and liabilities. Manda recounted the "herd instinct" theory she'd talked over with Joel.

Gwen nodded her agreement.

Manda talked about the behaviors she fell back on with Kristof that her mother had demonstrated around her violent, alcoholic father. "I've been standing up to people lately, even though it's really uncomfortable. Things go much better, and it's easier to do it now that I'm sober. I think I was on auto-pilot when I drank."

"'On auto-pilot' meaning you used old, self-defeating behaviors?"

"Exactly. I never learned to deal with difficult people."

Gwen noticed a troubled look pass over Manda's face, and she asked about it.

"Lyssa. My sister. I really believe we could be good friends if we were both sober and working the program. Part of me wants to jump on a plane and visit her and wave a magic wand to make us better. But you talked about detaching from Joel, and I think I need to detach from Lyssa until I know she's in the program and staying clean and sober." She told Gwen about Lyssa's "marijuana maintenance plan."

"You can pray for her. And be a power of example." Gwen asked the harder question, "Do you think you can detach from Joel?"

Manda shrugged. "He's my boss, my landlord, and my friend. I value his professional perspective, and he's been a huge support these past few months. I don't want to cut him out of my life."

"You could make your sponsor the 'bad guy' around not dating him, but I feel strongly that you should level with him about how much you're affected by his ongoing contact—relationship?—with Lorraine. If that's the only thing stopping you from having a relationship with him, you need to be clear with him about that."

Gwen shifted in her chair and draped her arm over the ladderback. "You know, I've been thinking about that. Knowing Lorraine, she's up to something, and for some reason, Joel's going along with it."

Manda looked bewildered.

Gwen explained, "If you recall Joel's story at the AA meeting, he said several times that he was doing what was expected of him.."

"What could Lorraine be expecting Joel to do for her and why?"

Gwen raised her eyebrows. "If I know Lorraine, she's out for Kristof's blood, and Joel is conveniently on the scene to follow through with whatever scheme she's cooked up. And I know for sure he's filled with guilt about her marrying Kristof on the rebound and ending up in such a mess. Maybe even guilt about your involvement with Kristof, which would not have happened if Lorraine hadn't married Kristof and hired you and yada yada."

"But he's not responsible for any of that."

"No. But Joel is overly responsible. It's a character flaw. We've all got 'em. That's one of Joel's, and he's sometimes blind to it, particularly when a woman is involved."

Manda sat back. "Way complicated. No wonder 'Keep it simple' is one of the slogans on the wall at meetings."

"Believe it, chickie," Gwen told her with a chuckle. "Let's leave all of that aside and get the focus back on you. What's clear from my side of the table is that you value Joel as a businessman and you want to continue to be mentored by him in that capacity. I'm going to recommend that you develop that relationship. Don't hesitate to ask him for advice about grad school decisions, financing your education, getting work experience, and so on. Also consider asking him about his business plans, past and present, and in general how he handles his fortune. I think you'll learn a lot."

"That feels right. He and I are on solid ground with those topics, and—you're right—I would learn a ton."

Gwen touched her hand, and Manda wondered what was coming next. "I also want you to keep in mind that Joel may be older than you, but he's still very young. He relies heavily on his sponsor Phil because he has no father, brother, or other close family to support and guide him. You know what that's like."

Manda nodded and swallowed a lump in her throat.

Gwen went on, "It's not easy being Joel Cushman, heir to a significant fortune. Women want Joel—not because he's witty and warm-hearted and smart—but because he's rich, and they'd be happy to produce the next heir. Lorraine is probably the only woman he's been with that didn't care about his fortune; nor did he care about hers. Now she's back but he's found someone else. She's not going to succeed in resurrecting the old relationship." Gwen drummed her fingers on the table. "I'm really, really curious what she's cooking up."

"You gonna ask her?"

Gwen tipped her head from side to side as if debating the question. "I might ask around."

"You gonna keep my name out of it, please?"

"Oh, you bet I am," Gwen assured her. "But I'll fill you in if I find out anything."

"Closing in ten," the coffee shop owner called to them. "Two o'clock we all turn into pumpkins."

They laughed and thanked him.

Gwen told Manda, "So now you've completed steps four and five."

"Fearless moral inventory, admitted to another person?"

"Yes. You had done most of your inventory already, and you added to it by looking at your experience with Lorraine and how that is still affecting you. And you shared all of it with me with honesty, open-mindedness, and willingness. Well done. How do you feel?"

"Lighter. And exhausted."

"We will move on to the other steps soon. I just want to say that right now I see your biggest amend being to yourself—taking time to choose your life's work and being open to a loving relationship. Giving Joel a fair chance, not rushing or being rushed into anything not right for you. For right now, I suggest you go home, rest, maybe go to the hot dog meeting tonight, take it easy the rest of the weekend."

"Sounds good. Gwen, I know you're a psychologist, too; should I be paying you a fee?"

"Not for working with you on the steps. But as your sponsor I do need your phone number. Here's mine," Gwen offered her business card and took the scrap of paper Manda gave her. "Are you okay to drive home?"

"I'm good to go. I will take your advice and will think hard about everything we've talked about." She felt tears brimming. "Thank you for bringing me to a much better place."

Gwen gave her a big hug. "That's what we do for each other in AA. You'll soon be in a place where you can do the same for others."

Chapter 7

Manda flew along the lakeshore, her feet circling rhythmically, willow fronds ruffling as she passed between the rows of trees. The sun was weak today, and the southern breeze off the water made the air temperature perfect for cycling. This was her second pass of the two-mile path along the lake; today she would log eight miles for her early morning ride.

Gwen had suggested more discipline in her exercise routine. "See what happens," Gwen challenged.

"I'll have a better butt?"

"That, too. Give it a month, and watch what happens, watch how you handle things."

Manda knew she was handling things differently. Even though she was still waiting for word from grad schools about scholarships, she had taken charge from her side. In addition to finishing the paperwork for loans—her backup plan—she had, in the last week, taken the initiative to visit St. Basil's and Syracuse University.

At both schools, she confirmed her interest and her qualifications and her financial need. Both schools were eager to have her start in the fall, but both were delayed with their scholarship decisions. If Joel was right, the small schools were worried about enrollments. So she told St. Basil's she was also waiting to hear from Syracuse about financial aid; that got their attention.

She was not going crazy in the meantime; she had plenty to focus on. As she did most mornings, after her bike ride she showered, ate cereal with berries, dressed in a tan or navy skirt and preppy shirt, fixed a fresh salad with chicken for lunch and packed it in her tote bag. By ten o'clock she was in her cubicle at the Manse working productively; after work she headed to the lakeshore for a walk to de-stress. A quick change of clothes and she was ready for a light supper and an AA meeting. Any awake time after the meeting went to coffee with friends, reading, or sewing. Her life worked today.

Her friendship with Joel felt like it was "on hold," rather than "over." She was not interested in dating anyone else. Her mantra "off men for life" had changed to "not yet." And her butt was definitely better.

Gwen found other ways to challenge Manda's thinking and push her into more grown-up behavior. Manda now saw herself as one of the staff at the Manse, rather than a student who was lucky enough to have an internship that turned into a part-time job. When Manda proposed asking Joel about continuing her position at the Manse after graduation, Gwen suggested she talk it over with her boss, Dan, instead. "That is the normal way to inquire about one's job," Gwen pointed out with a smile.

"Duh. I should know that."

Her discussion with Dan went well, and she was excited to hear that he and Joel wanted her to take on more responsibility, provided she agreed to stay with the job for at least a year at three-quarter time. She told Dan, "Yes!" and barely restrained herself from hugging him.

Part of fitting in as a regular employee, Gwen pointed out, was dressing the part. Manda now had clothes that fit. In the past month she had put together a simple wardrobe. By using the tailoring tricks her mother taught her, she improved the fit of her better-quality, baggy clothes. On a visit to a nearby fabric shop, she picked up two bargain pieces of cloth—one linen, one twill—to make tailored skirts.

She discovered one of her friends from the Manse, Sara, was a genius with consignment shops and bargain-backrooms. Saturday afternoons found them in the more affluent villages of the Finger Lakes checking out the latest goods. Manda's limit any weekend was twenty dollars; so far she had picked up an ivory silk shirt, a black pencil skirt, black ballet flats, and smashing belts and scarves.

Late in August, on one of their afternoon biking trips, Gwen asked Manda, "Are you thinking about dating?"

"Nope, not yet."

"Not even Joel?" Gwen tested.

Manda did not answer.

"Listen, if you're thinking about marriage in your future, you might want to consider dating a few men at some point. Dating is an approved way to find your 'soul mate,' as you call him."

That hit Manda where she hurt the most; she believed she had found her soul mate and lost him because of her own immaturity. She was still embarrassed about her meltdown with Joel after the dessert party.

"I'd just like to be friends with the men I know right now and any interesting men I meet."

Gwen gave her a skeptical look.

"For a while. While I'm in grad school. And anyway, I think a serious relationship should start with friendship."

Gwen agreed that was a good starting point. "Do you consider Joel your friend?"

"We have been friends. I'm not sure now." Manda told her, "I think for a serious relationship to have a chance, it's important to be honest with each other, and there have been secrets that still worry me."

"Does Joel know that? Have you been honest with him? Have you gone back to talk with him about it?"

Joel had been invisible since her meltdown. Manda heard him leave the house each morning on his way to the Early Risers meeting. She occasionally heard his voice in the hall at the Manse.

"I believe he does," Manda answered. It sounded false even to her.

Gwen speculated, "It's possible he's waiting for you to approach him."

Manda thought it over. "I guess," she conceded. "When it comes down to it, I'm afraid."

Gwen swerved and couldn't catch herself before she dumped the bike. Manda stopped to give her a hand.

"Are you hurt?

"I didn't see that coming." Gwen checked the bike for damage and, finding none, brushed dirt and willow fronds from her clothes and her hair. "I swear, Manda, when you get honest about something, you blow my socks off."

"Seriously, Gwen, I have a lot of growing up to do. It's not that I don't love—well, I don't know if I love Joel. I feel like I'm not ready for any next steps. Blaming it on Joel's secrets is just a cover, to be honest."

Gwen motioned to a picnic table by the lake, and they parked their bikes for a break. Manda took a long swallow from her water bottle and offered Gwen her bag of trail mix. Gwen ate hungrily.

"I have a bunch more questions for you," Gwen warned Manda.

"Like…"

"Do you want to marry into a large family? Do you want children? Is religion important to you? If you didn't have to work, would you still want to? Do you need to have interests in common or lead essentially separate lives? I want you to give some thought to those things and talk with me and other women about them."

"I'll give it a try." Manda response was halfhearted.

Gwen encouraged, "Another way to think about it is to look around the program at marriages that seem to be what you're looking for. Make note of what appeals and what doesn't. If you're comfortable, ask the women and men in those marriages how they make it work."

Manda was quiet.

"Does that sound like a good idea?"

Manda turned to smile at her but frowned instead when she saw the sky. "We need to go back now. Look."

The clouds in the west were black with rain.

As they mounted their bikes, the wind picked up and blew toward them. Gwen urged, "Let's pick up our pace. I don't want to get soaked out here."

Just as they reached Gwen's car, rain spattered them with big, cold drops. Forgetting that Manda had ridden her bike to meet her, Gwen threw her own bike on her rack, gave Manda a hasty wave, and peeled out of the parking lot toward her home on the eastern lakeshore.

Resigned to a soaking, Manda pedaled two miles in the downpour and, at last, climbed Lakeside Terrace to the last house on the bluff.

Joel was watching for her and ran down the stairs with a big towel. "I'll put your bike away. Get a hot shower." She nodded her thanks, too chilled to speak.

When she emerged from the shower, her apartment was silent and empty. The heat from the blow dryer warmed her as it dried her curls. She pulled on dry jeans, a warm turtleneck, and thick socks.

A light knock sounded at her door. "Joel?"

"Want food?"

Manda laughed and opened the door to him.

"I made a pot of chili. It's too hot to bring down. Join me?"

She smiled and nodded. "I'll bring celery and cheese."

Joel added with a grin, "You might want to wear your glasses." Manda grabbed her glasses, a bunch of celery, and a hunk of Monterrey Jack and trudged up the stairs behind him.

"Did Gwen call you?"

"I called both your cell phones when I saw the storm moving in. I caught Gwen just as she pulled into her driveway. We figured you were almost home by then, so I watched out for you."

"I was frozen. That towel saved me. Thanks for taking care of the bike."

He nodded and took the celery to the sink.

She sat cross-legged on a stool at the island.

"I'll slice cheese and make celery sticks while you dish up the chili," she offered.

He handed her the fresh-washed celery, a sharp knife, and a cutting board. They worked silently for a minute.

"It's nice to see you," she ventured.

Joel turned with a smile and met her eyes.

"I miss our friendship," she blurted out.

She saw pain flash behind Joel's eyes.

He cleared his throat. "Me too," he managed to say. "I just want to say I've been seeing my therapist, and I am taking responsibility for being so dense and hurtful when we talked after my anniversary meeting."

"I think that's a good move, Joel."

Joel looked at her, and she offered a troubled smile.

He looked away and made himself busy setting two places at the table next to the window, transferring food and glasses of water and a sliced baguette in its own basket.

They sat opposite each other and worked their way through the chili, silently watching the rain pound the lake.

"More?" Joel asked and pointed to Manda's empty bowl.

She shook her head. "It was great, thanks."

Joel said casually, "I've been wanting to ask you something that's really none of my business."

Manda saw the vulnerability in his gray-green eyes, and—for the first time—she saw his love reaching out to her. How had she missed it before?

She stammered, "Go ahead."

"I've been thinking about your grad school plans and how you could finance your degree. Okay to talk about it?"

Manda nodded and offered him a slice of cheese before taking one herself.

"I know both your parents died together in an accident, and I think you said your aunt, your guardian, also passed away not long after."

Manda nodded.

"Was there any inheritance you could tap for your masters program?"

Manda was startled.

Joel held up his hands and acknowledged, "Like I said, it's none of my business."

"It's fine. I have no idea how to answer that. I can't believe I never thought of it."

"You don't know if there was an inheritance?" Manda looked out the window, trying to remember. She'd put it out of her mind because all of it was too painful.

Joel let her ponder while he cleared their dishes and started a pot of tea. He came back to the table with a sweater and draped it around her shoulders before sitting across from her again.

"Thank you. I didn't realize how chilled I still am." She slipped his sweater over her head and rolled up the sleeves. "There's not much I remember. I know our family lived comfortably, and I thought there was money put away for our college expenses, but still we were expected to get scholarships. And we both did.

"Mom and Dad owned the house with no mortgage, and they both made good money as teachers. When they died, I don't think they had a will, either of them. Lyssa and I were both under eighteen. It was my father's sister Estelle who agreed—reluctantly, capital R—to take us in until we went to college. Aunt Estelle was allowed to sell our parents' house to meet the expense of taking care of us." Manda sat back and let out a big breath. "Does any of that tell us who inherited anything?"

Joel was thoughtful. "If your parents died intestate, any life insurance will have gone to funeral expenses. Probably a judge awarded Estelle custody—or twisted her arm by approving the sale of the home for her needs as guardian. I suspect she made out well if there was no mortgage. The judge probably put anything else—savings, investments, and so on—into trust for you and Lyssa until you came of age, at least twenty-one. You lived in New York State?"

Manda nodded. "Olean, and my aunt lived a few miles away in Allegany. I have a vague memory of Aunt Estelle saying something to the two of us one night when we'd been sassing her. Something about telling the judge he should make it thirty when we could claim our trust. Lyssa went off to Texas at the end of that first summer, so that scene must have been shortly after our parents died. I think the house had just been sold, and we were acting up about her selling all the books and record albums and things that mattered to us."

"And when did your Aunt Estelle die?"

"I had just started at Tompkins, so early fall one year later. She had a heart attack, they said."

"Did you hear from anyone about a signature to probate her will, anything like that?"

Manda thought about it and shook her head. "I don't remember anything like that."

Joel prompted her, "You mentioned once that you paid cash for your car. Where did that money come from?"

"That was money I saved from waitressing all through high school. And I went back to Olean every summer—

except last summer—to waitress. I always stayed with a friend from high school."

"Do me a favor," Joel said. "Ask your sister if she's aware of money in trust for the two of you. Even if it's not much, it's worth pursuing."

Manda nodded thoughtfully, her eyes on the lake.

"Are you okay with my asking about this?"

She turned to look at him and gave him a sad smile. "Yes, absolutely. It could really help us a lot, and I might never have thought of it. Probably Lyssa never thought of it either."

"Are you and Lyssa in touch with each other?"

Manda told Joel about the graduation card and told him they talked every few months by phone just to stay in touch.

"But you're not close?"

Manda shook her head. "The marijuana maintenance plan, remember?"

"How could I forget?" Joel said wryly. "Well, if there's money in trust, it may take some legal intervention to track it down and release it to you, but it's worth pursuing. Any effort to contact you probably hit a dead end, since you and Lyssa had both moved away and moved several times. Manda, I can see this is a downer for you. I'm sorry."

Manda felt tears threatening. "No, it's really helpful. I just haven't thought about their deaths. That got left off my inventory." Joel covered her hands with his, and she felt his warmth deep inside.

"I've really missed your touch."

He squeezed her hands. "Do you want to talk, or do you need to be alone?"

"I think right now I need to call Lyssa."

"Why not call from here?"

When she agreed, he handed her his smartphone and excused himself.

Manda heard his bedroom door close. She reached Lyssa on the first try.

Lyssa had not given any thought to an inheritance but she did remember the blow-up with Aunt Estelle. "She just gave away all our records and books and trashed the posters. Yeah, that was the first and only time I heard about our trust. Aunt Estelle threatened to block it until we were old and gray. Well, thirty, like you said. I totally haven't thought of it since."

Lyssa also remembered the name of the judge and gave it to Manda. "Hey y'all let me know what you find out, ya hear?" Lyssa said in her adopted Texas twang.

"I will. Thanks, Lyssa. I love you."

"Oh, gol', I love you too, lil sis. You know I want you out here."

"I'll come visit when I can. I'm sober now. I have a few months."

"No foolin'? How it is for you?"

"It's way better, Lyssa. I'm happy. I want you to be happy, too."

"Maybe. How y'all doing it?"

"AA. It's working. You okay, Lyssa?"

"Course I am. Don't you be worryin' 'bout me."

"Call me on my new cell" Manda gave her the number.

She stood staring out at the rain for a while until she felt Joel's hands on her shoulders. She turned to him and welcomed his strong arms around her. She breathed in the clean smell of him and rested her head against his shoulder until she found her voice. "She remembered the judge's name. Can you help me figure out the next steps?"

"I'll make some inquiries. We'll see where it leads."

Manda pulled back to look in his eyes. "Sometimes I wish you'd met me when I was grown up instead of at the beginning."

Joel's smile blossomed. "It's pretty fascinating this way."

Manda was a regular at the women's meeting in Clifton Springs on Fridays instead of Joel's meeting in Tompkins Falls. She rarely saw Joel at meetings, but, to her delight, she saw his sponsor Phil every Wednesday at his Big Book meeting.

Phil had founded the meeting several years earlier as a way for members to study and discuss the "bible" of Alcoholics Anonymous, which they referred to as the Big Book. She quickly learned that Phil was a local expert on the AA literature, particularly the Big Book, and she loved hearing him and the other old timers talk about it.

Most weeks, Phil invited Manda and a few other newcomers to join him after the meeting for cold drinks on his big back porch on the lake. Conversation freely ranged from summer concerts, to the fracking controversy, to the local economy, to Middle East hot spots.

One Wednesday, Manda was the only taker for the back-porch gathering. Phil shushed her when she tried to bow out, and asked her to carry the jug of iced tea out to the big round table. "I'm getting old, you know," he laughed.

"You don't look it, Phil," she assured him. "You look like you walk every day and probably play a few rounds of golf every so often."

"Well, you're right on both counts," he told her. "But I'm seventy-eight, and that boy of ours is wearing me out this summer."

Manda diverted her attention to the lake.

Phil tolerated her silence a while before gently prompting, "Are you going to ask me about him?"

"I haven't seen him very much."

"Do you want to?" he probed.

"When I see him, it's good—really good. But things got more complicated than I could handle, so I took my sponsor's advice and backed off Joel's and my relationship to focus on recovery for a while and work and, mostly, just growing up."

"Who's your sponsor, Manda?"

"Gwen Forrester."

"Good woman. Very experienced sponsor and counselor. Did she tell you to stop seeing him?"

"No, more like change the emphasis, back off the personal intensity for a while."

"Do you love him?"

"I think so, Phil. I care about him and admire him and enjoy him. I'm just not sure what love is or how to do it. Half the time I feel like a whacky teenager. Gwen says that's early recovery, and it will get better."

"You said the relationship got too complicated. What did you mean? Sex?"

Manda shook her head. "I didn't realize, until we argued after Joel's party, that Joel is somehow involved with Lorraine. Now, I mean, in the present, and I don't know how to sort out a relationship with him under those circumstances."

When Phil was quiet a while, Manda looked at his face. It was in shadow, and she couldn't read him.

Phil told her, "He feels guilty for what happened to Lorraine after he ended the engagement, and he's stuck there. He's letting her choreograph his role in her revenge against Kristof. It's wearing me out. I'm glad you have the good sense to stay out of it."

"Revenge," Manda said in a spooky voice. "It sounds like another bad movie with Kristof as the villain."

"That's a good way to put it. And our boy has no business playing out revenge fantasies; his own or anyone else's. But I can't get through to him on that point. He's not being a sober AA acting the way he's acting."

"What are he and Lorraine up to? Do I want to know?"

"It involves developing Cady's Point as a high-end gated community."

Manda laughed in disbelief.

"Why's that funny?"

"It's just stupid," Manda said. "I mean (A) it's not revenge, unless I'm missing something; how does that hurt Kristof? And (B) it's not consistent with Joel's way of doing business; he's a benefit-the-community, maybe-for-profit kind of businessman. And (C) Cady's Point is a place of spiritual healing and ought to be developed as a retreat center or rehab or something like that. What they're doing is just stupid."

"Well, Manda, you've got all the arguments, and I wish you'd sock it to him. I'm sick of arguing with him about it. As for their relationship, it's nonsense to think Joel is 'involved with' Lorraine. He's fronting her business deal, nothing more."

Manda pressed her fingertips to her forehead. "Gwen said something just like that."

"And what was that?"

"When I said Joel seemed to be having a relationship with Lorraine, she said probably Lorraine was planning something and Joel was just going along with it."

"Bingo!" Phil shouted. "Gwen's known him longer than anyone, and she's hit the nail right on the head. He's feeling guilty and he's going along with Lorraine's wishes."

Manda let out a huge sigh. "That makes me feel worse, not better. Joel told me he's seeing a therapist. Did you know that?"

"Yes. I kept after him to do that after the fiasco with you on his anniversary. It's not your job to save him from himself, Manda" Phil cautioned. "I guess it's not my job either." He was quiet another minute, and Manda could feel the weariness and agitation in the older man. It wasn't good for his health to be worrying about Joel.

Save him from himself? Is Phil being dramatic, or is Joel going off the deep end? Manda asked pointedly, "You think Joel is self-destructing?"

"Probably not. But I'm seriously concerned, just the same," Phil told her. "I took the liberty of putting in a call to his Uncle Justin."

Manda kept her voice light. "Where is Uncle Justin these days?"

Phil shook his head. "I only know he's not answering his voicemail. Could be taking walkabout through the Australian Outback, for all I know."

"Do you have an email or Twitter or Facebook name for him? Is his last name Cushman?"

Phil chuckled. "Manda, I have no idea what you just asked me, but his last name is Cushman, yes."

"I'll see what I can find out. And just maybe I'll have that promised conversation with Joel about his various business plans. See if I can bring the conversation around to this stupid one he's got going with Lorraine."

"You, young lady, have a good mind. And Joel is crazy about you, and he listens to you." Phil brightened. "I will plant the seed. I feel more hopeful now."

Manda leaned over to kiss his scratchy cheek. "It's nice when I can give back to you guys, even a little, for all you've done for me."

The next sunny day she took a walk on the grounds of the Manse after work instead of going to the lakeshore. Joel met her on the path, and she knew it was not a chance meeting. "Just wondering how you are," he told her and stood a few feet away.

She smiled and nodded. "I'm doing well, thank you. It's nice to be part of the staff. I appreciate the way you and Dan are giving me more responsibility. Any suggestions for me?"

The question surprised him. As the first part of his answer, he did a wordless scan of her clothes and demeanor and gave an approving smile. "No suggestions. You're doing a good job." He gestured to the path as an invitation to walk together. Manda fell into step with him. "You asked once about the business plan for the Manse. I don't know if that's something you still want to hear?"

"Very much." Manda knew they needed to use their formal voices at work, but it was a strain for her.

Joel told her, "I'm sure you've noticed that the Manse is not a big money-maker, nor was it intended to be."

"We almost operate as a not-for-profit?"

"That's a good way to frame it. Obviously we don't have that status and can't, but profit was not the motive. The impetus for the Manse was twofold; to do something useful with my family home and to do it in a way that benefits the local economy."

Manda looked at him sideways. "You grew up in this mansion?"

"I did. The mansion was not where I wanted to live when I came back to this area. I looked at the level of luxury and fine taste the place represented, and knew it would appeal to wealthy clients and to locals who wanted a very special venue for weddings and the like.

"In phase one, the house was the core of a luxury inn and spa. After a few years, we added the function rooms and more exercise facilities. At this point in time, the function rooms—large and small—represent the bulk of the income. Our largest expense is—"

"Buildings and grounds, right?"

"Exactly. Maintaining the façade is critical to the business, and the cost of that is factored into our packages for business meetings, corporate retreats, weddings, bridal and baby showers, wine tours, and so on." He turned to her, "Want me to stop?"

Manda shook her head. He was on a roll, and she wanted to hear whatever he had to say.

"Our catchment area is more than regional; we draw from New York City and the corporate headquarters in the greater New York metropolitan area. I don't think we've had a corporate training event or corporate retreat since you've been on staff, have we?"

Manda shook her head.

"The downturn in the economy impacted that aspect of the business, but we have one coming up in July. You'll see activity this month as we upgrade the training rooms with new technology. In fact, a technology specialist from St. Basil's has done the design for us and will be consulting through the implementation. You may want to stop by and introduce yourself."

"I will, thanks."

"We need to watch our time," Joel was still using his manager voice. "On the way back, ask me questions and tell me what you think we could add or do different."

The path back to the Manse was clear. Joel put his hand on Manda's back as they walked, and she relaxed under his touch.

"I've always wondered why there's no development of the lakefront."

"What did you have in mind?"

"At the very least, a gazebo and lighted paths along the shore would have romantic appeal for the weddings and weekend packages. The shoreline seems like a natural for a big dock for swimming, a few moorings for lake residents who come for dinner. I'm sure it opens up safety issues, but there are many possibilities for water activities for families."

"That last would move us into the 'resort' category, and you're right, it comes with a host of safety issues. To be honest, I never thought of the dock and moorings, because I'm not a boater."

"That surprises me."

"Sea sickness. I don't do boating, and I don't think about it."

"Do you swim?"

"I do and I love it. We're debating: build a pool or promote the lake?"

"You know my vote."

"Lake?"

"Lake."

"Your gazebo idea has real potential."

Manda laughed. "And it's not an original idea, right?"

Joel chuckled. "It's actually in the plans for this year, now that the fitness trails are in place."

"I'm hearing that you want exterior changes to be kept natural."

"Yes, very much."

"I take back the big dock, then. Maybe the gazebo should be a terraced garden with strategic lighting. Add a few, nicely landscaped, lakeview photo-op—benches, maybe."

Joel nodded thoughtfully. "Very nice. Harold will be all over the garden idea. Let me pursue that with him."

They were almost in view of the Manse.

"I'm going to check on a few things. Why don't you go on ahead?" He squeezed her shoulder and took the left fork in the path.

Manda gave him a wave. She knew he was making sure they did not walk into the building together. She sighed. They hadn't said a word about Lorraine or the gated community.

On the first day of August she received her long-awaited letters from St. Basil's and Syracuse with offers of scholarships from both. While it wasn't all she wanted, she believed she could make it work. She knew what she wanted to do, but she ran it by Gwen as a sanity check.

Gwen agreed with her thinking and added, "I'm glad you're not obsessed about finishing quickly, and you're willing to take your time with the school you prefer."

Manda took a deep breath and proposed, "Gwen, I want to run it by Joel, too. What do you think?"

"His opinion is certainly better-informed than mine. And I really wish you'd also try to talk with him about the situation with Lorraine. One suggestion: try to hook up with him at the Friday meeting, rather than scheduling with him at work."

"Sure. Why?"

"It tells him you are doing this in the context of recovery, that you are open to personal topics, and that you're not trying to go around Dan. It also says that you respect his time in the office and don't expect him to deal with personal concerns on the job. That's a big improvement over a few months ago."

"Amen. Good advice."

"And that's all the advice I've got for you, except 'Don't drink, no matter what happens'."

"I'll call you after."

"Not later than nine o'clock unless you're desperate." Manda thanked her and put in a call to Phil. He was glad to hear she was coming Friday night, and he would save her a seat.

Manda approached Joel at the coffee pot. He watched her cross the room toward him. His surprise gave way to skepticism and finally a smile as she neared him. "Nice to see you at the Friday night meeting again. Great haircut."

She gave him a big smile and fluffed her shorter curls. "Sara at the spa bartered with me for help with her taxes."

"This time of year?"

"Not everyone files by the April deadline." Manda shrugged. "None of my business."

"Not my business either. You're really getting this recovery stuff. Five months now?"

"Almost. And I owe my summer progress to my sponsor Gwen. She's helped me change my thinking and my clothes and my attitudes and many things."

He caressed her with his eyes. "It looks good on you."

Manda's eyes softened, and he could feel her peace.

"I'd like to talk to you."

He nodded cautiously.

"The results are in from my grad school applications, and I'm pretty sure of my decision. I want to run it past you. If you're willing."

"I'm willing, if we can also talk about us."

Manda studied his face and took her time responding. "Okay, except I'm confused enough that I want to keep them separate, and it would be easier to talk about the grad school stuff first."

Joel nodded his agreement. "It's still light after the meeting. How about a walk along the shore?"

Manda's face lit up with a smile.

Manda arrived at the parking area ten minutes ahead of Joel. She did some stretches and a few jumping jacks. A fickle breeze chilled her, and she pulled a hoodie out of the trunk of the Beetle. It was big and baggy and wrinkled; she threw it back in the trunk and did a few more jumping jacks.

Joel pulled in beside the Beetle. "Sorry I'm late," he said. "Sponsee with crisis."

"Sure you can do this tonight?"

"Absolutely." He stretched in place.

"You're smart wearing a windbreaker."

"How about a sweater?" he offered and pulled one from the front seat for her. "What's so funny?"

"It's not wrinkled. How do you do that?"

He laughed. "I just put it there when I left for the meeting. I had in mind taking a walk along the lakeshore and didn't know how cool it would get. Or maybe my Higher Power made me bring an extra one in case you wanted to walk, too. You never know." He wasn't going to tell her Phil had given him a heads-up.

They started down the gravel path along the lakeshore, their shoulders six inches from each other, hands not touching.

Manda started. "I like our walks, but we always seem to talk about how I'm doing. How are you doing?"

"Crazy," he told her. "The expression in the rooms is 'Stark raving sober.' I'm working it out with the help of my therapist, but it's slow going." He let his hand brush against hers. "Tell me about the grad school decision."

Manda laid out her three choices, starting with the full scholarship from UT Austin for a Ph.D. program, which she had rejected. She told him her thinking.

"Yes, good decision," Joel agreed. He sent up a private prayer of thanks that he wasn't going to lose her to Texas.

Manda told him about the master's program at Syracuse which came with a three-quarter scholarship.

"Your voice tells me that's not the winner. Tell me why."

"It's the best money, and it's a great program, but it's not the best fit for me. The emphasis is on for-profit organizations and entrepreneurial ventures. Very exciting, very 'now.' Very little emphasis on social entrepreneurship or ethics or not-for-profit, which are important to me. Also, at three-quarter time, I wouldn't have enough time for the Manse and would need to let go of the bookkeeping and the studio apartment."

Joel nodded his understanding without giving his opinion. "Door number three?" he asked lightly.

"St. Basil's offered me a half-time scholarship, which is really generous for them. The program emphasis is what I want. If I went half-time, they're cool with me using the all the scholarship money to fully cover the first year. I'd need to find funding for year two, but assuming I can, I would finish in two years. And I could continue with the Manse and the bookkeeping, assuming that works for you."

He nodded. "You're okay with stretching it out two years?"

"I am," she said with no hesitation.

"And how would you finance year two?"

"I have an application in for a loan, which I'm willing to do. In the meantime, I could save some toward tuition and books. I know I can't count on it, but maybe we'll hear something about Lyssa's and my inheritance."

Joel proposed, "And you could look around for other sources. A business might be willing to subsidize you. It's worth checking, and you'd have time to do that."

"I hadn't thought about that. Thank you."

He gave her hair a ruffle of approval and asked her, "Will the Beetle make that commute for two years?"

He saw Manda squeeze her eyes shut.

"I was hoping you wouldn't ask that."

"Because you know it's a problem."

"You're good."

"I can't be losing my employees on the highway, even if it's just a break-down for a busted tire. And it could be much worse."

"I planned to ask you for the name of a good mechanic and have the car evaluated for a ninety-mile round-trip commute most weekends."

"It's a weekend program?"

She nodded. "One weekend a month for each course."

"Please think about staying in Rochester overnight those weekends, even if you get a new car."

Joel knew her first instinct was to resist his good advice. He was quiet while she worked through it.

"I'll consider it."

"Really?" Joel's tone was skeptical.

"Really." Manda laughed at herself.

"Thank you. Ken Huntington will do a good job checking out your car. He doesn't have a website; I'll get you his number. What if he tells you to junk the Beetle, which I think he will?"

"I think the right answer is: have him find me a reliable used car, and I'll get a loan for it."

Joel put his hands in his pockets. "That's not a bad idea. Let's see what he says about the car first."

"So you think St. Basil's is the way to go, half-time?"

"Absolutely."

"And you're cool with my doing the bookkeeping and staying in the studio?"

"I am, but you may need to work in some internships, so let's keep an open mind about that and take it as it comes."

"You're making this easy for me."

"Did you think I would give you a hard time?"

"Just saying I appreciate it. And I don't take it for granted."

He paused on the walk and turned to her. "So, can we talk about us?"

"We did okay with my agenda. Let's go for it."

Joel tipped her chin up, brought his mouth close to hers, and waited for her to make the next move. Manda planted a soft kiss beside his mouth and slid her hands down his chest and around his waist.

When he'd pulled her close, she told him, "I want things to work out for us. I'm really confused and afraid about what's going on with Lorraine. And I'm still very emotional and very slow about growing up."

"I am not worried about you growing up, because you're working hard. I'm still working on my issues, too, as you have seen. It's a work in progress for both of us." He leaned back to see her face and saw tears brimming in her eyes. He let her go but took her hand and kissed it.

They walked hand-in-hand along the path another twenty yards.

"What's going on with Lorraine," he told her, "is a plan to develop Cady's Point. She owns it all, including the house, and she wants to be done with it."

"I thought she gave the house to Kristof in the divorce."

"She did, and that was renegotiated a couple months ago."

"He sold the house to her to cover his legal fees?"

"Got it in one."

"How could anyone own Cady's Point and want to sell it off for development?"

Joel shrugged. "Lorraine is a Cady on her mother's side. She inherited the Point. For her it is just something she owns."

"And you and she want to develop it how?"

Joel gave a heavy sigh. "Her idea is to make it a gated community, very exclusive homes, docks, an area for supervised swimming, boating lessons, and all that."

"And you endorse that?"

He laughed and stuffed his hands in his pockets. "I don't think it's a good business plan, given the tax rates on lakefront properties. She'd be building the homes on speculation, which is at odds with what people in that tax bracket want. She has terrific taste, but so do they."

Manda asked, "And she can afford to build several million-dollar homes on speculation, even though she's been advised they may not sell?"

"Yes, she can afford it."

"It's none of my business, I know."

"I'm making it your business."

"In that case," Manda asked him, "how would you develop Cady's Point, if it were up to you?"

Joel took a minute to answer. "If I owned Cady's Point, I'd level the house, leave the rest alone, and let people use the Point for recreation. If the community wanted facilities and transportation and supervision, I'd work with them to make it happen."

Manda reached for his hand. "It is that kind of place. It was very healing for me, in the beginning."

Joel turned to face her and put his hands on her shoulders. "So, what about you?" he challenged. "If you could develop it any way you wanted, what would you do with it?"

She smiled warmly, and Joel could see her savoring the idea. "I'd want some of it designated as public land, just as you said. I'd like to see the rest as a rehabilitation or retreat center of some kind, a place for people to heal and walk and play and swim." She laughed. "How's that for practical and realistic?"

"It sounds like heaven for the lucky people who go there."

"Maybe you should buy it from Lorraine and be done with— sorry, I'm overstepping my bounds here."

"Be done with my affiliation with her?"

"Affiliation?"

"We have a business affiliation," Joel told her, but even he could hear the waffling in his tone.

"That's not all, is it?"

Busted. "Well, between you and me, Lorraine has a not-so-hidden agenda to revive the relationship with me. She has her two children now, which I did not want to give her."

"And is that what you want to do? Revive the relationship?"

Joel was baffled by the question. "No, of course not. Lorraine just doesn't hear 'no.'"

Manda let her tears fall. "Is that really all this was about?" she said, her voice shaky.

Joel folded her in a warm hug and held her close. "Did you really think something was going on? Something other than business?"

Manda nodded against his shoulder.

"I am so sorry for not understanding that. Manda, I love you. No one else. I need you in my life. You make me laugh. You are my friend and my soul mate. You are the only one I listen to when I mess up. I know I get angry sometimes, and it scares you. I promise I will keep working on that. Working on all my stuff."

Joel cradled her face in his hands. "I cannot lose you from my life. Not to a car accident. Not to Texas. Not to another man. Not to my own stupidity."

"Joel, I need you to end your affiliation with Lorraine." Her eyes were hard.

Joel finally saw what Phil had seen immediately—that his guilt had blinded him to the impact of his actions on Manda. Letting Lorraine call the shots had poisoned his relationship with Manda. It was the source of Manda's pain and the wedge that had been driven between them.

"I've been a fool."

"You think?"

"I do."

"I need you to tell Lorraine you are done with any kind of relationship—business, personal, advisor, anything. I'm not sharing you with her, not even a phone call or an email. Are you done or not?"

"Done," he vowed.

Manda studied his face, searched every corner of his eyes, and was satisfied with what she saw there. Her mouth curved in a smile, and her eyes were soft with happiness.

Joel looked into her heart and saw the love burning there for him. "Manda, let's make this work. A day at a time."

Manda's face clouded suddenly with doubt. "Can we?"

"Tell me what you're worried about."

"That I love you and you're my best friend and I want you in my life as more than a friend. Much more than a friend. I know I'm past being a basket case, but, Joel, I know so little about loving partnerships or negotiating serious disagreements. I have so much to learn."

Joel grinned. "Me too. That's why we have Gwen and Phil and a host of professionals. And we love each other."

"We do. That part I'm sure about." Her laugh was pure joy.

Joel ruffled her hair and kissed her mouth, warmly at first. When his passion grew, Manda matched it.

Without warning the wind slammed them, and they saw that the path was growing dark. Arms tight around each other's waists, they headed back the way they came.

Chapter 8

Manda slipped and slid toward her gently used, five-year-old Volvo. "See you in January," her classmate Lynda called across the parking lot.

Manda gave a happy wave and called back, "Drive safe."

With the new car, Manda had not minded driving back and forth to St. Basil's in Rochester two weekends a month. Joel liked the Volvo safety record; Manda liked the killer sound system.

Tonight Joel would have a pot of chili waiting for her to celebrate the end of the first semester. She hoped they could catch up a little before she crashed. Sunday was their day together, without fail. Manda hadn't felt the sun on her face for a month. Maybe they'd get out for a walk if the weather improved.

She switched on her cell phone and saw four messages, all from Tony in the last two hours. What was that about? She fumbled with the car key, deposited her books and laptop on the passenger seat, and speed-dialed Tony.

"Where have you been?" he yelled.

"Class just ended. What's wrong?" She could hear him breathing hard. "Tony, for heaven sake what's wrong? Is something wrong with Joel?"

"I need you to come right now."

"Where are you?"

"Strong," he choked out. "Emergency Room. Get here, honey." He disconnected.

She looked around for help, someone who could give her directions. "Mitch!" she yelled across two rows of cars,

"Mitch, help me! How do I find Strong Emergency Room?"

"Hold on." Mitch slid his way to her, pushing buttons on his phone. "One map, coming up," he said lightly. He held out the phone for her to write down the information. "Told you, you need a smartphone, Manda."

"Don't rub it in!" she snapped back.

Mitch said calmly, "It's going to be all right. I'm making bad jokes to pretend I'm cool. I'm pretty freaked myself."

"Sorry. Something's happened to Joel and I need to get there. I can't even think."

"I see that. Let me lead. You follow right on my tail."

Manda caught a sob before it could get started.

"Let's go," he commanded. "Just stay on my tail. We'll be there in fifteen minutes, I promise."

They made it in twelve.

Mitch walked with her into the hospital, his hand on her back as they made their way through Saturday night chaos to the information desk.

"Joel Cushman?" Manda said to the attendant.

"Are you the fiancée?" Manda looked at her dumbly.

"Yes, she is," Mitch said behind her. Manda knew he knew she and Joel were not engaged.

The attendant looked to Manda for confirmation.

"Nod," Mitch prompted, and she nodded.

"Through those doors," the attendant told her. "Ask for Rachel. You can't go," she pointed at Mitch.

Manda turned to Mitch, trembling, and accepted his reassuring hug.

"You'll be all right. Breathe and pray. I know Rachel from Bill and Bob's." He waved to the woman with the long black hair peering at them through the double doors.

Manda laughed a little hysterically. "All this AA code. You'd think we were spies."

"We're family. Call me if you need anything; a place to stay, anything. Now get in there." He walked her to the double doors and gave her a little push when they swooshed open.

Rachel came toward her. "Manda? I'm in the program, too. That's why I stayed after my shift to help you."

"Thank you—" she couldn't finish the sentence.

"Come with me. It's very bad. We're going upstairs to surgery. I need you to know that Joel may not make it."

Manda refused to take it in. She stammered, "Please tell me what happened."

"I was going off duty when the call came in from LifeFlight. I didn't want you to be here alone. A lot of us in Rochester AA know Joel. We're organizing for others to come and be with you as long as you need us. Can you tell me your sponsor's name and phone number, too?"

Manda said Gwen's name and rattled off the phone number. She let out a breath of relief at completing one sentence.

"Whatever happens, you're going to be all right, Manda," Rachel told her. Manda wasn't so sure. She wanted to be home with Joel, eating chili and laughing and making plans. She couldn't lose him now. They had their whole lives in front of them. They hadn't even made love yet. The elevator doors closed on them. Manda grabbed for Rachel's hand in panic.

"Take a deep breath," Rachel ordered. "Good girl. And another."

Finally out of the elevator, they passed a waiting room teeming with people—some talking on their cell phones, some pacing, some weeping, some numb—and continued to a smaller conference room, which was mercifully quiet.

"Thank you for doing this." Manda took another deep breath and let it out calmly before asking, "What happened to Joel? What's wrong?"

"Joel and his friend Tony P. were driving back from someplace on the lake."

"Cady's Point. He's thinking of buying the land."

"Whatever, on the way back they hit black ice and went off the road into a stand of trees. Tony was hurt, and he's being treated downstairs right now. He'll be okay. Joel was severely injured. No side air bags. Head trauma and fractures down the right side of his body. Undetermined internal injuries. Tony called right away for LifeFlight and got him here, which gave him a chance. He's in surgery now."

"What are they doing?"

"The main thing is to treat the skull fracture, and—"

Manda collapsed in on herself. *God, no.*

"I know it's a terrible thing to hear. Joel's a young man, in good physical condition, and he may do all right. It's too early to tell. They're also going to set the fractures to his arm and leg if they can."

"You mean, if his body can stand up to it?"

"Yes, that's what I mean." Rachel put a warm hand over Manda's. "I need you to drink some hot tea and eat a little something. You have a long night ahead, and you need some nutrition. What can you keep down? Yogurt and toast, maybe?"

Manda had no interest in food, but she was dizzy and she knew she needed to take Rachel's advice. "Sure." She spotted bottles of water on a low table and asked, "May I?"

"Absolutely. The doctors won't be in to tell us anything for hours."

Manda finished the sentence, "unless it's bad news." She stood frozen in the middle of the room, clutching the bottle of water.

Rachel took the bottle from her hands, opened it for her. "Stretch out on the sofa while I make a cafeteria run for us."

As she left, Rachel turned off the glaring overhead lights. A small lamp on the low table kept Manda company. She took a few swallows of water and lay back against the pillows. *God, what's up with this? I don't want to lose him. But I don't want him to lose himself either.*

The small lamp seemed to flicker; Manda thought it was because her eyes were tearing up. *I don't know why I said that. I just know this could change him—his body, his mind. I need you to help Joel. To help his body.* She choked on a sob and let the tears flow.

She must have dozed. She floated awake when Rachel set dishes on the table.

"Tea is nice and hot. Yogurt with fresh fruit, and there's a buttered English muffin. See if you can get some of this down."

Manda came to the table, and Rachel squeezed her hand. Manda felt warmth and strength flow in past her defenses. "You're an angel," Manda told her.

They ate together and talked a while.

Rachel watched Manda's face carefully as she dropped the second bomb. "We need to reach Joel's next of kin, Justin Cushman. His office phone says the office is closed indefinitely."

Manda had no explanation for that.

"Do you know how to contact him?"

"I found his professional Facebook page last summer, and he gave me a couple ways to get through to him directly. One was the office. What do you want me to tell him?"

"That it's urgent. He needs to come right now."

Manda searched Rachel's face for more answers.

Her only answer was, "It will help Joel to have him here."

It was still dark when Manda woke to an insistent tapping. An older blond woman stood up from the chair Rachel had occupied. She flipped on the lights and gave Manda a reassuring smile as she opened the door to admit a scruffy physician in bloodstained scrubs.

Manda scrambled to her feet, swayed once, and leaned on the table for balance.

"Doctor, this is Joel's fiancée Manda. I'm Lucy one of the aides. How is Joel?"

"Alive. Holding his own. He did well enough that we were able to stabilize the fractures, though he'll need more surgery soon. His internal injuries do not appear to be life threatening."

He turned his attention to Manda and gave her a weary smile. "Joel may or may not be able to hear us, but it's important that you to talk to him. Briefly. Tell him what happened. Tell him any good news you can think of. I will see you again later this morning." He gave a curt nod and left as abruptly as he'd arrived.

"That's good news," Lucy told Manda's stricken face, "the best we can hope for right now. Finish your bottle of water and I'll take you to ICU."

"Where?"

"Intensive Care Unit, dear. They're monitoring Joel's condition constantly."

Manda couldn't take it in, but she could follow orders.

As they walked down an endless hallway, Lucy told her, "The arrangements are all made for you to shower and sleep and get a change of clothes and some decent nutrition today and tomorrow. Your sponsor Gwen will be here later this morning with some of your things."

"What time is it?"

"Three a.m."

Manda said over a sob, "God, I could never do this alone."

She felt Lucy's arm come around her. "Get that crying under control now," Lucy ordered and handed her a box of tissues from a nearby cart. "You need to be strong for Joel. Remember what the doctor told you to do?"

Manda nodded, took a steadying breath, and walked into a room filled with monitors, tubes, and IVs, all attached to the body of the man she loved.

"You can do this," someone whispered.

Joel lay broken on the bed, half of his face wrapped in bandages, the rest discolored and distorted with swelling.

"You know what to say," the whisper repeated.

Manda went to Joel's left side, perched on a chair, and touched the part of his hand that was not bruised or invaded by an IV line. "Hey, Joel, so much for our Sunday date. They said you and Tony had an accident, and you were on the side that hit the tree. Tony's doing okay. They're only letting me see you for a minute right now, and I want you to know I love you, and I'm in this with you. It's going to take hard work, and we'll do it together." Manda took a worried breath and let it out.

"I'm in touch with your Uncle Justin, and waiting to hear which flight he's on." She tried to calm her voice. She hated lying to Joel, but it was what he needed to hear.

Someone touched her shoulder.

"That's my cue." She leaned closer and said softly, "They think I'm your fiancée. Don't blow my cover, okay?"

Lucy swept her out of the room and down the hall. "You did great. You said exactly the right things." She held Manda close and let her sob her heart out.

"What are all those tubes?" Manda choked.

"They're making sure he's hydrated and nourished. The line into his arm has the drugs he needs. And did you see? Joel's breathing on his own, which is a really great sign that his body is handling the stress."

"And the wires?" Manda's voice was much calmer this time. "I want to know so I won't freak the next time."

Lucy rubbed her back and told her, "They're monitoring the activity in every part of his heart, and they're watching some brain waves."

"And that little clip on his finger?"

"That measures his pulse and the level of oxygen in his blood."

"What I said to Joel in there. I was really stretching the truth, but I believe it, too."

"You need to believe everything you told him and work to make it come true. Don't waste any energy worrying or doubting. Just believe in Joel's recovery and do your part."

That became Manda's mantra for the next week, "Just believe. Just do it."

Joel's condition was more or less stable from one day to the next, but not stable enough to do the follow-up surgeries for his lower leg. Manda gave up trying to understand the drugs they were infusing into his blood stream. She knew it was critical that he not get an infection, so she imagined an army of miniature bug fighters pouring into his veins along with potent pain killers.

She moved to the rhythm created by her visits with Joel, seeing Joel for a few minutes, spending a couple of hours with Gwen or another woman from AA, walking and showering and getting a meal, seeing Joel again, and resting or exercising until the next visit. Without help from Gwen and the other women she was sure she wouldn't be eating or exercising or taking care of her appearance.

"Gwen," she told her sponsor at the end of the first week, "Joel's still completely unresponsive when I see him, and Justin has not been in contact at all. I keep saying the same things over and over to Joel. I keep trying to contact Justin. Am I crazy?"

"That's all you can do right now, chickie, so just keep doing it. If Joel's able to hear you at all or even sense your presence, he's getting hope and love from you. Try wearing that perfume I brought, the one he always comments on. And right now, eat," Gwen ordered.

Manda went back to her salad.

"I'm plugging in your cell phone and your laptop while we talk; looks like they're running low."

Manda laughed. "I know the feeling. Thanks."

"Did you just laugh?" Gwen teased. "See how much it helps to get a good meal and talk to a friend?"

"Why is he still unconscious?"

"Did the doctor say he shouldn't be?"

Manda shook her head. "But I think he's concerned. He used the word 'coma' this morning, and I freaked. He said it's not unusual, that people with head injuries can take a long time to return to full consciousness."

"Have they been able to assess the damage?"

"As far as they can tell, they don't think the head injury caused major damage to the brain. But there's only so much they can test while he's unconscious."

"Are you worried?" Gwen pressed.

"Maybe I'm just impatient."

"I get that," Gwen teased. She added, keeping her voice light, "Maybe Joel wants to be in a coma for a while."

"What do you mean?"

"I'm just thinking from my experience as a psychologist, sometimes it serves people to be distant for a while, to withdraw."

"Like to heal from some trauma?"

"Yes, or sometimes to avoid some major problem in their lives. There are other reasons, too, I'm sure."

Manda pushed the salad away, stood up, and did some stretching, using the back her chair for balance. "I keep thinking of the other accident, when he lost his family. Maybe he's afraid that's where he is now, and he doesn't want to face what he faced after that accident."

"Maybe. He needs to know that was then and this is now. You can help him."

"How?"

"Give him the news. Tell him about Tony's recovery and the new truck he's buying. Bright red. With side air bags. Tell him your grades. Tell him about the decorations at the Manse and how many people are spending time there over the holidays. Anything he'd like to hear."

"Get him interested in what's he's missing?"

"Exactly. You can do that."

"Only if you bring me up to date," Manda said with a laugh. "I'm not exactly getting out to see what's happening in the world."

"Good, that gives me an assignment. I'll get the Friday night group on it, too. Who's having a baby? Who's getting engaged over the holidays? What's Santa bringing everyone for Christmas? People can really get into it, instead of sitting around worrying. I'll have them record some things, too. A stroke of genius, Manda."

"Except you thought of it," Manda pointed out. "Please have some of them email me, too. I need the contact with them."

Gwen cheered, "You and I are a good team. I'll bring the recording with me next Saturday. In the meantime, you keep the faith and call me every day."

During week two, without her lifeline Gwen by her side early each morning, Manda realized she needed a daily AA meeting. She found two, a noontime meeting in the hospital's alcohol and drug rehabilitation wing, and an after-work meeting in a large conference room next to the cafeteria. Depending on how her visits to Joel fell, she could make one or both meetings. The daily contact with "her people," as Gwen called the AA fellowship, gave Manda's spirits the boost she needed each day. And meetings got her out of her head.

She needed all the courage she could muster on Tuesday when Joel had a bad day. He was fretful but still unconscious. "What's going on?" she pumped the doctor after her visit with Joel. "Is this a bad sign?"

"We can speculate, but I've seen patients do this when they're at the point of rejoining us and not entirely happy about it. I wouldn't take it as a bad sign, but he may need more incentive to be present. Any word from the missing uncle?"

"No. I have to believe he's on his way, but I'm really annoyed he hasn't communicated. I keep checking his Twitter feed, but it's been silent for almost three weeks. There are no changes on his corporate Facebook page. I think he's been in Africa, but none of the places he posted show up in searches on Google or anyplace else I've tried."

From the bafflement on the doctor's face, she realized he had no idea what she was talking about.

She summarized, "I'm doing the best I can."

"And you have a lot of support. Your need to connect Joel with everyone who cares about him. I need you to keep doing a good job with that."

Manda sighed and nodded her agreement. At least the doctor thought she was doing a good job.

That night Joel was quiet again, his breathing steady and his heart rate rock solid. "Listen, Joel, the doctors know you can make it, and I know you've never been afraid of hard work.

"I will be so angry with you if you leave the planet without us having a seriously hot night of stormy sex. That night I slept on your sofa during the storm, I had the greatest dreams about us together. I want that for real. I know how good we'll be together, and I want that for us.

"I want a life with you. I want to dream and plan with you and spend our days and nights together.

"And I'm not just saying that because these people all think I'm your fiancée. I mean it. I know it will be a lot of hard work for you getting well, but you can do it, and I'm in it with you. We all are. Phil and Gwen and Tony and the Early Risers. We'll make sure you have what you need. I promise."

"Time, dear," the nurse told her with a gentle hand on Manda's shoulder.

"I was really hoping he'd hear me."

"I know you're upset, dear. He'll rest now, and you should, too. You both need your strength."

Manda gave Joel a gentle kiss and whispered, "Sleep well. I love you."

Both Manda and the nurse missed the flutter of Joel's index finger just as they turned to leave.

The next day she told Joel about two newcomers who came to their first few AA meetings that week. "Remember the emotional roller coaster ride? I do. And these guys are really hungry for a solution. That's where I was last March when you outed me in the shower. Remember?"

On Thursday she realized she would be nine months sober the following day. She wished she could celebrate the milestone with one of her groups and most importantly with Joel. When she visited Joel's room just after midnight, she took his left hand more firmly than usual in both of hers and told him how happy she was to be sober for nine months. "Two hundred seventy-five consecutive days. I did the math."

She thought she saw a corner of his mouth curve. "Joel?" she gasped.

She felt a little pressure—his right index finger pressing up against her hand.

"Hey, you're back." She put her lips carefully against the corner of his mouth where he had tried to smile. "I love you," she whispered, but she sensed he had already slipped back. His heart rate had increased a little and then settled back into its slow, steady beat.

She looked out at the nurse on duty and signaled for her to come in.

"I saw a change in his vitals for about a minute," the nurse confirmed. "This is the first real sign of consciousness, and it's encouraging. We'll see how he is through the night. If he's ready tomorrow, the doctors will want to test his brain function and mobility."

"That sounds stressful."

"It will be, for you as well as for him. You may want to give yourself the day off. If I were you, I'd get my hair done, buy a holiday outfit, and maybe throw in a massage and a facial."

Manda's smile brightened the room.

"I know just the place for all of that. I'll get on it first thing in the morning."

She turned back to Joel and saw one eyelid flutter.

"Hi again," she said and took his hand gently in hers. "You're going to make it, Joel. We're all in this with you."

She asked the nurse, "Can I stay longer?"

"Another few minutes won't hurt. We just won't tell anyone."

Manda watched Joel's face for a while, but there was no further movement. Exhausted, she lay her head near his hand and slept. Sometime during the night, he worked his fingers into her curls.

At the Manse, Remy embraced her and rushed her into the spa. "We have everything set up for you, *ma petite*. The rose body wrap, the pedicure, the manicure, the facial, the haircut. Everyone is so glad you are here today. We know that means Joel now will be well soon. This is true?"

Manda had a little trouble following his English, but she smiled and kissed his cheek. "This is true, Remy, my good friend. Joel is improving. Is there anything I need to tell him?"

"That we carry on and wish him a quick return. You are too thin, *ma petite*. I bring you breakfast?"

"Croissant with—"

"Jam and butter and coffee, *mais oui*. It will be waiting for you." He snapped his fingers. "Gianessa, Manda is ready for the body wrap."

Manda shook the hand of a graceful, serene young woman and followed her into a fragrant room. Within minutes of starting the treatment, Manda was sound asleep and woke only when the ninety-minute treatment ended with a spritz of rosewater over her face and shoulders.

"Forgive me for waking you." Gianessa's melodic voice coaxed her to sit up and drink a small bottle of mineral water. "How do you feel?"

"Amazing. Are you a healer?"

Gianessa smiled enigmatically. "Some tell me I am."

"I know someone who needs your healing hands. Soon, very soon. Did you just start at the spa?"

"Last month, just for the holiday season to help with the increase in business."

"I know we'll talk again," Manda promised.

Gianessa gave her another enigmatic smile and drifted out of the treatment room.

Remy was waiting to usher Manda to her pedicure. She found her croissant and coffee waiting as well. Two hours later —exfoliated, moisturized, buffed, painted, and hairstyled— Manda paid a short visit to Dan's office. "Anything I can do for you, boss?" she asked.

Dan wrapped her in a hug. "Does this mean Joel's improving?"

"Yes, it does." Manda beamed. *I hope. I believe.*

Dan quizzed her for half an hour about the systems she'd been working on. She answered his questions and talked with him about the work he needed her to do as soon as she could.

"I can log in once a day from now on," Manda promised him. She knew having familiar work to do would give her stability going forward.

"Let Joel's money make it easier for you," Dan advised. "At a minimum get a decent hotel room with a secure network connection if you plan to do any work."

"I can't believe I didn't think of that. Dan, is there anything I need to bring to Joel's urgent attention?"

Dan shook his head. "We're all set with the end-of-calendar-year activities and holiday bonuses. Joel is always ahead of the game with things that affect the staff. Across the organization, winter is the time we do our inventory and adjustments to the strategic plan. If he's gone longer than March I would be concerned, but we can float along pretty well for a few months."

"You're really on top of things."

"Our function crosses every department, so I need to have pretty deep insight into operations and exceptions."

Manda quipped, "I understood what you said. "I thought I'd lost my brain back there in the surgical ICU. Seriously, thank you keeping an eye on things and for all the good mentoring you do for me. What am I missing today?"

"Check your voicemail while you're here. Your phone's been ringing every hour on the hour since late yesterday afternoon. Either it's an automated telemarketer or someone's trying very hard to reach you."

Manda was already punching in her access code, desperately hoping it was Justin calling her work number.

It was. He had been delayed by storms, he said, and unable to connect to any communications for several weeks. He gave her hourly updates on his progress. The final message told her, "I'm departing Cairo momentarily, leaving from Stockholm this evening, arriving Chicago at midnight. Don't ask. Flight to Rochester arrives six fifteen Saturday morning your time. Unless you pick me up at the airport, I will come directly to the hospital and will need to speak with Joel's team as soon as possible." Click.

Manda turned to her boss and said quietly, "Dan, can you listen to this last message with me? I don't know him, so I'm not sure how to react." She replayed it on speaker with the volume too low for others in the office to hear.

Dan listened and offered his opinion. "I know Justin. He's normally a hearty soul. He sounds ill, not just sick of plane travel."

"By 'Joel's team,' he must mean the team of doctors on Joel's case, right?"

"I'm sure it is." Dan gave a wry chuckle. "Good luck assembling them on a Saturday morning."

"I will do my best." She laughed, "I have one whole hour before my personal shopper expects me at La Bella."

Dan smiled and teased, "You didn't know what you were getting into with Joel, did you?"

"I had no clue."

"You sorry?"

"No. It will be a rough road for a while, though."

Dan handed her a slip of paper and pointed to a four-digit code. "Make your phone calls in privacy from your cubicle." It must be the long-distance code for her phone. He winked. "The rest of us have a mandatory one-hour meeting right now that I'm about to call."

"I like the jingle bells!" Manda told Anita, closing the door firmly enough to set them jingling one more time.

Anita held out her hand in a warm La Bella welcome. "How is Joel doing?" Anita had not seen Manda since her graduation day, but now she greeted her like a valued customer. Manda knew it might have something to do with large gift certificate Joel had set up for her for Christmas.

"He's much better. Thanks for making time for me this morning. I want to look my best for Joel right now and bring some holiday cheer into the hospital with me."

"You are thinner, you know, and I don't think you mean to stay that way. We'll need to be smart about sizes and styles." Manda took that as a caution that she didn't look good a size smaller and that she looked pretty bad on the whole. And this was after a spa facial and haircut.

"I am in your hands, Anita."

"Let's start by finding the right colors to brighten your face."

After La Bella, Manda spent quiet time at Lakeside Terrace. She started in her beloved studio apartment, pulling together casual clothes and supplies for herself for the next two weeks.

One of Justin's messages told her he had reserved a suite for the two of them at an elegant small hotel in center city Rochester. Manda was glad to take him up on the offer. Sharing a suite would be a challenge, but it promised her a comfortable bed and secure WI-FI. Besides, Justin wanted to get to know her, and she needed him as an ally during Joel's recovery.

Up in Joel's apartment she went first to the porch where they'd shared a mushroom omelet months ago, the day of their first fight. So much had changed since then. Increasingly Joel asked her opinion about business at the Manse. She knew he was troubled about the college, but he was keeping that to himself. Maybe that was the reason he wanted to stay in Limbo land for so long after the accident. It must be a huge mess. Maybe Justin could help him with that.

The porch was bare on this winter afternoon—no table, no chairs, no tubs of flowers. Manda had felt about thirteen years old the day she and Joel first talked out here. She would turn twenty-three in a few weeks, and today she felt like a twenty-three-year-old woman with a purpose and a foundation. She thought about her bold statement to Joel that day, that he needed love in his life and someone to share the day. Now she was that someone. *Please, God, give us days to share. And nights.*

The wind from the frigid lake forced her back inside. She double-checked the locks on the French doors and wandered into Joel's bedroom. With a longing look at the bed, she wondered when they would be able to share it, how long until Joel was well enough to make love. She couldn't think about it now; thinking made her frightened of how damaged his body was. She didn't want to worry about the tests they were doing today and how he was holding up.

She wished she could be in Tompkins Falls long enough today to see everyone at the Friday night AA meeting. Instead, she was having a snack at Phil's house with Gwen in half an hour. Then she needed to get back to Rochester, to Joel.

A stack of books on Joel's bedside table caught her eye. A meditation book, a book of Celtic spirituality, and a thriller. She picked them up and went looking for a small suitcase to hold them. She added his terry cloth robe, some socks, and his laptop. She appropriated the body lotion and soap from the guest bathroom. On her way through the living room, the framed photo of Joel's sister, Christie, caught her eye; she tucked it in with the robe. *God, I need you to do this with me. You know how scared I am. I need to believe in Joel's recovery, and I need to do it with him.* With one backward glance at the cold, gray lake, she locked up.

Manda knocked at Phil's front door and before she could say hello, Gwen and Phil enveloped her in hugs. They bombarded her with questions she couldn't answer, except to say, "He was conscious enough this morning for them to do lots more testing, and they advised me to take a break. I confess I indulged in a little retail and spa therapy. And Justin is coming in on a plane from Chicago at dawn."

Phil growled, "It's about time. Where has he been?"

"Someplace in Africa, I think, but his itinerary was through Stockholm. He said not to ask."

Phil shook his head just as Gwen called to them from the kitchen.

Manda smelled succulent roast beef. She raced Phil to the kitchen door and saw a feast laid out on the scarred wooden table. There lay a platter with the roast flanked by bowls of steaming potatoes, fresh cooked green beans, mashed butternut squash, and a jug of apple cider.

"Some 'snack,' eh?" Phil chuckled.

Manda stood with tears in her eyes until Phil pulled out a chair and ordered her to sit down. "You need this. Eat."

"I need this." Manda blotted the tears from her cheeks. "I need you guys. Phil, I've missed you so much."

"So, eat, chickie," Gwen commanded. "Not another word.

The dishes were piled high in Phil's big old sink ready for washing when Manda heard a car door slam in the driveway. She looked out the window and spied a shiny new red truck.

"It's Tony!" she yelled and made a dash for the door.

"Wear a coat," Phil barked.

Manda heard him but didn't care about a coat. She'd been longing to see Tony, to make sure he was okay, and to thank him for everything.

Tony stepped out of the truck, but at the sight of Manda flying at him he shrank behind the door of the cab. "Don't hurt me. I know you hate me. Please don't hurt me, honey."

Manda skidded to a stop. "What? Hate you? Are you crazy?"

They faced each other in disbelief. Tony broke the spell with a grin. "You don't?"

"No way. I'm so glad to see you. You look like, what's with the beard?"

"It's a great beard. But you look like a ghost, honey. I know thin is in, but Joel's not going to like this."

Manda teared up at the teasing.

"Hey, I'm just getting back at you for the 'beard' thing. Joel's going to be thrilled to see you, however you look."

Manda's tears spilled over.

"Aw, honey, I'm making it worse. Come here." He reached out for her with one hand and slammed the door shut with the other. Manda jumped at the noise, and Tony drew her into a tight hug. "It's all going to be okay, honey. Relax."

"You're really okay, Tony?"

"I'm really okay. And I have a great new truck. Want the grand tour?"

"Come inside, you two," Phil barked from the kitchen doorway.

"She wants a tour," Tony yelled back.

"She wants pie, you fool."

"Pie? Why didn't you say so? Come on, let's go get it." Tony kept his arm around Manda's shoulders as they picked their way over clods of ice and snow and pounded up the stairs.

"It's seriously good apple pie. Gwen made it, I think."

Tony's eyebrows met over the bridge of his nose. "More like Wegmans, honey. But I'll take your word it's good."

Phil ushered them into the steamy warmth of the kitchen and wrapped Manda in an afghan. He scolded Tony, "And you thought she wouldn't have anything to do with you. I told you accidents happen, and it's all in what you do about it."

Manda nodded, her teeth chattering.

"You sit close to the oven," he ordered Manda. "And eat another piece of pie."

"I need ice cream," Tony told Gwen.

With an indulgent smile, she deposited a smoking-cold scoop of vanilla ice cream on Tony's steaming slice of apple pie.

"You made this?" Tony asked skeptically.

Gwen shook the ice cream scoop at him. "The pie, yes, the ice cream, no. Eat before you insult anyone else."

"Yes, ma'am." Tony dug in.

Manda picked out the apples and nibbled at them. "I am so full. I don't know why I'm eating this. Is there more coffee?"

Gwen poured a fresh mug for each of them. "Decaf. You're buzzed enough to stay awake."

"You're driving back tonight?" Tony sounded worried.

Manda nodded. "And staying at a hotel Justin reserved for us."

Tony gave a loud, long whistle. "Bet it's fancy."

"If it has a good bed and a decent shower, it will feel like heaven to me."

"Manda, seriously, why don't you stay with me tonight?" Gwen urged for the third time that evening.

"I need to be back with Joel. And speaking of, Tony are you the one that fixed it so I could see him all the time he was in ICU?"

"What do you mean?"

"Somebody told them I'm Joel's fiancée. Otherwise I wouldn't have been allowed to see him."

"Wasn't me, honey. Maybe your Higher Power is trying to tell you something." He winked. "I'll bet somebody had a ring all set for you under the Christmas tree."

Manda gave him a soft smile and blew him a kiss. "Bet we're waiting until I get my year."

"You've already got—no, you don't, do you? When did I twelve-step you in the old white truck?"

"Nine months and one day ago."

"Very cool. Congrats. So how's Joel doing? Phil says he's conscious."

"They're doing a whole bunch of testing today, and I should find out tomorrow how he really is. Justin will be with me."

Tony fussed with the last bite of crust, moving it back and forth his plate. "Wish it had never happened, honey."

"I know. I do, too. But you saved his life, Tony, and—we hope—his brain." Manda shuddered. "I can't think about that right now. Hey, how are you? You were pretty banged up, too."

"Ribs mostly. They're still a little sore. Shoulder needs some more physical therapy. I'm glad you didn't launch an attack on me out there." He grinned. "You came flying at me, and I ducked for cover."

"Are you hammering and nailing again?"

Tony flexed his fingers. "Good as new. Got work for me? I'm out until January."

"Joel will need a ramp for a wheelchair for a while."

"Up to the third floor?"

"Good point."

Phil told them, "Maybe you can let Justin deal with all that, Manda, now that he's finally deigned to make an appearance."

They were laughing their way through the dishes when Manda thought to ask Gwen, "Were you able to get anyone to record a greeting or some good news?"

Gwen pointed to two DVDs beside Manda's tote.

"Joel will love these."

Phil ruffled her hair. "Getting dark, Manda. Time you hit the road, if you're going to." He held her coat, and she shrugged into it.

"Love you, guys. Keep those prayers coming tomorrow."

"Always," Phil promised.

Manda buttoned her coat, gathered her take-along bags for the hotel mini-fridge, and turned for one last hug from each of them.

"We're with you all the way, kiddo," Phil said in his gravely voice. "If I could drive, I'd have been camped out with you at the hospital."

"The food's way better here." Manda kissed his cheek. "Joel knows you're with him in spirit."

Gwen added her parting thought, "Tell Justin that Gwen sends her regards. And don't let him con you."

Manda thought about that all the way to Rochester.

Manda studied Justin as he directed a burly porter to stack four jumbo suitcases on a cart. Taller than Joel, his brown hair going gray, Justin had the same confident stance, the same handsome profile, the same decisive gestures, and the same air of entitlement. Dan had called him one of the Good Old Boys. It fit.

Dan was right, too; he must be sick. In a sad counterpoint to the privileged demeanor and mountain of jumbo luggage, Justin's custom-tailored suit hung on him.

The bags secured, Justin looked around him, and Manda waved wildly to catch his attention.

His eyes brightened and his voice boomed in the early morning quiet. "You're the spitting image of her, do you know that, lass?"

Manda laughed. *Where did the Irish brogue come from?* "And who might 'she' be, Justin?" She couldn't believe she'd just met him, and here they were laughing together.

Justin lunged for her and gave her a bear hug he didn't seem capable of. "Bridey Tompkins, of course. Joel's grandmother. We all adored her."

Manda stammered, "Wasn't that the grandmother named O'Donohue?"

"Indeed. Bridey O'Donohue married Roland Tompkins. Their daughter Mairead Tompkins married my brother Joshua Cushman. Joshua and Mairead had two children Christina and Joel. There's your genealogy lesson for Saturday morning. And as you know, all of them except Joel died in a crash many years ago. Joel has bad car karma, especially in winter. Do you know your mouth is open?"

"So Joel is Joel Tompkins Cushman. As in Tompkins Falls and Tompkins College?"

Justin rolled his eyes. "He tried to tell me you didn't care about the money, but I didn't believe him until this moment." He sized her up. "We're a couple of scarecrows, aren't we? What's next, Miss Amanda?"

"Just Manda. My sister is just Lyssa. Our parents were teachers, and they expected us to earn our A's."

"And I understand from Joel you did earn your A's." He signaled for the porter to follow them. "Show us the way, Just Manda."

Fifteen minutes later Manda eased the Volvo to a stop under the portico for their boutique hotel. A doorman sprang to their service, and a bellhop followed on his heels.

"Welcome back, Miss," the doorman greeted her. He gave a smart heel click to Justin. "Welcome, sir."

Justin set about dispensing tips, something they had not enjoyed from Manda.

A valet materialized, accepted Manda's car key and gave her a half bow, just as the bellhop hauled the last bag from the trunk.

"Did you bring all your worldly possessions?" Manda joked.

"Everything packable."

"Fortunately I saved the larger bedroom for you. I moved into the suite last night."

"Good girl. You've saved me from a decision. I can't make a single decision before noon."

"Better rethink that. Joel's doctors are meeting with us at nine o'clock."

Justin regarded her seriously. "Well done, Manda. How shall I reward them for talking with us on a Saturday?"

"You mean, like, build them a cancer research center?"

"Something along those lines. What do they have for a rehab for my nephew?"

"The only thing I know for sure is there is a masseuse with healing hands right there at Joel's spa at the Manse. She's magic. I want her on Joel's team."

"So we'll make him a suite there, put in a heated indoor saltwater pool, and—"

"Justin?"

He stopped and looked at her.

"Did you sleep last night?"

"Yes."

"Shower this morning?"

"Yes."

"Eat breakfast?"

"No."

"Then you're as hungry as I am." Manda directed their steps to the cozy breakfast room.

"Do you intend to take care of me?"

"I am taking care of me," she clarified. "Yesterday six people told me I was too thin. I feel like I haven't had a good night's sleep in a year. And I'm trying not to obsess about Joel's injuries or about what they'll say to us at nine o'clock about his recovery. So thank you for the suite. It's quiet and comfortable, and it has the best shower this side of the Manse. I'm just taking care of me, Justin, and you're welcome to come along for the ride. But please don't fight me about anything or I'll cry. You don't want to be there when I cry. Just ask Joel."

Justin let out a comical sigh. "And I was just starting to think you'd make a good secretary."

Manda's laughter bubbled up. "You are so different from Joel."

"How so?"

"You're a solo drama production."

"Why thank you."

"I look like your Grandmother O'Donohue?"

"Not mine. Joel's. My honorary Aunt Bridey Tompkins. She was a redhead, not a brunette, but she had your curls and your sparkling blue eyes. You'd have thought she ate sapphires on her breakfast cereal."

"Why didn't Joel tell me he's a Tompkins?"

Justin sobered unexpectedly. "Ask him sometime. Except for Bridey, I think he'd rather not be part of the Tompkins family."

Manda had to ask, "So, do you know what's happening at the college?"

Justin was quiet. Judging by the cold, hateful look that passed over his face, he knew. She let him stay quiet all the way through their omelets.

Manda was the first to speak. "Thank you, all of you, for meeting with us this morning. Justin Cushman is Joel's uncle and his only living relative. He arrived this morning from Africa." She tried not to roll her eyes. She totally didn't buy that story.

Justin requested, "In laymen's terms, doctors, what are we dealing with?"

The four physicians exchanged looks. The one Manda knew as "Joel's doctor," took the lead. "Medically, Joel is in for additional surgery on the leg over the next month. Then he'll need intensive rehab, rest, and quiet for about six months. He is fortunate that the pelvis was not fractured, although it is contused and will be painful for a few months. The ribs are bruised, not broken, and his lungs are clear. Internal organs have some bruising but will heal with rest."

Justin praised, "I so appreciate your concise response, in words we can understand."

The lead physician nodded and turned to his left.

Information from the next doctor in line was positive. "His brain function looks excellent, and we can expect full cognitive recovery."

Justin and Manda let out their breath simultaneously.

"Some motor skills have been impacted in ways you would expect," he continued, "nothing severe. We feel confident those will fully recover in concert with his physical therapy."

Justin commented, "As you can imagine, that's been a major concern." He reached for Manda's hand and gave it a squeeze.

The third physician, a woman, added, "One area for particular concern. We're watching his right eye, which is not moving or tracking as it should." Before Justin could respond, she told him, "In cases like this, there's a good chance it will self-correct. We're encouraging him to do some simple exercises, and he's taken up the challenge." She gave a graceful fist pump that garnered a hearty laugh from Justin.

Manda waited a beat before asking, "Does Joel have sight in the eye, doctor?"

The ophthalmologist nodded, and Justin gave Manda's hand another squeeze.

"What would you do if the tracking didn't correct itself?" Manda wanted to know.

"It's likely we could correct it surgically, but we wouldn't attempt that for a few months while the brain and skull are healing."

Manda winced.

Justin changed the subject. "And the right arm and hand?"

The fourth physician in line answered, "The hand is badly contused, but miraculously there are no fractures. The upper arm took the impact. The humerus is well set and should not require any further surgery. Both the arm and the hand need time to heal before physical therapy. To reiterate my colleague's point, he will need at least one surgery on the leg soon. However, assuming his recovery progresses as we expect, we can release him to a physical therapy facility later in January. That gives you time to find the best center for you and for him."

The silence that followed told Manda they had no recommendations. Maybe it was time to build one at Cady's Point, even though that would not help Joel now.

Justin tested the silence. "Are we to assume you have no rehab here that would meet my nephew's needs?"

The same physician answered, "Certainly, there are fine facilities in and around Rochester, but he's likely to do better closer to friends and family. A qualified physical therapist dedicated to his case would communicate with us, and we'd also suggest a warm-water therapy pool accompanied by aquatic therapy for the first few months of his recovery."

"That gives us good, clear direction, doesn't it?" Justin praised with a look to Manda for agreement.

Manda nodded and smiled. But she wasn't finished with her questions. "Doctor," she addressed her remarks to the doctor who had taken the lead, "you qualified all of this by saying 'Medically'. Why was that?"

She saw Justin sit back wearily. She realized he was more stressed than she was. She gave him a confident smile, and he rallied.

The doctor was saying, "It was obvious Joel was mentally stressed throughout our conversations yesterday, even when we gave him the good news about his condition. He acknowledged that a professional situation is weighing heavily on his mind, but he would not share the details. We wonder how much you know?"

The doctor was looking directly at Manda; panic paralyzed her. She was supposed to be Joel's fiancée; she was supposed to know these things. "The college," she stammered and could not continue.

Justin took her hand in both of his. "I can tell you in confidence that Joel's been dealing with very serious problems at the college that bears his family name. As chair of the board of trustees and the major donor, he feels personally responsible for fixing it, and he has come to the conclusion it cannot be fixed. On the one hand, resigning his position and withdrawing financial support from the college would certainly cause it to fail, putting many good people out of work.

"On the other hand, purging the thieves and pretenders and rebuilding with new personnel would be a monumental undertaking and would almost certainly bring the scandal to the attention of the public. Which, in turn, would destroy the college's reputation with donors and potential students. I have given him my blessing to resign and withdraw his support, but my nephew is a warm-hearted soul, committed to the economic health of his community. He is agonizing." Justin folded his hands.

Manda was stunned. She stared at Justin in disbelief. She'd never guessed the extent of the problems. How could Joel be dealing with all of that and not ask for her support? What kind of life partner was she? She heard someone clear a throat.

"Perhaps he needs to delegate this particular business decision to you, Mr. Cushman," the lead doctor said sternly. "We are in agreement that the degree of stress Joel demonstrated yesterday is a serious complication. His recovery will be both delayed and compromised if he continues to carry this burden. In short, Joel cannot afford it, medically or mentally."

Justin asserted, "I will insist on taking responsibility for that decision and all it entails, doctors."

"I support that, Justin," Manda added.

All of them stood as if on cue. Justin, Manda, and Joel's team shook hands all around. Manda repeated their names with each handshake, then put their business cards in order and tucked them in a pocket in her tote.

Justin made overtures about a donation, and the second doctor, the neurologist, suggested they talk again in the near future.

Justin asked them, "Can I visit with Joel today?"

The neurologist assured him, "Joel will be immensely relieved you're here. I recommend you spend a quiet ten minutes reassuring him you're taking responsibility for his affairs while he focuses on his recovery."

Manda did a slow burn. How clever of Justin to throw around his money and take over as Joel's only visitor.

The lead physician added, "One visitor at a time may be enough for today." He smiled at Manda. "Nevertheless, he will want to see his fiancée, I have no doubt. I'm sure he's grown accustomed to hearing your voice several times a day without fail, every day since the accident. Perhaps a short afternoon visit."

Manda wanted to kiss him; she settled for giving him a radiant smile.

However, Justin's head had swung toward Manda, and he nailed her with a look. "Fiancée?" he mouthed.

"You've been away a long time," Manda said sweetly and paused for emphasis. She knew her statement gave every appearance of being a gracious acquiescence that Justin's visit to Joel ahead of her was exactly the right thing. "Joel will be relieved you're here."

As they rode down the elevator—just the two of them—Justin asked sharply, "Since when are you and Joel engaged?"

"That was a myth perpetrated by Joel's AA friends at the hospital, since it was the only way I would be allowed to see him. He had no one," she snapped.

Justin hesitated. When he spoke, it was to say, "We were a good team back there, you and I."

Manda thought it sounded as much like a warning as a concession.

Chapter 9

They had gotten through the meeting with the four physicians okay, but Manda had an uneasy feeling Justin did not regard her as his ally. Maybe she was being paranoid. They were both stressed. She suggested they decompress at a coffee shop she and Gwen had found that had a first-rate barista, salads, and desserts.

Justin sipped something called a *doppio con panna* while Manda stirred honey into her green tea. She saw Justin eyeing her hand; her spoon rasped against her stoneware mug. "Sorry." She set down her spoon.

Justin pondered, "How can we get Joel to release his hold on the college?" He was hunched over the table, as though the burden pressing on his shoulders was too much.

Manda thought it was another dramatic ploy. She corrected him, "It's the college that has the stranglehold. Joel is the one in agony."

Justin countered, "You must admit, Manda, it is an agony of his own making." He stole a look at her and raised an eyebrow at what he saw.

Manda felt her face flame with anger. *How dare he say that about Joel?*

"I didn't expect that would get a rise out of you."

She smiled sweetly. "You're completely right, Justin. If Joel had no heart and no conscience he'd walk away and let the college self-destruct."

She saw something menacing flash behind his eyes. She figured she had the same look in her eyes just before she smiled and slammed him.

"Let's start again, shall we?"

Manda said calmly, "The way I see it Joel will turn the college over to you, but only if your strategy includes ousting the bad guys and watching out for the economic needs of the good guys."

Justin's eyes were slits. "I underestimated your interest in the college."

"I don't know much, honestly. I'm just thinking that's what Joel would be most interested in." Manda felt him watching her. She looked around the coffee shop thinking of all the coffee and salads and bagels she'd consumed here with Gwen since Joel's accident. *I need to talk things over with her. What did she mean about Justin conning me? Can I trust anything about him?*

"I want to visit the Manse," Justin was saying, "after I see Joel."

"Are you going to run it while Joel's out of commission?" Manda's tone was sharper than she intended. Out of the corner of her eye, she saw Justin's head jerk as though he'd been slapped.

"Nonsense. I'm on the hunt for an area we can turn into an apartment and therapy suite for a few months."

Manda backed off. She took a deep breath and said a silent prayer. *Help me find a way to work with this guy.* "Harold will help you with that," she offered. "Buildings and grounds. There's a roster of names and emergency contact numbers at the main desk."

"Very helpful," Justin conceded. "Any other advice?"

"Tony Pinelli is a good carpenter, and he's available over the college break. I'll give you his phone number. Tony is Joel's good friend; he was driving the truck when they had the accident."

"Has he recovered?"

"That's what I heard yesterday. I think it would help him to be part of Joel's recovery this way."

Justin blinked in surprise.

"What?"

"You're snapping my head off one minute and making compassionate recommendations the next."

Manda looked down at her tea. "Sorry. I'm so tired and so stressed. And confused. I want to be able to trust you, but…"

Justin reached a hand toward her, then pulled it back. "Manda, I want us to work as a team for Joel."

She nodded her understanding. She felt him watching her again, heard him take a noisy sip. She wished he would let it alone.

"I know you're upset with me, and I need to know what it's about."

Manda leveled him with a look. "I don't believe the whole Africa fabrication. Why did it take you two weeks to show up?"

Justin drew in a breath and sat up to his full height. He held the breath and then blew it out as if he had reached a decision. "I've been ill. I was undergoing diagnostic tests and receiving treatment, and there was no way anyone could reach me."

Tell me about no one being able to reach you. Manda was glad she only thought the words. The pain on Justin's face looked genuine, partly physical pain and also emotional pain. It dawned on her that Justin regretted he hadn't been available for Joel when he desperately needed him. She also sensed that right now Justin needed Joel pretty desperately, too.

"I'm sorry," she choked.

Justin grabbed both her hands and hung on tight. "You were here for him, Manda, and I'm profoundly grateful. I mean to make up for it. I mean to be here for him now. And for you."

Tears flooded Manda's face. She pulled one hand away and reached for a brown paper napkin from the holder on the table.

"You'll need more than one of those, lass." Justin made his way to the creamer bar for a fistful of napkins and a glass of water.

Manda worked her way through eleven napkins. When the flood was under control, she gave him a self-conscious laugh. "I warned you." She watched her hand shake as she brought the glass of water to her mouth.

"Careful there. Yes, you warned me. And I fought you anyway. My apologies."

"I probably I needed that. I've hardly cried since the accident."

"You were overdue."

"He is going to be all right, isn't he?"

Justin nodded. "With you at his side, he'll come through this."

"He needs you, too. Not just to get the college off his shoulders."

Justin tapped his glass mug with a nervous rhythm. "What's your advice about the college?"

"I have none, other than what I've said already. Joel and I haven't talked about the college. I don't know why? Maybe he was protecting me. I acted like such a dunce about what happened to me. He was probably never going to bring it up again. I feel so bad that he was carrying it alone."

Justin winked at her. "He does that sometimes. It's a serious character flaw, you know." He went for another glass of water, dipped a napkin in it and tipped her chin up. "You have a little mascara on your nose."

Manda figured she had mascara everywhere except her eye lashes.

Justin set about dabbing off the mascara. He told her, "He's shared some with me—the nature of the problems, the extent of them, and a few words about who can be trusted. I'll clean it up, one way or another."

"But that means you'd have to stay a while."

Justin pursed his mouth, and his eyes twinkled. "Would that be such a bad thing?"

"For you, I would think?"

Justin was shaking his head.

"You'd stay here? In Tompkins Falls, I mean?"

"I need to be here. Live here again, be part of this place. Not just while Joel's recovering. I can't explain it any better than that."

"Justin, are you—?"

"I'm not dying, if that's what you mean." He gave a chuckle and set down the damp napkin. "Good as new."

Manda pulled out a compact and scrunched her nose. "Clean anyway. Thank you. You'd be a good dad, you know."

He waved it away with a dramatic flourish, but she could see he was touched.

"So what's in it for you, returning to Tompkins Falls?"

"We'll find out. I know I'm ill, though the doctors don't know with what, and I will continue that investigation the best I can from here. But more important, at the moment, anything I can for Joel I will do."

"Thank you."

His features softened, and his eyes sparkled. "You'll be a beautiful wife for him."

Manda felt her face flame.

"Now you look like a blushing bride. Joel will like that look."

"But first, he'll wake up to you. He needs you."

Justin checked his watch and took one last sip of his espresso. "I'll call you later. We'll have dinner tonight, shall we?"

Manda nodded needlessly, as he was already out the door.

She listened until his rental BMW surged away from the curb. She met the barista's eyes and signaled that she'd like another tea. Then she speed-dialed Gwen.

"Hey, chickie, I'm halfway to Rochester and realized we never set a meeting place."

"Our favorite coffee shop?"

"Sure. You okay?"

"Yes. So is Joel. We have a lot to talk about."

"You're stressed. Walk around the block and then order me a market salad. See you in twenty minutes."

"Nice celebration," Gwen decided, buttering the last slice of Italian bread. "I don't need that chocolate cake that's calling to me from the pastry case."

"But I might." Manda eyed the two tiers of tortes and cheesecakes. "They have Joel's favorite Turtle Cheesecake."

"You go right ahead, chickie. I'm glad your appetite is back."

"Now that you know everything about Joel and about me, I need to talk about Justin. I don't think I get him."

Gwen put her fork and knife in the middle of the salad bowl and pushed the bowl away from her. "Has he tested you six ways to Sunday?"

"Tested me?"

Gwen nodded. "He's not going to let just anyone marry his nephew."

"What do you mean?"

"Look, Joel is his only living relative, and he loves him beyond all reason. He's been Joel's surrogate father for most of his life. Even Lorraine was not good enough in Justin's eyes. So, Justin is going to make very sure you're compatible with Joel, make sure you're in love with him and marrying him for the right reasons."

"Which I am."

"Which you are. The other thing is, you'll be heir to Joel's fortune if anything happens to Joel, and you'll carry the Cushman name, so he has some interest in that."

Manda thought about it. With a rueful smile, she told Gwen, "I should have realized."

"So, chickie, have you passed so far?"

Manda shrugged. "I guess."

"And do you think you two can be allies for Joel's recovery?"

"I think it will be a challenge, and we'll just keep working it out. For Joel. We had a scene right here, right before I called you."

Gwen thumped her hand over her heart. "I saved you?"

"By the time I called you, he had already left in his too-cool Beemer."

"When did he have time to buy a car?"

"He had the concierge at our hotel arrange a rental."

"The man has too much money."

"The man is ill. Seriously, from the look of it."

Gwen sat back heavily. Manda watched a succession of emotions pass over her face.

"Do you have a thing for Justin?"

Gwen's eyes opened wide. "*Moi?*"

When Manda continued her eagle-eyed stare, Gwen shrugged.

"I suppose every teenage girl in Tompkins Falls flirted with the idea of growing up to be Mrs. Joel Cushman or Mrs. Justin Cushman."

"And isn't Joel more your age?" Manda teased.

"Justin's fascinating, that's all. He has a genius for manipulating people and making them smile the whole time. As a psychologist, that has always fascinated me about him, even before I became a psychologist."

"That's what you meant about not letting him con me?"

"Did I say that?"

"Your very words. It kept me awake the whole drive last night."

"Yes, I suppose that's what I meant."

"He's going to stay in Tompkins Falls, you know."

Gwen snorted. "Lord help us." But she was smiling.

Manda told her, "I think it will be good for Joel to have him here. And for Justin to be here with us mere mortals," she added with a grin.

Gwen reached her right arm over the back of her chair. "You don't like Justin?"

"Like him? I don't know, but sometimes it feels like we're old buddies. He says I remind him of Joel's grandmother."

Gwen grinned. "The one that read tea leaves?"

Manda nodded. "Did she ever read yours?"

Gwen thought back, frowning in concentration. "I think mine said, 'you will see deep into the heart and soul.' And I grew up to be a psychologist."

"She was good."

"What was Joel's?"

"Joel's tea leaves said, 'You will kiss many women before you find the one.' Pretty cool, huh?"

"Wonder what yours would have been?"

"Wonder what Justin's was? I can't imagine him giving up his life's work and moving back here."

Gwen shrugged. "It's not like Justin to be idle. He must be planning something."

"Well, first he's going to take over for Joel at the college."

"Why would he need to?"

Manda slapped her hand over her mouth and mumbled, "Can't tell you."

Gwen narrowed her eyes. "Sure you can. We'll play 'Pay the lawyer a dollar and then everything you say is protected by confidentiality.'"

"You're not a lawyer."

"That's just the name of the game, silly. I'll pretend to be the lawyer." Gwen winked.

Manda sat a moment longer, sizing up Gwen, thinking about how desperately she wanted to confide in her. Finally she pulled her hand away from her mouth, rummaged in her purse, and slapped a dollar on the table. "Let's walk. I don't want to talk here."

On their frigid walk over the Genesee River bridge and back, Manda disclosed everything she knew about the unfolding drama at Tompkins College, liberally mixed with speculation from both of them.

"Suppose Justin decides to resurrect the college in his own image?" Manda wondered. "Do you think Joel would have a fit?"

"Probably not. Probably Joel will just be glad to be done with it. If people still have jobs, he'll be fine with it. If the whole thing implodes, it won't be on Joel's head anyway."

Manda blew out a forceful breath. "You're good!" she told her sponsor.

"That's why you pay me the big bucks." Gwen joked. "And I want you to work very hard to forge an alliance with Justin. If he's going to be around a while, you can learn a lot from him."

"I'm not sure he's the kind of businessperson I want to be. Throwing his money around and dashing off to places that aren't even on the Internet? Oh, except he wasn't."

Gwen gestured her impatience. "Manda, I repeat, you can learn a tremendous amount from him. And you can make his money work for you. Think about it. If you spend a few of his millions and lose it all, it makes no difference to him, and you learn some valuable lessons."

Manda squawked. "Lose a few million and not care?"

"Really, think about it, Manda. You repeated to me a conversation you had with Joel about Cady's Point, right? I remember you said you had a great idea with no funding. Instead of being terminally annoyed with this guy—and even though he probably looks to you like an egomaniac wheeler-dealer—you can put him to work for you. How's that for a challenge?" Gwen pushed open the door of the coffee shop.

Manda's laugh filled the shop as she and Gwen burst back in after their walk. The barista set down his homework.

"Ready for that Turtle Cheesecake?" the barista asked Manda.

"Make it two," Gwen told him.

Hours later, Manda slipped through the door to Joel's hospital room and let it close softly behind her. Joel was asleep, his face peaceful. She noticed the visitor chair had been moved around the bed to Joel's right side. She wondered if Justin had done that and why.

When she took her seat she nudged the chair a few inches closer, and it scraped the linoleum. Joel's eyes fluttered open.

Manda smiled and touched his hand. "I didn't mean to wake you."

Joel's smile was lopsided, hampered by a bandage covering his cheek. "You're beautiful," he rasped.

"I love you so much." Manda leaned forward to touch his face and his lips with tender fingers. "Would it hurt if I kissed you?"

Joel laughed. "Are you kidding?"

Manda carefully planted one hand on either side of his body and leaned down for a soft kiss. Joel cupped her breast with his left hand and she sighed happily.

"Justin is crazy about you," Joel told her. "He wants us to be married tomorrow."

She chuckled. "You're kidding, right?"

"Only a little. He said he thought he was seeing Bridey when he met you at the airport. All you had to do was smile and you captured his heart forever."

Manda sat back in the chair and exhaled in disbelief. "That's pretty cool. I'm really glad." She gave Joel a bright, happy smile. "He's full of surprises."

"He is that. He said you were here multiple times a day, day after day. I knew you were here, but I didn't know how long I was out." His voice trailed off for a moment and his eyelids drooped. "You brought me back, love of my life."

"You're falling asleep again, aren't you?" Manda watched his eyes close. She kissed her index finger and touched it to his lips.

"I promise," Joel added, struggling to open his eyes again. "I am going to get well for us. No matter what it takes."

"Of course you are, Joel. We're doing this together. Close your eyes now. It's time to rest."

Manda closed her eyes, too, and said a prayer of thanks. She listened as his breathing deepened and the beeping of the heart monitor slowed. At last, she stood up. She swayed slightly and reached for the back of the chair to steady herself. *I need to rest, too.*

Manda was putting the finishing touches on her makeup when she heard Justin return to the suite. She had dressed carefully in a new outfit, the one Anita thought brightened her face. She listened to Justin moving around the suite. The shower started, and a few minutes later his wardrobe doors squeaked open and banged shut. He was humming, or maybe that was a poorly tuned radio station.

When he was quiet again, Manda called cheerfully, "I'm almost ready, Justin. Thanks for making the reservation for us." She put a smile on her face and came out to their shared living room. "You're looking dapper," she told him. In truth his face was drawn, and his hand-tailored Italian suit hung on him.

He rubbed his hands together. "So, where shall we begin?"

"Please, with dinner," Manda implored.

Justin gave a hearty laugh.

She could do this, she told herself and took a calming breath. Who was she kidding? She had passed out in her car when she returned to the hotel and come to with her head resting on the steering wheel. She'd taken a long nap and felt fine in the shower. Maybe she was just hungry. A hot meal was what she needed.

"I understand," Justin told her, his hand on her elbow as he led the way to the grill, "they have the best steaks in Rochester."

"Sounds perfect," she agreed. She had no energy, so she decided just to listen for a while. She had a lot to learn about Justin.

Over their dinner of onion soup, sizzling steaks, steaming baked potatoes, baked squash, and crisp salads, Justin told her about the places he'd lived and the places he'd done business. He'd been based in Switzerland and London and had traveled the world, evaluating and financing new ventures, making a fortune. He said he was done with it. "I've closed my office, and I'm slowly divesting myself of my responsibilities. I won't say why. It's unimportant."

Manda instinctively reached out her hand and covered his. Justin sandwiched her hand in both of his. "This is where I need to be—back with Joel, sharing his life, making a life for myself in Tompkins Falls, looking out at Chestnut Lake every morning and evening."

Manda beamed. "I can identify with that."

"Are you going to finish that?" he asked, pointing to her half-finished potato.

Manda shook her head, watched him lift it onto his plate and sat back to listen to more tales of his travels. She didn't hear any separation anxiety. He seemed to be saying goodbye to that life.

She was surprised when he told her he'd been teaching throughout his career, for his alma mater University of

Chicago, at their London campus and online. His voice was excited when he talked about his students and about conducting a class online with students from around the world. "That's what it is, you know—conducting. When you're never in the same room, the professor is a conductor making all the students perform at their peak in concert with the others. Tell me about your studies."

She told him about her program of study at St. Basil's. He seemed genuinely interested in her commitment to not-for-profits.

Before long, the waiter was back, whisking away their plates. Manda asked, "So how was Joel when you visited this morning?"

"Our visit went pretty well. In true Joel fashion, he has insisted they withdraw the morphine as quickly as possible. I can see he has pain. Of course he has pain. But he is determined to manage it. I told him not to be foolish about it."

"How much did you talk with him about the college?" Manda asked. Justin's response was delayed while their waiter delivered dessert and coffee.

Manda took a forkful of her triple chocolate torte, moaned as the silky bittersweet chocolate coated her tongue, and closed her eyes to savor the experience.

"One of life's pleasures, eh?" Justin asked and raised his coffee in salute.

"It certainly is. Did you propose taking over the college problem so he could focus on recovery?"

"I did. He is relieved. There was no argument."

"Tell me what you're thinking, Justin. Do you plan to get rid of the thieves and pretenders—as you so aptly call them—and then what? Look carefully at the employment picture for the faithful and capable?"

"You are on solid ground with that."

"And if you decide to close the college," Manda began and made a sudden decision to speak from her heart "I want to know if you intend to do the right thing for people who are within one year of retirement and those on disability."

"Of course. Assuming they're not among the thieves and pretenders, they would have a separation agreement to carry them to retirement. Those on disability would be counseled and their cases handled professionally so as to continue benefits as needed. Would you agree?"

"Yes."

"And what would you recommend, Manda, for the good guys who don't want to finish out the year?"

Manda took a deep breath, gathered her thoughts and answered, "Well, the people who want to take other jobs before the end of the academic year would be free to do so, and have reasonable time off for interviewing. Also, knowing that other colleges may be leery of hiring Tompkins employees—not knowing who's a good guy and who's a bad guy—you and the board might want to provide letters of reference on a case-by-case basis in response to employees who request a letter and who provide a current resume and tell you their job-search strategies. Does that make sense?"

Justin was turning his coffee cup around and around. "You have a head for this. Of course, I may want to see how things go once the thieves and pretenders are gone. Suppose the college is viable in some form after the purge? Wouldn't that be the best possible solution?"

"Do you really think that's possible?"

"It remains to be seen. In that case, will you want to continue to advise me?" Justin's eyebrows were raised as far as they would go.

She took another forkful of her torte. "Actually, no. I think Joel and I should just let you take over the whole college mess and handle it however you see fit."

Justin stifled a laugh and watched Manda lick thick chocolate off the fork. "You mean to say I could not expect any advising from you or Joel?"

"I'm afraid not." She winked. "Nor any arguing or interference."

"Do I hear correctly that you're in favor of turning over the whole college disaster for me to handle as I see fit?" he restated.

"I actually think that's asking a great deal of you, Justin. What would you want from Joel and me in return, once he's well enough to reciprocate?"

Justin drummed his fingers on the table and looked into the far corner of the room for a few moments. "Interesting question. What little project do I have that Joel could do better than I could do?" Justin kept a straight face, but Manda could see his eyes sparkling with mischief.

"Let's say I take over the college. Clean it up and close it down, or whatever I choose to do with it. Perhaps you and Joel should take responsibility for his charitable fund. It's been parked with me too long, and it would benefit from his attention."

Bingo. "Interesting possibility. You know, I always wondered why you agreed to handle it for him."

Justin sighed dramatically. "I set it up according to his wishes when he was still a teenager, with the expectation he would take it over in due course. But Joel, as you know, warmhearted as he is, has immersed himself in his community and has become too deeply involved in the moral issues of his college to have time for the foundation. If I free him of the college, by rights he should pick up the responsibility and do it his way."

Manda's smile was brighter than morning sunshine on the lake.

"Bridey smiled just like that, you know, lass. And you don't fool me for a minute."

"Justin, I love you. I believe that trade—college for charitable fund—will make Joel smile even brighter than I'm smiling right now. That's where his heart is, Justin."

"And yours, Manda? Where is your heart?"

"With Joel, of course."

"Goes without saying, doesn't it? And what of your own business interest?"

"I'd like to build a rehabilitation center on Cady's Point. At first for wealthy clientele, to get it off the ground." She was amazed how easily the words came and how right they sounded.

"What kind of rehab? Drug and alcohol, I presume?"

"No. Heart and chronic illness and physical rehabilitation—people who are ready and willing to change their work habits and their thinking, start eating for health, and find exercise they want to do and will commit to for a lifetime."

"Sounds like something I need myself. Say more."

"Justin, Cady's Point has healing energy. Whether you believe it or not, the Indians knew it, and I've experienced it myself. And I'm sure you know there are medical schools and alternative-medicine institutes all over the Finger Lakes. The Chiropractic College, the School of Massage, two doctoral programs in physical therapy, the whole concept of Clifton Springs, naturopathic physicians, energy workers, herbalists."

In her excitement, Manda pressed Justin's hand. "Some of those professionals are open to working with the other professions. I'm talking a holistic rehab facility. And with any facility like that, there are management and accounting and clerical and hospitality positions that need competent people. Builders and electricians and grounds persons. Jobs, Justin. And plenty of capable people in this area to fill them.

"And plenty of baby boomers in the northeast with heart problems and lupus and arthritis and joint replacements and sports injuries and money to get the best treatment they can find. And some of them are smart enough to know it's not a quick fix. They need to change. They're willing to take the time and find the quiet and the expertise to facilitate that change. I want to create that place and make it a success. That's my business interest."

"How much will you need?" he asked her.

"I need you to help me figure that out and to make it happen. You're the venture capitalist, and I need your mentoring to make this fly."

"You've got the passion and the vision. I've got the money and the entrepreneurial expertise. Is that the ticket?"

She studied his face, saw past the signs of his illness, saw a spark of interest lighting his eyes and a genuine smile softening the hard lines of his mouth. She pushed past her own fear, held up her hand to him and said, "That's the ticket."

"Sold." He gave her a high five and a big grin. "By the way," he asked her, "it is your intention to marry my nephew, is it not?"

"Of course it is."

"I can't understand why he hasn't asked you yet."

"That's easy. We've both been trying to follow our AA sponsors' suggestion to wait until I have a year of sobriety. I just celebrated nine months."

Justin chuckled. "Joel and his rules. I predict there will be an engagement soon and a wedding long before you finish graduate school."

Manda felt herself blush. "Well, give me a little warning so I can get a smashing dress. I want to be a bride and a wife Joel will be proud of."

"Let's split another chocolate torte. I don't want to look like a scarecrow in my tux, or you in your lovely dress."

When Manda pushed open the door of Joel's room the next day, Joel appeared to be sleeping. He was starting to look like himself again. The swelling in his face was down.

She wanted to kiss away the worry lines that had reappeared. She came quietly to the bed and touched his left hand.

Joel smiled without opening his eyes. "Love of my life," he said, his voice raspy.

She laughed. "You're awake, but those worry lines are back. Are you toughing it out without pain meds?"

"Trying. I wanted to be lucid when you came today."

Manda took his hand in hers, and he opened his eyes. "You're wearing my body lotion."

"I know you like it when I do that."

He looked at her with the relief of a man in the desert who had seen the oasis.

"How are you dealing with all of this?"

"Meditating a lot. Using all the tricks I learned my first year of sobriety."

"I really thought I'd lost you. Tell me how I can help you get well."

"This is how. I need you at my side. I wouldn't have come out of the coma if you hadn't been here."

Manda had to clear her throat. She rallied a smile and asked him, "So, where were you before you came out of the coma?"

"Hanging with my sister."

"You went toward the light?" Manda guessed.

Joel nodded.

She kissed his hand. "Did you really see Christie? How is she?"

"Misses me. Asked me if I could stay."

Manda's heart hammered in her chest. "Were you tempted?"

"For about a minute. To be away from decisions I didn't want to make."

Manda gave his hand a squeeze. "I heard you talked with Justin and will turn the college mess over to him. I'm so relieved, Joel."

He nodded. "I have to. I can't fix it. He knows how to clean things up and close things down. We need to let him do it his way, Manda. I need you to help me stay out of it." His breathing got more and more anxious as he talked.

"I will," she said decisively. "It's out of our hands, and Justin will handle it. Just rest, Joel." She pressed his hand against her cheek.

Joel smiled as his palm caressed her soft cheek. He closed his eyes for a minute.

She soothed, "We have many good things ahead. Your recovery is the most important thing, and I won't let anything compromise that."

The worry lines began to fade from his forehead. Joel's serenity seemed to enfold her. She sat very still, watching him rest. She closed her eyes and enjoyed the silence, broken only by the beeping of the heart monitor.

In a few minutes he opened his eyes. "It's not the same as the grandfather clock, is it?" Joel joked.

"The beeping?" She laughed. "So, what else did you and Christie talk about?" Manda asked him.

"She likes you."

"She knows about me?"

Joel nodded.

Manda looked around. "Good, they brought her picture over when they moved you." The framed photograph was on a stand just to Joel's right. Manda wondered if they'd placed it there as incentive for him to exercise the weak right eye. "Does she look the same as you remember? The same as in the photograph?"

Joel moved his head a little, and she could see the eye seeking and connecting with the photo.

"She's more beautiful now. There are no scars, no burns. Her hair is like sunshine, and her eyes are like the sparkles on the lake in the early morning. Her laugh," he broke off, as if hearing it again. "Her laugh is musical."

Manda guessed, "So, you aren't worrying about her anymore?"

"She never blamed me," Joel said. He shifted on the bed, grimaced at the pain, and found a comfortable position. His full attention was on Manda now, and his voice was stronger. "She was watching me all the time I was drinking and using. She saw me get sober and graduate and start the business at The Manse, and all of that. She's very proud."

Manda smiled into his eyes. "She'll see you recover from this, too. That's very cool."

Joel nodded. He was looking intently into her eyes now. "What?"

"I know we wanted to be married next year, after your program is done."

Manda felt a wave of panic. "And you've changed your mind?" She heard her voice rise in anguish.

Joel tried to calm her down. "Just about when."

Manda finally realized what Justin had meant last night; he was probably giving her a heads-up that Joel might want to move up the timeline. But her understanding came too late, and her panic was stressing Joel. His heart monitor set off an alarm in the hallway.

God, I'm making him worse. You've got to help.

A nurse pounded into the room. "Out!" she ordered Manda.

Manda stumbled to the door and turned to see the nurse injecting something into the IV line hooked to Joel's left arm. *What have I done?* Manda stood with her hand over her mouth, looking at Joel with wide eyes. His eyes closed, and the alarm stopped, as Joel's heart rate returned to normal and leveled off a little slower than she was used to.

She sobbed into her hand and turned to walk down the hall. One of the aides came to her side; it was Rachel from her first night in emergency.

"What happened?"

"I got really stressed, and it made him really stressed."

"It happens. Now you know you have to use the same strategy you used before. Keep it light, even if he doesn't."

"How stupid could I be? I thought it would all be okay now. I totally blew it in there."

"He's got a long way to go, Manda. You both need to take it one day at a time."

"I think I'm going to pass out."

"They don't think I have a bug or anything, but they can't take a chance with Joel stressing out or getting sick," she told Gwen. "I've passed out a couple times now, and they want me to take a few days to rest and eat and stuff."

"I know, chickie. And Joel wants to see Phil and Tony. They're going to drive up to the hospital tomorrow. Justin will be back the next day."

"Back from where?."

"Justin's in New York City for a couple of days," Gwen said slowly.

"He is? How do you know that?"

"I know it because he asked me to keep an eye on you. He wants you to come to the lake with me for a couple of days, which I think is brilliant."

Manda started to protest and then realized, "It is brilliant. You're both right. I can go to my regular meetings and stop being a lunatic."

"And you do know—from what Justin told you and from what he told me—that Joel was really just trying to move up the wedding date, not call it off. Right?"

"Yeah, I do. I was so stupid. But I want to talk about the date with you."

"At the lake. We can talk about everything. Wedding plans, your next semester, anything you like."

"I can't even think about school."

"Calm down. See how much you need a break? So, am I driving us, or can I trust you to follow me to my house without passing out?"

Sydney Shorey shifted her breasts closer to Justin, sucked the olive off its toothpick and winked. "Were you looking for a stroll down memory lane, a roll in the hay while my husband's away or something a little more professional?"

Justin let out a belly laugh and took in the curvy, classy woman across the table. "Syd, we had our moments, didn't we? I remember it with great pleasure. How's the marriage working out for you?"

"Good this time around. We divorced and remarried, you know."

"I did not."

"He had a mid-life crisis around forty, and I sued the pants off him. Then I made a push into the highest level of college administration. When I was named president, I knew I needed a proper escort, and Danny was back and ready to commit. So we're making it work this time."

"With an occasional fling, do I hear?"

"Actually, no, but I wanted to know if you're still interested."

"I'll always be interested in you, Syd, but I make it a policy not to sleep with married women. I'm glad it's working out for you and Danny."

"You've never married?"

Justin winked. "There's only ever been one Sydney."

"Poppycock. What are you up to, Justin? What's brought you back to American soil?"

"I am coming to the aid of my nephew, who—"

"Joey?"

"Joel. His ancestors—not the Cushman side—started a college a century or so ago, founded on ego and dedicated to personal glory. It recently took a nosedive of the smelliest kind. Joel was on the verge of resigning his post as trustee and withdrawing his backing when he was seriously hurt in an accident. He will recover." Justin stopped to clear his throat and swallow some water.

Sydney reached for his free hand. "That's why you're back."

"Part of it. The rest is my health, but let's leave that aside for now."

"Here comes our salmon," Sydney announced. They sat back while the waiter delivered sizzling salmon, mounds of Au Gratin potatoes, and asparagus in Hollandaise.

"Cheers," Sydney toasted with the last sip of martini. "I've never understood how anyone could toast without alcohol."

Justin raised his water glass. "All it takes is a glass with some liquid in it." He moved his appreciative gaze from her body to the table setting. "Beautiful table. Good choice."

"So you're taking over Joel's responsibility at this college of his. Are you going to close it down?"

"If that's the right course of action, I will heartlessly put half the town out of work. Naturally, I want to know if there are viable alternatives."

"Let me eat for a minute, and I'll have some suggestions."

After a few mouthfuls and moans of approval, Sydney asked, "How serious and how widespread is the corruption, do you know yet?"

"Joel says about a third of the personnel. Faculty, administrators, and staff have been implicated. Is it absurd to try to make a college work with two-thirds of the employees?"

Sydney shrugged. "Some colleges purposely downsize that much for economic reasons. Or at least that's the public explanation for major cuts like this one at Joel's college. The first move is generally to abolish tenure. That allows the college to bid farewell to faculty who are no longer serving the students or the college's best interests, in favor of those faculty who have stayed at the cutting edge or are not jaded or corrupted."

Justin thought about it, while Sydney dug her fork into the asparagus.

"Succulent. I wonder where they find asparagus this time of year."

"South America, I suppose."

"One-third of the employees, really?"

Justin nodded. "Syd, this is not my field. If I were looking at the viability of a business or a bank or a utility, I'd know where to start, what data to pull out, what to measure. Help me out here. What are the dimensions I need to pay attention to?"

"That's the right question." She nibbled at a slice of potato.

"I want whatever you don't eat," Justin told her.

Sydney teased, "You're telling me not to take a nibble from every piece, is that it?"

She shoveled half the potatoes onto Justin's butter plate.

"What a woman."

Sydney rearranged her curves to show her pleasure, and then she got down to business. "For my money, there are six or eight dimensions, as you call them. First is curriculum. Does the college have, or potentially have, current, marketable, relevant programs?"

"Such as?"

"Global economics, rather than ancient history. Professional programs integrated with liberal arts, critical thinking, and a range of internship or study-abroad experiences."

"I get the idea."

"And talented faculty for those programs. Collaborative faculty, not armed camps or backbiters."

Justin nodded his understanding. "What else?"

"Infrastructure. How well maintained are the buildings? Is the technology cutting edge and supported? Do the administrative systems streamline the flow of student records and accreditation data and other reporting functions?"

"I don't suppose it matters that the campus is green, manicured, and picturesque?"

"That could be a bonus, and it could be the deciding factor between shifting to mostly online delivery versus catering to undergraduate student development."

"Interesting."

"You'll want to find out about the students. If the ones you've been attracting are not bright and motivated, you have a problem. It may be a failure to market properly, an outdated curriculum, a lousy reputation. Do you see what I'm getting at?"

"Yes, very helpful." Justin enjoyed the last bite of his fish.

"And the remaining two-thirds of the administration and staff. Are they competent? Committed to the students and to the fiscal health of the college? Do they work together? Are they organized efficiently? Some things can be fixed."

Justin set down his fork. "So it's not all about income and funding?"

"That's important, but as I've said there are many factors." She silently counted them on her fingers. "I forgot the library. It's got to be a hub for student research and collaboration with faculty, multimedia production, heavily connected with other college libraries for resource sharing. A library makeover goes a long way toward revitalizing a college, if the college is worth salvaging."

"If I can summarize, I hear you saying the trustees should study all those dimensions and make a decision: reinvent the college or fold it. To reinvent it, we'd need to abolish tenure, slash and re-imagine the curriculum—all the programs and how they're positioned. Overhaul recruiting and retention, re-purpose facilities and staff, resurrect the library, and overhaul systems, probably bring in a chief information officer. What are the odds that any of the high-level administrators will survive?"

"My guess is there are one or two gems. You'd want to identify them quickly and protect them. Make them key players."

"I may want to circle back for recommendations for consultants."

"Happy to help. Buy me dessert, and let's talk about you."

"Why talk about me?" Justin signaled for the waiter.

"I'm worried about you."

"Nonsense."

"Not nonsense." Sydney ordered two decaf coffees and a trio of sorbet with two spoons. "You're not happy. You should be married, happy, and passionate about your work. You look like you're dying."

Justin sat back and drilled her with a look. "I may look like I'm dying, but I believe I'm being reborn."

At her stunned look, he gave her a big smile and reached for her hands.

She grinned. "You always knew how to shake me up."

"Why didn't we marry, Syd?"

Sydney cocked her head and thought a moment. "You wanted wealth. I wanted a life partner, a couple of kids, and work I felt good about. We had different agendas. On different continents. You went off to study in London and never came back."

Justin had a sudden memory of the phone call telling him his parents' flight had gone down in the Atlantic. "No, I never came back. I just ran. I'm finally done running, Syd."

Sydney kept hold of his right hand while the waiter set down their dessert and coffee. When they were alone again, she looked at him across the table. "You know, in the old days we'd get close like this." She shook her head, remembering. "And then you'd get this fear in your eyes."

"But we were good together, weren't we? Or was I the only one that thought so?"

Sydney gave a throaty laugh. "You speak my truth. But you were scared about intimacy—the deep sharing two people are capable of when they know each other's secrets and care deeply about each other's happiness."

"And that scared me? I wonder why."

Sydney shrugged. "I guess I always figured it came along with wealthy families, distant parents, no one to model for you what true intimacy was and how it worked."

"That tallies, yes." Justin's smile was a warm caress. "I always loved you, Syd. Let me know if Danny boy steps out of line."

"You've got a deal. But I'm betting you'll find someone else now. And I insist you invite me to the wedding."

"What do you suppose Justin is doing in New York?"

"He could be meeting with some woman, interviewing consultants to save the college, or just seeing a few Broadway plays. If we need to know, we'll know. That's enough stalling."

"Okay, the problem is I don't know how to talk with Joel about the wedding."

"There's a problem?"

"Duh!"

"Now wait. I'm hearing that you want to marry Joel and you want to be by his side through his recovery and for the rest of your lives. Where exactly is the problem in that?"

"The problem is I want a wedding, and he wants to be married in his hospital room so we're not 'living in sin' when he comes home. I know I'm being selfish. But it really matters to me. When I found out Lyssa and I would be getting our inheritance and it would pay for my second year at school and more, the first thing I thought about was a wedding dress. Me, the girl with no fashion sense. I want a really beautiful wedding gown, and I want to walk down the aisle and stand up with Joel in front of everyone we love and say our vows and celebrate with them."

"And you can't do that why?"

"Because Joel will want to be married before we live together, which means we'd be married in his hospital room." Manda dissolved in tears.

"Chickie, it's time you got those tears out." Gwen went to Manda's side with a box of tissues, pulled out half a dozen and handed them to her. "Weep and blow, sweetie. Then we'll make sense."

Manda let the tears flow. Halfway through the flood she choked out, "I guess I'm just feeling sorry for myself."

"Keep the tears coming. There's more than selfishness and self-pity going on here."

Gwen sat quietly while Manda cried herself out. She watched patiently as Manda blew her nose. When she saw the misery on Manda's face change to calm and then to happiness, she knew her sponsee was coming back into balance with herself.

"You've been through an exhausting, frightening time these few weeks, sweetie. You nearly lost the man you love; you've found yourself forging an alliance with his larger-than-life uncle; you've been sleep-deprived and undernourished; you've been away from your meetings and your people. Don't beat yourself up for feeling a tiny bit disappointed about a radical change in wedding plans."

Manda drew in a deep, cleansing breath. "Okay. You're right."

"Of course," Gwen quipped.

Manda managed a weak smile. "And I'm so thankful for that. I need your help to do the right thing here. I love Joel, and I don't want to mess things up by being a twelve-year-old. I've done that once."

"Do you really think Joel is so rigid that he won't consider living together for a few months while you plan the wedding you really want?"

Manda nodded. "He doesn't want me to be the target of gossip again—or him either—by doing anything people will disapprove of."

"Are you so sure of that? I mean is that really what Joel's thinking? Or is it you thinking that's what Joel's thinking? Or is it you thinking, and you want it to be somebody else's thinking?"

"Well, he hasn't actually said anything like that."

Gwen rubbed her back and told her, "I think you're being overly sensitive about public opinion, Manda, and I can see from your experience why you would be. But I don't think Joel's worried about judgments other people are making about you or about him or about the two of you."

"You don't?"

"I don't. Joel felt awful that he couldn't protect you any better than he did, but all of that is in the past. Are you opposed to living with him during his recovery, without benefit of marriage?"

"Not at all."

"It doesn't feel like you're shacking up or being taken advantage of?"

"Of course not. Does it to you?"

"No. If people need to gossip, that's their problem. Don't let that stop you from doing what you know in your heart is best for you and Joel. Joel works very hard at being true to himself. You need to do that, too."

Manda nodded, gathered all the soggy tissues, and dumped them in the cute little wicker wastebasket on Gwen's four-season porch. She looked out at the lake—slate green under a weak winter sun.

Gwen let her be still for a minute before asking, "Manda, from your heart, what is best for you and Joel right now?"

"I believe the right thing is for us to be married. We're soul mates, and we're good partners. I can help him with his life's work, and he can help me with mine. Even if he doesn't want children, we have so much in our lives, so much to offer each other and others. I don't just mean Joel's money, you know that."

"I know, sweetie. Here's a wild thought. Suppose Joel, all of a sudden, says he wants to have a couple of kids?"

Manda's smile lit the porch, seconds before the sun broke through the clouds to warm the room. "I'd be thrilled."

"And it's okay with you if he doesn't?"

"It's okay with me if he doesn't."

The sun did not waver. Nor did Manda's smile.

"You sound very clear about both those possibilities."

Manda nodded.

"How about telling Joel all of this?"

"Do you think it's okay for Joel and me to be talking about serious stuff while he's still so fragile?"

"You've thought it all the way through, so, yes, I do."

Manda looked out at the lake again. "Justin really wants what's best for Joel, doesn't he?"

"Yes. And he's convinced you and Joel belong together. And just between you and me, Justin's got his heart set on buying your wedding gown as his wedding gift to you."

Manda squealed with joy and made a grab for Gwen.

Gwen hugged her tight. "Which means my job is to fatten you up."

"Good, because I'm starved."

Manda decided to take the stairway up all five floors. When she reached the top step on Joel's new floor, she felt the last of the fear blow out of her with an exhale. *That felt good.* She stood still for a moment, took a deep breath, and exhaled again. At last, she was ready to navigate the hospital corridors to Joel's private room.

Joel's eyes opened the moment Manda walked through the doorway. He reached out a hand to her, and she moved in for a kiss. Joel wasted no time on preliminaries. "I want us to be married and maybe have a family."

Manda caught her breath. She sat heavily on the bedside chair.

"Manda?"

"Yes!" She was stunned. "I thought you didn't want children?"

"I didn't. And I don't have to, if that's not right for you."

"What changed your mind?"

"I've been thinking about it for a while. I've been learning about love with you and about tenderness. Watching you grow and change has been fascinating. I'd like to be a father, and I think I can be a good one."

"I know you can."

Joel seemed to hold his breath. "Do you want children?"

Manda grinned. "With you? Absolutely."

Joel kissed her hand. "So let's get married and see what happens."

Manda laughed. "It's a plan."

"You like the idea?"

"I love the idea. Let's make it happen."

"I was going to propose for Christmas, but I think Christmas might have been last week. I've had the ring for a while. Justin is trying to find it in my apartment. Did he tell you he's going to live in my place and oversee renovation of the first floor for us?"

"I thought the plan was to create a suite for you at the Manse and add a therapy room and a pool."

"Two plans. A one month blitz at the Manse for the therapy suite, and three months construction at fourteen Lakeside Terrace, the whole first floor."

"So you and I will be living together as soon as you get out of the hospital?"

"Which is why I want to be married now."

Manda took a deep breath. *I can do this.* "That would mean I don't get to wear a beautiful dress and have flowers in my hair and have my sister stand up with me."

"Is that really important to you?"

"It's really important to me, Joel. How would you feel about being engaged and living together for a few months?"

"I'm fine with that." Joel reached for her hand. "Are you sure you are?"

"Yes, as long as we have a date for the wedding and our plans are moving along."

Joel face creased with a smile. "Why do I think you've started making plans?"

"Busted." Manda gave him a quick kiss. "I asked about dates in June, and the Manse can hold a reception for fifty on the third Saturday. If it's a nice day, we can be married in the new garden. Harold says the roses will be in bloom."

"That makes my heart sing," Joel told her with a glance at the heart monitor, which had not wavered from its beat. "I'm getting good at faking out this machine."

Manda let out a belly laugh that brought the nurse rushing in. Joel waved her back, and Manda apologized for both of them.

Joel stroked her cheek. "There is one more detail we should discuss, if we're going to be living together sooner than we planned."

Manda raised her eyebrows.

"I heard you say you wouldn't let me leave the planet without a night of wild sex."

Manda blushed hotly. "You heard that?"

"You got my attention," he teased. "One question."

"What?"

Joel ran his thumb along her lower lip. "Just one night of wild sex?"

She gave him a saucy smile. "How about one night at a time?"

"I can get into that." He gave her a long, slow kiss. "We might need to work up to wild and stormy." Joel's smile told her he wasn't terribly worried about that.

Manda went back for another kiss, a little more playful this time. "I think that could be fun."

"I agree, we should have as much fun as we possibly can." The next kiss was deep and long and punctuated by soft laughs from Manda and satisfied sighs from Joel.

Manda felt her heart opening and widening and flowing into Joel's. She pulled back and looked into his smoky green eyes. "I love you with all my heart."

Instinctively, Joel reached out with his right hand to play with the curls that had fallen onto her forehead. He held her gaze for a moment before touching her lips and kissing her all over again.